ORIENT ESPRESSO

by Edward Flaherty
The fifth novel in "The Landscape Architect" series

You may ask what is the landscape?
To which CJ would answer,
"When we get out of bed in the morning and put our feet on the floor,
we are in the landscape".
What? My apartment, my flat, my house, my town, my city?
To which he would simply answer, "They all sit in the landscape...
and the landscape?
It may not be your friend."

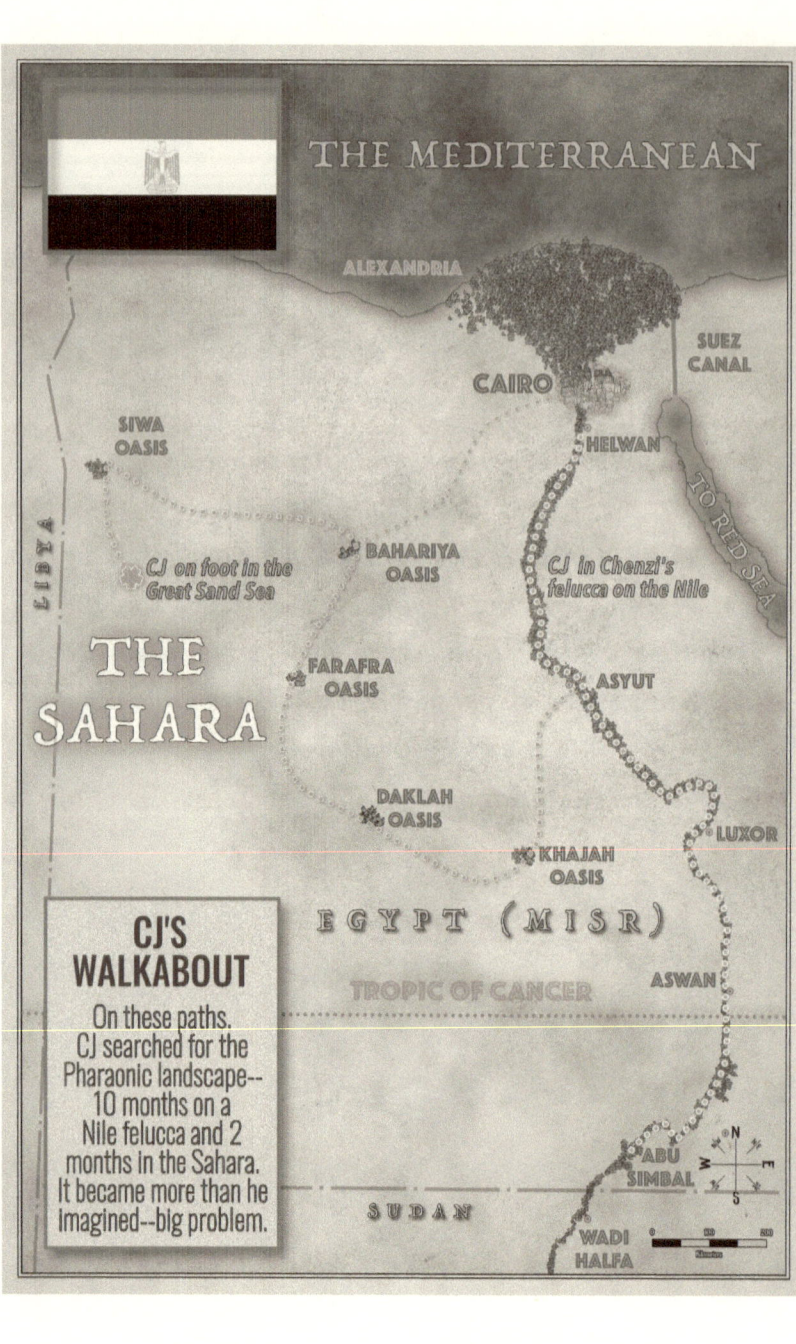

THE MEDITERRANEAN

ALEXANDRIA

SUEZ CANAL

CAIRO

HELWAN

TO RED SEA

SIWA OASIS

CJ on foot in the Great Sand Sea

BAHARIYA OASIS

CJ in Chenzi's felucca on the Nile

LIBYA

THE SAHARA

FARAFRA OASIS

ASYUT

DAKLAH OASIS

LUXOR

KHAJAH OASIS

EGYPT (MISR)

TROPIC OF CANCER

ASWAN

CJ'S WALKABOUT

On these paths, CJ searched for the Pharaonic landscape--10 months on a Nile felucca and 2 months in the Sahara. It became more than he imagined--big problem.

ABU SIMBAL

SUDAN

WADI HALFA

N W E S

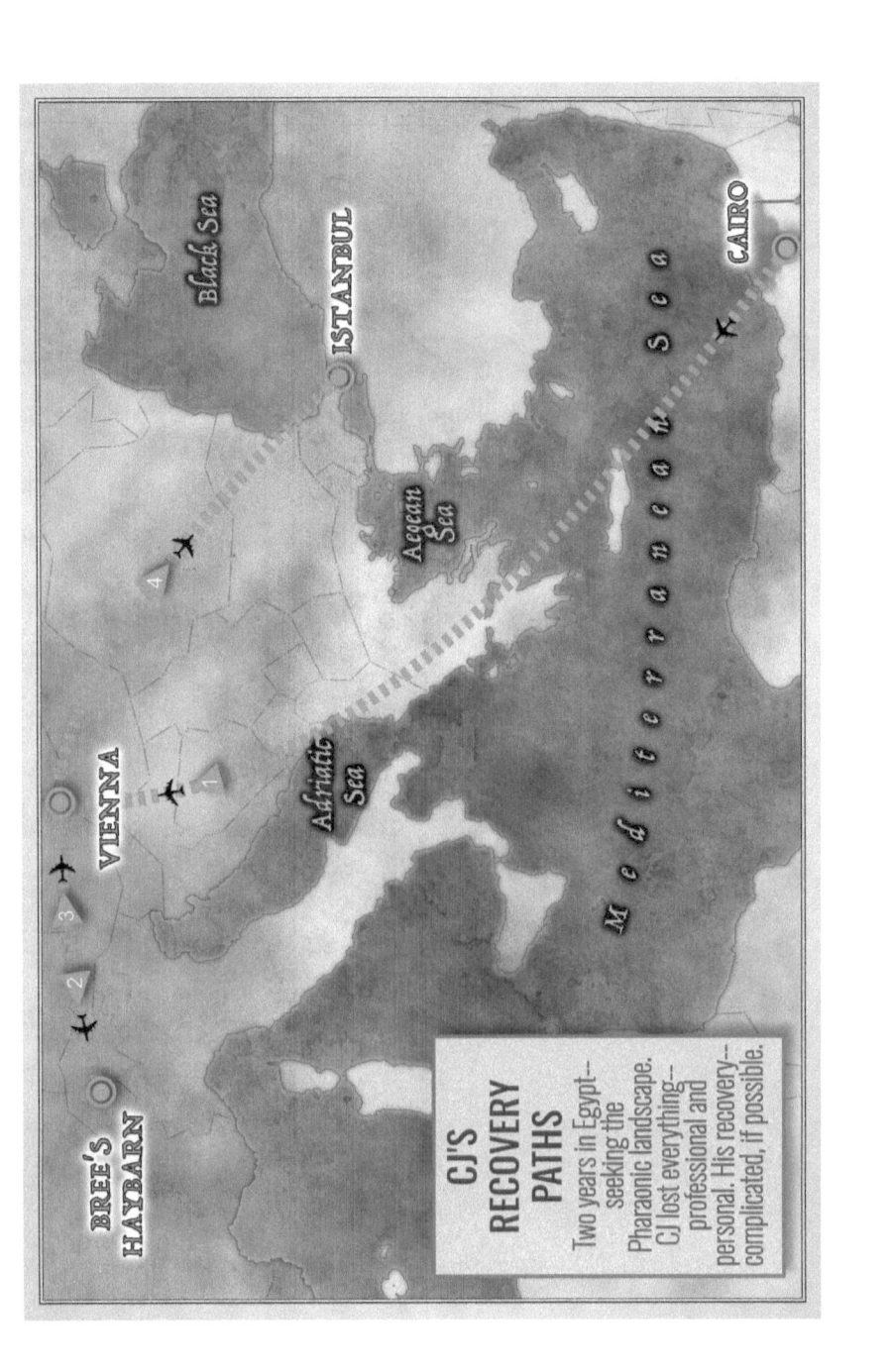

BREE'S HAYBARN

VIENNA

Black Sea

ISTANBUL

Aegean Sea

Adriatic Sea

Mediterranean Sea

CAIRO

CJ'S RECOVERY PATHS

Two years in Egypt—seeking the Pharaonic landscape. CJ lost everything—professional and personal. His recovery—complicated, if possible.

HELVETIA

CJ's quest for Kaytee
ended with a shock in
Geneva, Switzerland.
But after, in the Alps, he
experienced what?
... the "holy grail"
of landscape design?

Since 1291

Zürich

Bern

INTERLAKEN

Geneva

Preface

Previously in *Yenbo Palms* and *Crystal Vision*, W. Kurt Milligan, CJ's old friend and boss, had to narrate the stories. Why? Because he had been told CJ was dead. Kurt struggled to get details because he did not believe it. Even though Kurt didn't know it, he was correct in his conclusion.

In *Orient Espresso*, CJ finally tells what really happened to him in Cairo, Egypt—a difficult story.

Edward Flaherty

Foreword

Friends,

Hey! I had been looking forward to my new job in Cairo. I had been without work, without a home since the RIF (Reduction in Force) in Yenbo, Saudi Arabia... but... my Cairo job and the aftermath? A long story, another landscape battle.

Here's the background. Following my spectacular landscape and jodelling experiences in the Swiss Jungfrau Region, I had hoped in Cairo I might broaden those Swiss experiences by gaining some universal perspective from the Egyptian (Pharaonic) landscape, culture and music.

My enthusiasm for the Pharaonic landscape and the roots of Umm Kalthum's music? That was part of a professional cocoon that I had always used to hide from the emotional hurt, the loss of my wife Sachy and our kids in that horrific auto accident two decades ago in Albuquerque—the hurt always felt like yesterday.

My personal life had been crippled for decades until in Switzerland where Bree, an acquaintance from my student time in the Morocco landscape, took me by the hand and helped me create some new and healthy personal memories.

In *Orient Espresso*, I struggle trying to balance my personal and professional lives. Life is hard. For every ounce of sweetness there are pounds of suffering.

From two years of my Egyptian diary and design journal notes, I have compiled my landscape discoveries in the first chapter of *Orient Espresso*.

Everybody is going to be asking me—what have you done?

Why throw away your career? What were you thinking? I owe people some answers.

Christopher Janus aka CJ

Contents

1-Egypt

Doorstep

I stood on the doorstep.
  The Nile.
  Cairo.
Egypt.
The Sahara.

Over decades I'd heard so many stories about this landscape—so many good, so many more bad.

All strange and stranger.

And the stories kept coming.

And the people telling them even stranger.

Was this the landscape of my lifelong quest? Was this the landscape of my dreams...

Eleven months ago I walked away from my job in Cairo.

Today I am hitching out of Bahariya on my way to the Great Sand Sea. I am already surrounded by Egypt's Western Desert, the Sahara.

Overwhelmed by the Sahara—dehydrating, suffocating, the wind like sandpaper—coarse sandpaper on my skin all day, fine sandpaper on my skin at night when I slept. And in the sunlight, blindingly bright. My skin raw, burning. That was the Sahara.

To reduce the Sahara effects, I had a plan. I kept my carpet bag filled with survival essentials for a couple days, dried fruits/ nuts, water, small tent, blanket, first aid kit, knife, sun creme, compass... I moved oasis to oasis by hitching at the last gas station on the edge of town, waiting for *fellaheen* (country folk) filling their farm truck gas tank, telling them my destination and offering to pay for their full tank of gas.

It worked most of the time in the weeks as I moved oasis to oasis—Kharja, Daklah, Farafra... Sounds easy? It wasn't. If there was one truck per hour that would have been busy. I had lots of thinking time; and the Sahara captured my thoughts, my memories, my hopes. When I couldn't find a ride, I paid for a local taxi. Before I started on this Sahara quest, I had my clothes and local dialect working for me.

Clothes and local dialect? Years ago when I was in Morocco, I took a Peace Corps-sponsored crash course in the Moroccan dialect of Arabic—it made street exchanges easy; but that dialect didn't work here in Egypt. How did I get around it? I spent many months on Chenzi's *felucca*, his small wooden sailing boat—just him, me, the *felucca* and the Nile.

After a couple days with Chenzi, I started going ashore with him when he did his shopping. Shopping? He knew a network of farmers along the bank. Most often his shopping was a barter or favours for whatever fruit/veg/meat was in season. Language was hard at first. But I walked with Chenzi almost every time he went ashore. He was good with that.

My clothes had rich tourist written all over them—and they were not practical for *felucca* life. I saw how to dress myself as a *fellaheen*, with *gallabiya, kamis*. Chenzi showed me where and how to get them—then how to wear them. Subtle changes in my mentality helped me to gradually leave behind the modernity of Cairo, of Egypt.

Little by little, building on my past Arabic language basics from Morocco, I started to pick up Egyptian "street", or rather "*fellaheen*" Arabic with Chenzi. He saw my fascination with plants—stopping along the shoreline at beautifully regal groves of date palms (*Phoenix dactylifera*) and the rare blue lotus (*Nymphaea caerulea*) found in quiet eddies close to shore.

That was the Nile. Those were my memories, my distant dreams.

Desiccated by the Sahara and on the edge of an oasis waiting for a ride, I longed for those water-filled days. But I am on a quest. I have a thing called the Pharaonic landscape—I figure deep in the Sahara are the roots of this strange ancient culture and the *fellaheen* music of Umm Kulthum. Those roots have been overgrown by modern, bucket-list, Disneyland-style tourism. My months on Chenzi's *felucca* up and down the Nile were me trying to rid myself of fast-paced modern time, fast-paced modern pop-life. It worked.

Now I am on my own in the Sahara, waiting for a ride. Sandpaper, coarse sandpaper blowing over and burning on me. Dreaming of moisture, of water.

And why? Why the hell am I doing this? Through first-hand immersion, I have, throughout my career, searched those subtle existential relationships flittering between music, landscape, culture and the evanescent portals from material to spiritual. I have dedicated my life to an examination of the realities of the outer landscape becoming the transcendent landscape.

Thus I decided to disappear on the nourishing edge of a river whose source has always been dark... on the arid edge of the Sahara... on the aged edge of Pharaonic culture. The music was pulling me. I had hoped these experiences would enhance my design and career efforts as a landscape architect to produce for people a life more intriguing, more interesting, more enriching via enhanced association with plants, gardens, landscapes.

So, absorbed in my landscape cocoon, I put aside my most dear girlfriend and emotional lifeline, Bree and my professional reputation when I went on walkabout in Egypt, the Nile, the Sahara.

Mistakes? You decide.

***

Sand Surfing

Hitching out of Bahariya at the last gas station on the road to Siwa, I got lucky. A young guy with desert-sun brown skin was filling up a Toyota 4x4. The huge SUV had Sand Surfer advertising all over it. I did my thing—offered to pay for his gas if he would give me a ride to Siwa.

Deal!

Mohamed, told me to call him Mo, and I shook hands. Before we left, he asked to check my passport because tourists were not allowed through the military check points along the way. I still had my 36-month work visa sponsored by our joint-venture partner, a well-known top-ranked Egyptian AE (architecture/engineering) company. Mo said shouldn't be a problem. And off we went, as the crow flies, 300km till Siwa.

On the way, I learned that Mo, born in Siwa, had graduated from Cairo University majoring in modern languages—German, French, Italian, Spanish and of course English. He asked me what I was looking for.

"I am not interested in the national parks, the White Desert or the Black Desert..."

"So, is it sand-surfing or just a taste of its lifelessness—that covers just about most of the non-standard tourists?"

He made me think. I had pictured myself not at all as a tourist. What I intended to do... I had given it much thought while hitching... was about exploring the lifelessness and the storied shape-shifting cultural landscape roots in the Great Sand Sea... maybe uncovering the essence of what I called the Pharaonic landscape.

"I want more than a taste, but I don't want to endanger my life."

I was feeling a bit self-conscious now. If I described any more of my motivations, I'd sound even more like a green-horn tourist wanting to get a feel... wanting to experience the nature, the aura of the Great Sand Sea. Isn't that what the camping in all the Great Sand Sea tourist packages is for?

Mo said, "I don't know exactly what you want but I can outline how we can help... for a fair price."

"I am not looking to take photos or anything like that. I just want some alone time amongst the dunes."

"Being alone in the Great Sand Sea is a danger to human life—you understand, right?"

"Mo, I have the basics in my carpet bag—ultra light tent, solar blanket, almonds/dates for a couple days, first aid kit, knife, sun creme, compass..."

"Water. What about water? And you know how easy it is, compass or not, to get disoriented out in those dunes. And should a dust storm arise? Kiss your life goodbye."

"Okay, what do you suggest?"

"Look, it's almost dark, why don't you spend the night in our Sand Surfer Centre. We can talk this through in detail tomorrow."

The next day Mo introduced me to his no.2, Chisisi. He said, "My no.2 is my older cousin, he also graduated from Cairo University. He knows, as much as anyone can, about the Great Sand Sea around Siwa. Chisisi is a warrior, a warrior who saves people from the angry Sahara."

I asked Chisisi, "Warrior?"

"The angry Sahara is not just about its fabled dust storms. Here is how I look at it. There is a passive angry Sahara and an aggressive angry Sahara."

"How so?"

"You know, everyone knows about the dust storms that move in like a weather front. But on the passive side... the weather might be good clear or even cloudy but calm... mirages... I am not talking about the Hollywood-type of water, oasis mirage... something more passive but life threatening... it is subtle—

almost internal, mental... mean and silent... disorients your sense of direction, ability to discriminate and your will to problem solve."

"Let's get on with it—what are you looking to do—spell it out?" Mo said.

Mo put me on the spot. I asked myself what I wanted to do, was it or wasn't it just a typical tourist request?

"Okay, this is not a bucket list for me. I'm a landscape architect, a fan of Umm Kalthum, lived in Morocco, and six years in Saudi Arabia. The Great Sand Sea has history and mysteries. I ask myself why. I have no answer. So, I want to spend a couple days on my own in the Great Sand Sea to feel it, to assess it, to sensually analyze it. I know it's dangerous but you guys know how to protect humans in the Great Sand Sea. Let's work something out. I have no death wish. Do you understand?"

"How much window do you need?" Mo asked.

I guessed. "Three to four days—I don't know. I'll start with that. See the results and review what happens."

"Okay, here's what we can do.

"You've got many of the basics already—your clothes, the ones Chenzi set you up with, are good—just need to add loose-fitting trousers—we can arrange them—and don't use any of your American/Chinese made stuff—they don't work in the Great Sand Sea. You need nothing tight; but you need to have all of your skin protected. Clear?"

I nodded.

"And the rest of your gear... we figure... for four days... we need to set you up, just to be safe and sure, for six days with water and small, very light-weight packets of ultra-fuel cereal and endurance mixes—just mix with water. You'll need to budget one litre of water/day—it looks like you are austere that way—that'll help. We'll give you a backpack with six one-litre plastic bottles of water."

"I've carried five bottles before. I can do it."

"And most important, we will provide a small satellite messaging device, a Garmin mini. It works in a few important ways. As a beacon it lets us find you when you are ready to come back. Plus we can track your walking path in real time. And if you have a difficulty, you can message us directly. It is essential for what you want to do. We can guarantee you won't see or hear any other people."

I had already trashed my mobile and laptop. I had no watch, only a compass. I had tried to cut all my modern world tethers. Now they wanted me to carry the Garmin. In my mind I hesitated but it was essential—like I told them, I had no death wish.

I tucked the Garmin deep in the bottom of my bag and I was getting into it.

***

Infinite Threats

Three days later, just before sunrise, we were on our way out of the Siwa Oasis into the Great Sand Sea, the Sahara. I felt nervous, excited but also confident because of Mo and Chisisi's careful and complete preparation. Mo and I in one 4x4 and Chisisi behind us in a second 4x4—both with wide, large sand tires under low pressure.

I had asked not to be near any tourist camping or sand surfing spots. So Mo drove out of the oasis south on a track for 30 minutes. We were already out of sight of the oasis. Then we went SSE off the track for another hour up and down dunes I don't know how many times. Finally we stopped in a flat surrounded by the Great Sand Sea.

I felt confident because yesterday we had done a dry run with all equipment—everything worked. I liked my setup. It was safe and in the background. Mo and Chisisi hugged me and said goodbye, then drove off. I listened. The sound of their vehicles faded as they disappeared over the closest dune.

Then it was quiet. No mechanics. Only the sweeping sounds of the breezes moving sands over the dunes. I felt small—like a young sparrow—uncertain—flittering. I took a deep breath and turned around, surveying 360 degrees of my new landscape. Now what? I felt like the desert was surveying me—a strange new bird—in an unknown place—sizing me up as I was sizing it up.

I saw the sand. I felt the intense heat from the sand below and the sun above. I needed shelter from the sun's blinding brightness. And a rasping-sand-filled wind scratched at my exposed skin. I wrapped the cloth over my face and pulled my hands inside. The Sahara took control.

I couldn't think about plans for survival, where to walk, where to pitch for the night. Sand and overhead sun drove my thoughts. I wandered, I don't know where. In a brief moment of self-consciousness I asked myself, is this my penance? Is this what I must go through to find the Pharaonic landscape?

My first night—calm and clear.

Clear? No city lights. No electricity at all. No sounds.

Silence.

No moon.

A gazillion brilliant stars.

I should have realized that I was on a downhill trip to depression—but I didn't. At first I was amazed by all the stars from sand dune horizon to sand dune horizon—360 degrees of sand dune horizon—360 degrees of night sky clarity. And then my mind tricks began.

Endless stars, endless sand and me in the midst. I observed— what was I observing? The observer, as finite as I was—was surrounded by endlessness, by infinity. And I couldn't stop observing. There was nothing else.

My mind was relentless. I couldn't escape, my stomach churned—lack of understanding—I choked on infinity—I had no respite—I could not run away—all I could see was entrapment by something I didn't understand.

On a cool desert night I was sweating a storm. Then the strangest pop-culture respite—*The Truman Show*—it was all a stage set. That respite lasted as long as it took me to visualize the words. And then my existential anxiety overcame me again. Infinity and eternity danced over my soul, jumped on my very existence. There was no exit door. Driest mouth and throat but I had already drunk my daily quota. I had to tough it out. I became recurrently sick to my stomach before my bodily systems just gave out and I lost consciousness. Sleep—a blessing.

Until I woke up.

Then the rising sun, returning in all its glory burned my eyelids. The day had begun. Sand sea? The sand desert is the opposite of water. It is no water, no life, no hope.

The water, the ocean—there is hope that land is there. The sand desert is land but no hope. My water bottles are like a fuse. Drinking them is like the fuse burning down. And at the end... of the fuse... of the water... there is death. Might it be welcome? And is that death not a portal to infinity, eternity... that never-ending uncomfortable weirdness? Depressing thoughts smothered with existential uncertainties... endlessness of endlessness.

Sun getting hotter. Heat from the sands getting hotter still. No shade. Wind picking up. Sandy grit in my face—no time for existential thoughts. Shelter. I needed shelter. I had no shelter.

The day had been clear, hot and always too bright, as the sun is on the arid Tropic of Cancer. As the sun set the clouds moved in and I was glad not to be confronted with star infinity. I pitched, covered up and...

The Sahara sun and sand had done me in. I couldn't ask any questions. I couldn't answer any questions. I closed my eyes. Memories filled my head like dreams. They flitted through like rolodex cards one after another—so real life. I still can't be sure if I was sleeping or not—if I was dreaming or hallucinating—the entire daylight sun/sand/heat experience had been too much. But the following happened.

I had been living in Giza at the foot of the Great Pyramid walking distance in the neighbourhood of the Sphinx. These built wonders of the world came with their own baggage. It was not a clean, clear story. I asked myself, can it be that Ancient Egypt is being smothered by dense modern tourism? Has the Egyptian Disneyland paved over the ancient spirit I sought?

Late one night, long after the pulsating *son et lumiere* final tourist pitch sent the crowds home, when I was walking the perimeter of the Great Pyramids, I chanced upon another "lost soul" or so I thought.

I saw an older man, limping, a cripple. Looked European. And he wasn't being hassled by any dragomen. I approached him out of curiosity because I had never seen another explorer during my late nights at Giza.

Thus began a friendship that took me to the starting point

of my Egyptian walkabout. We met regularly in Giza on our late-night walks among the pyramids. Over months I came to know the Professor, a Jesuit, cultural anthropologist academic dedicating his life to field research. He became my local source of information.

In my talks with the Professor, I revealed all my Egyptian experiences, preconceptions and quests. He was on a similar quest—what really happened in the landscape on this planet before written history. Same but different, as I learned. While I looked for cultural roots in the landscape, the Professor, through his gemmology quest, sought to unravel landscape mysteries, seeking threads, clues to pre-Mesopotamian civilizations embedded in gemstones.

Born in Malta, he was affiliated with The Griffith Institute at the University of Oxford, spoke academic English, French and the local Arabic dialect. He was a "hair shirt" kind of guy (a person in touch with the locals, not inclined at all with packaged tourism). He suggested I get away from the masses, let the S'h'ra (he used Arabic pronunciation, never pronounced Sahara as it is spelled in textbook English), let the S'h'ra sands seep in. I was ready for that. My Sahara experiences on the edge of Big Cairo had been strangely unsettling. There had to be more.

He invited me to visit him in Helwan, next to the Rokn Farouk Museum on the bank of the Nile. There, I could always find him in a small coffee house, at midday. He said the environment would be more conducive for talks about Ancient Egypt.

I was wrapped by the inescapable sands and their existential threats. I needed something to hold onto. These memories, they became my handhold—hallucinations, dreams? These were memories and in the Great Sand Sea they became my cocoon.

***

Sakkara

First night, second night or third night, I can't remember which—same as the days. As I looked back on those nights, the prominence of the Professor reflected how I had valued his input before I walked away from my job and began in earnest my search for the Pharaonic landscape.

Ancient Egypt? More ancient than the Sahara? Really? The Sahara must be able to tell humans their existential story. But in which language? Music? Culture? Were their roots discoverable in this strange landscape?

But that landscape overwhelmed me. I was seeking something to grab on to. I was dreaming about how I got to this place of my dreams that was turning out to be my own existential hell. Together the Professor and I had walked the banks of the Nile. The Nile? Oh the relief of green and water— the thoughts, the memories were so real—but wait—this must be the formation of a mirage—none of which I could touch— yet was so real in my mind and I was hankering so intensely. The Professor visited me or I visited him. We did it together. It began on the shore of the Nile. He told me about a guest house not on any tourist map.

"Let's take a short walk to that guest house I told you about. We can have a drink, relax and talk about the future."

"I'm good with that." We walked west in the direction of where Madinat al Badrashin meets the Sahara. After 15 minutes slow walking, we arrived at the Sakkara Guest House—two stories of old mud brick construction scratched by blowing sand and burnished by the sun.

The inside felt the same—old, scratched and burnished construction—cheap looking, ill-maintained. The owner was not at the front desk. We walked right in. Just off the entry, beside the owner's desk was a commons room. In it I saw five plastic tables, each with two, three or four plastic chairs, high ceiling, no fan and behind a small serving bar, a refrigerator, a sink, a cabinet of glasses, a single gas burner and a coffee grinder. No AC, no TV, and surprisingly in a far corner, a piano.

The owner was in the common room, behind the bar making tea and coffee for his guests. Before we sat down, the Professor said to the owner, "*Salam alaykum, Daka, jooj chai* (two teas)."

The Professor turned to me and said, "Let's discuss a plan to get you together with the *felucca* owner Chenzira, known as Chenzi."

"Let's talk about what I want to do, first, and how the *felucca* could get me there—this is not supposed to be a tourist trip—it is about the Nile and the Sahara—I'm not into names or dates. I want to get out of the day-to-day contemporary rush—don't get me wrong, I don't want anything like Paul Bowles' Moroccan *Sheltering Sky* story. I'd like to absorb myself in a non-mechanized exposure to the Nile and the Sahara—is Chenzi the guy?"

"Christopher, let me share with you the last time I was here with Chenzi when he talked with a man who had just spent six months in his *felucca*.

"The subject was music... not as cut and dried as those 4 words... Daka heard it all too. The guy... if I remember correctly, his name was Muhleman... probably European... or South African... he sat down at the piano... he was accomplished on the keyboard.

"He'd play and then he'd talk and then he'd play more... it was all S'h'ra and Ancient Egypt."

The Professor then spoke Arabic to Daka, "Most amazing—do you remember, my friend?"

Daka, looking out the window on the S'h'ra... appeared distant... somewhere else... It was as though Daka was willing the hugeness of the S'h'ra into our small commons room. Something fit but didn't fit... awkward.

The Professor continued, "It was the music. His music carried something. Muhleman played contemporary Arabic music—like the intros to an Umm Kalthum number... then he would subtly shift to tunes from Ancient Egypt... accompanied by his monologue, designed to take us on some kind of voyage... a trip... a path into the S'h'ra... into the past. And on that day Chenzi was in the room with us.

"Chenzi had been in the Upper Nile with Muhleman for six months. And as Chenzi told me later, during those six months, days at a time would go by without a word spoken between them."

I liked what I was hearing about the *felucca* up the Nile. It sounded like Muhleman had the Sahara sands get into him—at least that's what it sounded like.

"And what's happened to Muhleman?" I asked the Professor.

"Nobody knows."

I twisted and turned under my tent, sand scratching my every movement. Just like that story, the gritty Sahara sand got under my skin... and every grain of sand, though small, had an immense aura, boding an irrepressible frightening.

***

Hauled Out

I used a plastic bag to contain my inorganic refuse. I buried all organic refuse deep in the sand. Weather was calm, clear. Sun was bright. No trees, no shrubs, no grasses. Wildlife? No tracks.

Peaceful? I think why most people say peaceful is because there are no mechanical noises—no humming engines, no whooshing tires on asphalt, no whining AC.

Peaceful? Me and my thoughts. Same every day.

And my mind—not peaceful but restless. Running from one topic to the next at a speed just as fast as modern civilization— even faster. Same every day. Took me a while to slow it down— if I ever did.

No wonder it is called the Great Sand Sea. It is like being alone in the middle of an ocean—confronted by an infinity in real life. Endlessness surrounding me. All my senses caught in infinity—an uncomfortable, depressing weirdness. I couldn't stop thinking about it. Every day the same. Before I knew it, the meaninglessness of my existence got squeezed by eternity—over and over ad infinitum. And what I was doing meant absolutely nothing.

I shook my head, my shoulders, my whole body to bring my here-and-now senses back to life. I had to shake myself from that deepest fear that only suicide could relieve.

I tried thinking of Bree and her Jungfrau Region haybarn— oh the richesse and simplicity of our life together in the Swiss Alp highlands, but under the S'h'ra influence all that I could see were her warnings about something strange and horrific buried in the Sahara. I tried ever so hard to see my beloved Bree working with plants in her haybarn garden—nothing, just the Great Sand Sea. Infinity closing in, my throat drying up.

The daytime was too much. No matter how many dunes I climbed over, it was the same. Crystal clear sky, my infinity blanket. The sun rose higher, the sky was clear. The brightness of the sun overtook the sky. And the reflected brightness and heat off the sand were intolerable. The sun and the sand had no romantic attraction anymore—just a daytime version of the night star infinity.

The S'h'ra had erased the Sahara. I had lost my Bree. That was weird—not just weird but deeply uncomfortable. Couldn't analyze. I didn't know where I was going or what I was supposed to do... then I got a beep from my Garmin. I dug it out of my bag. Mo and Chisisi were coming to haul me out.

They picked me up. They asked me questions. I couldn't talk. I climbed into the back of their vehicle. They stopped asking me questions, talking quietly only between themselves. I was in a strange daze. I could hear them but it was in the distance—like a dream. They were speaking Arabic. They were whispering. I heard some words—it almost seemed to be my native language, but it wasn't in English—sand fever-sand fever. I felt relief, fatigue... fading, under mental anaesthesia for days until I could organize and plan.

***

The Long Walk

At the end I returned from Siwa, hitching via Bahariya to Cairo. I had been almost a year on my Pharaonic landscape quest. I had enough searching. I bottom-lined it as a dead end. I ran away from the S'h'ra. My head felt like it was the desert itself. The sands had taken me. I didn't like the feeling. I was on my way back; but I was empty.

Hitching from the gas stations, I was dressed in the clothes Chenzi had helped me pick out to blend in. I never blended in; but I looked the part.

All I had left from my year in the Pharaonic landscape was my carpetbag—the outsized shoulder-strapped jack bag that I had picked up in the Khan Khalili before I set out.

While waiting for a ride, I looked at the insides of that bag—looking for what? What I had left behind? Some clues to my past before going off the grid—walkabout?

I rummaged through its contents—a couple bottles of water, some hygiene stuff, my one-man REI coop emergency tent and my special box—a small mother of pearl inlay, large enough for my number 2 pencils, Swiss army knife and A6 size note papers.

I can't remember. I think I kept my memories in there too. But I'm foggy on that. I had not written one word in it while I was wandering in the Great Sand Sea.

The desert—it had used silence to vacuum my energy. Its presence undid my intelligence, scattered my thoughts with such intensity that all I could think of... The desert forced me to be too close to the existential thoughts that always depressed me. Took away my life force.

I was on foot. My last ride from Bahariya took me close to Sixth of October. I was back in the aura of Big Cairo. It would be a long walk and I had more to go before the Sphinx/Great Pyramids, Mena House in Giza. I was beat.

My thoughts depressed me. I had hoped to get into the music and landscape links as existential fundamentals... but... the Sahara had left me with nothing. My examinations of Umm Kalthum's Nile Delta? Again nothing. Two years in Egypt and nothing. Emptiness—no result—no fun at all. Algernon Blackwood's *Descent into Egypt* had seduced me then misled me. Nothing—big-time mistake.

And now I walked through one of Cairo's new towns. Oh, the Sixth of October had its street trees and parks—*Jacaranda, Delonix, Plumeria,* how many different *Cassia,* palm trees in varieties—but I was always in battle with cars, busses, trucks and their roads.

Such aggressive sounds, smells, horns—so damn noisy. Cairo was originally a pedestrian-only city and now pedestrian access had been impeded by multilane, limited-access vehicular networks. They had it nicely, once before. Hell, Cairo was, once upon a time, walkable, no different than the Moroccan medinas. No longer.

***

Welcome Back

I finally got to Giza and the Mena House. Had used up the last of my *fluss* (Egyptian cash) on food and water on my way in from Bahariya. At the Mena House hotel check-in desk I discovered none of my credit cards, including my trusty AmEx card, were usable. My first digital re-entry into the modern world—I hadn't thought about these kinds of things since I dumped my iPhone and computer into the Nile 12 months ago.

I wasn't really shocked; but I was numb. I just stood there in my Egyptian hitch-hiking clothes for a couple, seemingly endless, moments. After all, I had been a year on the Pharaonic landscape quest, and the S'h'ra was still in me. The speed of the S'h'ra and the speed of modern Egypt? Cultural opposites.

The desk clerk ignored me. I looked at him, not sure what would happen next. He wasn't looking at me. He was intent on his computer screen and said, "Excuse me, I'll be right back." He turned around, opened a door just behind him and entered a back-of-house office.

That gave me time to try to figure out what to do. Some internal lights slowly began to turn on. So, by the time the desk clerk returned, I remembered my emergency traveller's checks. Used them for the hotel check-in.

Okay, things were working. But my head? Slow as molasses in January. Everything was slow motion. I certainly wasn't at Big Cairo speed, nor was I dressed in Big Cairo 5-star destination style. The S'h'ra had taken all from me.

The desk clerk, impatient with my transaction speed, handed me off to a young trainee girl. Finally, I got some words out. I asked, "A room on the garden side, please?"

She looked at me strangely then said, "We do have some rooms with Pyramid views if you'd like?"

"No, thank you." The most popular rooms facing the pyramids? No way, I'd had my fill. My infatuation with the Sahara and Giza Pyramids had run its course.

I had been to-ing and fro-ing with the people at the front desk for what seemed like an hour when somebody's movement nearby caught my attention.

An older guy... he looked very familiar, tall, white hair, grizzled, square jawed, well-dressed. At first, his name failed me.

He looked both imperious yet welcoming... finally, I remembered his name... Will Clendenon. He was sitting in the lounge close to the reception desk.

I'd been one year walking the Egyptian landscape, the Sahara, the Nile. I forgot about a lot of my professional life.

He stood up and walked toward me, did I see a hint of a smile? I wasn't ready to talk to anyone; but I had no choice. Will, looking me up and down, reached out to shake my hand then invited me to sit down with him in a quiet corner of the lounge.

"Why didn't you complete your assignment?" he asked.

Though I should have expected it, his question hit me like a glassful of ice water thrown in my face. He was the guy whom I worked for in Yenbo and he was the guy that got me the job in Cairo almost two years ago. At least I remembered the context; but I had no answer to his question. I needed something to drink and not alcohol.

He called a waiter over. I asked for a bottle of still water. The waiter brought it back immediately.

Will looked me over again as I opened the water and took a couple slow drinks.

"Take your time. Tell me what happened."

"Let me have a moment—you want me to start from the beginning?"

"Tell me everything, yes."

"Will, it's a difficult story to tell. It is mixed up. I'll try but it

34

will be a strange flow." I was having trouble knowing where to start and what details to tell. I drank some more water.

"I am waiting to hear why you walked away from your job."

"The desert. The desert talks clearly. Black and white. Water is there or water is not there. Life or absence of life. White or black. There is no in-between. Do you follow? But black and white is not enough. We humans live in the in-between. In between black and white. For us it is all grey, confusing shades of grey... you asked why I walked away? The grey and Alan—too much.

"The job was a joke and the desert was too strong. The job? Make-work by the Egyptian administrators using a small percentage of their international grant funds—the balance from what they hid in Cyprus. They weren't going to design and build anything here. My days were spent measuring my paycheck against my tax liabilities, swatting flies and shovelling through Alan's damnable word salads. The desert was strong. And my job as diaphanous as the decorative silks inside a Cairo whorehouse."

"Jesus, CJ, is that all you've got after a year? We had to declare you dead and you weren't available for any assignments. What the hell were you doing? What was so important that you threw away our work, our relationship and your professional career?"

I could feel myself warming up—the synapses had been encrusted by endless dry, sandy days in the Sahara. The waters and humidity of the Nile never reached my synapses. It wasn't until Will's repeated direct questioning that I started to feel my internal electricity flow.

I asked Will, "How did you know I was here and why?"

He looked at me, hard and long. Too long. "Let me be clear, CJ. The only reason I am here is because you successfully gathered information from members of the Saudi Royal family, saved us and the Client money in Yenbo and gave a dependable and respectable image to your landscape architecture profession on a huge project of international importance, Yenbo New Town. Give me the bottom line. What happened last year in Cairo?"

I was getting clearer. "Two things. Alan was asshole. And the young technical staff provided by the Egyptian consultants had no energy. Never turned up before 11 in the morning, drank an espresso or two over their mobiles and disappeared the rest of the day. On site the project was just a time-wasting façade—was never going to be built. And me? I had to learn about this ancient landscape."

I surprised myself with the directness of my answer.

Will didn't give me any time to think. He asked, "So, what's your move now?"

"I've had too much thinking time and I'm damn near skint."

"More than that. You don't officially exist anymore. Your Executor closed the books. Everyone you knew, your family, your landscape architecture colleagues—they all think Christopher Janus is dead. That's a quandary of your own making."

He paused again to let his last comments sink in deeply then said, "What's your move?"

I had no answer. Dead? I was flummoxed.

"Listen CJ, I want JeanClaude to de-brief you before I make my decision. So, for now, finish checking in and JeanClaude will contact you."

I was feeling sheepish but rose and was able to firmly return Will's handshake as he got up to leave. I sat back down for a few moments before getting up to finish my check-in... dead? Hadn't settled in fully; but the implications? Huge, I was sure.

***

Decompression

I passed my next few days without leaving my room. Had the Sahara overwhelmed my lungs? Had it overwhelmed the Nile? I was filled with uncertainty about what I had done. About my purpose. About where I was going.

But there was one small bronze bell crisply, yet ever so softly, ringing in the background of my thoughts, as it had sporadically the last couple months. In my mind, I unconsciously had grabbed a hold of my days and nights with Bree in her Swiss Alps Jungfrau Region haybarn—but was that an emotional mirage? The uncertainty was strong. Gut wrenching. Too much wrenching.

I forced myself to think it through. I had found comfort with Bree—emotional comfort—something that for decades I had missed. That was the pleasant, peaceful ringing—the soft yet crisp sound of the Jungfrau Region bronze cow, sheep and goat bells. I had hoped to see her again; but the mirage of my Egyptian job, the Pharaonic landscape had nearly wiped out those memories of emotional well-being that I felt with Bree.

I was still thick in my head. I stayed in my air-conditioned room. Didn't want to smell the Sahara or see the pyramids. I needed peace. I needed clarity. I wanted no more sands of time slowly drifting like honey in my thoughts. But, how can I say it... an ache of the heart had been displaced and had lodged in my head... I did not understand... the Pharaonic landscape. Once I ran to it and now I was running from it.

My room had a bath and a rain-fall shower. And did I need them! Bath, shave and shower. But more than deep cleaning,

I needed peace. I needed clarity. After a couple days of air-conditioned solitude and room service meals, I called the concierge and told him I needed some clothes. He told me a shop in the hotel might be of service.

I called them and they sent up warm-weather shirts and trousers. I selected long, beige linen cargo pants and a papyrus-patterned crème-coloured cotton, long sleeve, wear-out-of-the-pants shirt. Then I went downstairs to buy new sandals and a hat. I was feeling better. It had taken me four days to get this far. I was ready to be social.

The hotel had an Indian restaurant. I hadn't eaten vegetarian or Indian in a year. Their buffet was just what I needed. Was normality returning? Not sure but Will's words about my official death still did not seem to be anything but a dream. Dream? And Bree? Was she a dream, too? And my emotions when I say her name... are they but a mirage... an illusion?

Finally, one night I gave in and visited the courtyard garden with an aspect on the pyramids of Giza. The view still had an aura of mystery; but it did not have the magnetism that had pulled me into the Pharaonic landscape. I paused, looked deeply. I didn't retch. Their impact on me was shallow now. Somehow, I had turned the page.

I returned to the other side of the hotel where my room fronted on a water garden. Before going into my room, I took a turn around the water garden.

Water. Even along the Nile I felt I was short of water—always in deficit. I never drank from that life-giving river. Only bottled water. That certainly accounted for my good health as I was searching for roots in the Pharaonic landscape, only to be lost in their shape-shifting reality. Was it all a mirage? Of the type Chisisi had warned of in the Great Sand Sea?

I slipped off my sandals and dangled my feet in the garden pool. Water. Refreshing in so many ways. When I returned to my room, the light was flashing on my phone. A message.

***

JeanClaude

Culture and religion—people identify with them because there is no actual answer to the most fundamental existential questions—who am I, why am I here and what is here? This was no doubt the root of my landscape searching—at least, that was Vrndadevi's Vedic take when I was in Ban Muang, northern Thailand. That was another of the thoughts that kept popping into my head. It was the S'h'ra and thoughts. The thoughts blew through like the wind blows the desert sands. I needed "reality".

On my room phone was a message, two hours old, from JeanClaude. He wanted to meet me in my hotel lobby tomorrow morning at 11.

I thought whoa! Back in the real world, big time. The next morning I was in the lobby at 10:45. JeanClaude, also of Analysis Corp., and I had history—we had talked a lot in Yenbo where, after Alan, he became my handler. As I recall, we had similar botanical and landscape interests; and he had always been helpful.

He arrived at 11. We looked at each other, paused, then shook hands. He smiled warmly and asked where we could speak privately. Without ado, I led him upstairs to my room. I dialled room service and they delivered two Virgin Mimosas. The room balcony was in the shade and pleasantly overlooked the ornamental water garden. We took the drinks out on the balcony and sat. He spoke softly.

"CJ, what have you been doing?"

I thought I was ready but wasn't ready with an answer. I

couldn't answer. Then a flood of thoughts filled my mind—as if I had accessed a file of data in poorly organized folders—suffering, gardens, design, Egypt, Cairo, landscape architecture, date palms, gold, lapis lazuli, *felaheen*, cartouches, scarabs... I actually felt dizzy as these images roiled through my head.

JeanClaude reached for my arm and asked, "We talked before you left. I kept my word. I told no one. Even when they declared you dead, I said nothing. Now you have to tell me, *mon ami*, what did you find? What did you learn?"

This time answers came out of my mouth. I stammered, "Too much noise... and Alan didn't help... he was all noise."

"You should know that's finished. The project fell through and Alan is back in an office pushing papers."

Then my words flowed like a river. "That was all he was good for. Those bureaucrats like him and I never get along. That's me. He was climbing all over me."

"So is that all?"

I recalled all that JeanClaude and I had shared, ethnobotany, ethnomusicology, and that gave me the foundation to answer his question.

"Pharaonic landscape, music and design, that's what got me started. I didn't know what I would find, so I just dove in."

I continued, "Something about Egypt and its Pharaonic landscape. There was a music... it had a magnetic melody. I had to follow it. I had to search for its roots. The pyramids, the Nile, the Sahara. It had to be beyond tourism, beyond a bucket list... I was looking for the basic stuff of the landscape and a human civilization millennias-old mystery that beckoned. The job was stalling and I needed to go off the grid. It was time for me to search. Do you follow?"

"But that's old news, CJ. That's what you confided to me before you left. I already knew that. What I want to know is what you found. Did you discover anything worthwhile?"

I really didn't know what or how to say... finally... "I couldn't get free of that constant drumbeat of tourism... but the very few times I did... an infinite meaninglessness crept in... so disturbing... nothing beautiful or sweet... The worst was the Great Sand Sea—it robbed me of... I don't know what...

emotions, logic, intelligence. It was weird—the worst of everything."

I sat in silence. JeanClaude just looked at me. Then words returned to my mouth.

"I was left with only my professional analysis of desert landscape and the presence or absence of water."

JeanClaude still said nothing.

I continued, "So, I was left with the awkward, artificially enhanced tourism and my own realisation of overused resources, diminishing arable lands and increasing salinity of groundwater—so much for the Sahara—nothing mystical... except humans were still trying to squeeze more out of it while it was driving humans out. And the plants—subsistence level—I had no transcendental portals—I saw, I felt, I sensed... nothing. I've had my fill of this place. But that is only half of the story—the rest? My personal life... I don't understand... it went missing. I found no answers. No landscape roots. Just losses."

"Off the record I understand, you found nothing and feel you have lost something. We can discuss that later. Right now, try to understand this reality, CJ. You put me in a tough spot when you took off. I've got to know, are you in the game or not?"

***

Next?

I sat... sat... and sat while JeanClaude, waiting for my response, said nothing. I slowly sipped the sprightly taste sensations of this liquid, my Virgin Mimosa. A taste extravagant indeed, compared to the carefully measured lifesaving drops of water that had sustained me in the Great Sand Sea.

In the game? I had no answer. I wasn't sure. I had felt my professional and emotional attachments slipping away the deeper I had gone into that Pharaonic landscape. I had dragged myself out. I wanted life not death.

In my return to Cairo, I had felt like my brain was slowed down as if numb. I was thinking maybe now that I was back to my starting point in Cairo I could recover my sharpness, my professional drive, my emotional commitment. But it wasn't happening.

JeanClaude interrupted my thoughts.

"Are you with me?"

"What? I think so."

This Sahara landscape and especially the Great Sand Sea felt like a dry quicksand that surrounded and reduced the firing of my brain's synapses.

"I am still slow. What were you asking?" I said.

"What did you do with your phone and computer?"

"I offered them to the Nile. I was looking into the past. I undid my connections with today, with the future. They made so much noise in my life. I needed to free myself of the speed of modern present-day life."

"But CJ what was really going on?"

"Suffering... JeanClaude. I'm no different than any other person—we are all suffering and looking for relief. Me, I think it is in the landscape but the landscape and its artifacts have been consumerised, commercialised—we have forgotten the innate depth and breadth landscape wealth. Yes, even in Egypt—might as well be SoCal—landscape has become a thing." I paused. More words followed.

"I thought I could find something deeper here. I found loss. That's all. As odd, as numb as I feel now, that hurtful reality is clear from my 12-month Egyptian walkabout."

I paused again. I could understand that JeanClaude was listening.

Then he said, "I think that that relief is in the plants. My international ethnobotanical research showed me that every culture, no matter how small, no matter how isolated, has somewhere in its past, used plants in some form or another to get relief. I learned there is nothing fair in life whether living in first, second, third world or off the edge—everyone gets hard done by—people live with it and seek relief in sustainable means—most often plants are involved. Now tell me, what brought you back to Cairo?"

I answered, "...it was a hunt for the wumpus or the snark. Seriously. The deeper I got into that Great Sand Sea desert—the closer I guessed I was getting to the 'timeless understanding' I hoped was embedded in the Pharaonic landscape. Maybe I was... but I felt I was losing contact with the daily life things that had meant something to me—I sensed I was having to make a trade off—my professional and my emotional attachments for that something hidden in the Pharaonic landscape—the desert. I wanted to know what was behind the door... but..."

JeanClaude said, "I understand you need clarity... and confidence, but you have been off the grid for a year; what have you got to show for it? Uncertainty—not good enough. Let me tell you how I see it—you had the freedom to make that search. Do you understand what that means?"

I wasn't sure. I just sat quietly.

JeanClaude continued, "The idea of changing the world, the country politics, or those people you meet while you are working for food and shelter... that is freedom, that is normal, can we agree on that?"

My thoughts were moving so much slower... but his question I could understand. I agreed.

Then JeanClaude said, "What you have had that is extremely valuable is international professional credibility and know-how. Does that mean anything to you?"

I said nothing. JeanClaude, looking straight into my eyes said, "Your silence is dangerous. Let me ask you differently. Do you know that your actions in the last twelve months have destroyed your professional career?"

Those questions struck the issue that Will addressed when he told me I was officially dead. That dreamlike reality was shocking to my core and I didn't know what to say.

I was looking out on a garden of ornamental plants. The last year all I had seen were food plants (fruit and veg for people)—maybe I was coming out of my desert sand daze as I was thinking—there was a massive gulf between food for subsistence and landscape architecture work. And design? Design? Pop culture—Los Angeles—nothing to do with what I saw in those oases. All those thoughts... nothing was fitting together yet. I was internally stumped.

JeanClaude must have been reading my mind. He asked me, "Ethnobotany and landscape architecture, does that ring a bell? Are you still into that now?"

I was there and I wasn't there. I was confused about real life and dream life. I thought I was speaking to JeanClaude in a dream. But in reality he was pulling me out of a dream into real life.

I don't remember if he even asked a question—but I "answered". Or was I thinking... it was about the strength of the waters of the Nile as displayed in the health of the date palms... and that—that was a victory over the swelling sand-filled fears whipping over the Great Sand Sea to threaten all that was human.

I said to JeanClaude, "This urban 21st century Cairo has lost everything. It has its own aura and that aura has none of the tranquillity of the landscape—none of the peacefulness of healthy plants. Pedestrians are in constant battles just to walk to buy the daily food stuffs—bread, or to meet with friends over coffee. Something is out of place and people like me, landscape architects, have work to do."

JeanClaude looked at me as if he understood. I asked, "Why are you nodding your head?"

"I hear you talking about landscape architecture. I am glad to hear that," he said.

I continued but inside it felt like I was rambling, "From my walk across Cairo, I saw the frustration of humans over their condition in life—their attempts to find a way to make their time on earth better."

JeanClaude turned the discussion to governments controlling people. He talked about people afraid of what freedom may bring, government downfalls, loss of their power. He turned government and those governed into survival of the fittest. All was going over my head; but I caught the drift of it. The governed should not lose their freedom. I had heard something like this from *felaheen* when I was out among the oases in the Western desert.

Then as I remember JeanClaude said, "A key area of agreement is that plants have extrasensory perceptual effects on humans, providing means for calming the dystopian realizations that are part of human life, especially urban human life."

That sounded familiar. Then JeanClaude changed the subject.

He asked, "You offered your digital life to the Nile?"

I said nothing.

He asked, "How do you move forward from that? And more, *mon vieux ami*, you have been officially declared dead by Egypt, the US and your company. We've work to do, if you're still in the game..."

He had again put that question to me. I felt things tighten in my head. Tighten? It was a good sign—fundamental sequence and maybe even logic began working. Something more than wind drifting sands.

During my walk across Cairo, I had already felt my old

landscape architecture fire begin to rekindle. Get plants and gardens accessible to everybody. But... in the game? I had no answer for him.

JeanClaude sat in silence looking at me. Then he asked, "You have no answer? What's holding you back?"

I thought I knew; but it was so difficult finding words.

Maybe I wasn't back to normal. My thoughts went slow as an ant in honey. I finally responded.

"JeanClaude, I hear the soft ringing of a brass bell in the back of my head... maybe it is lodged in my inner ear... emotions... I think the Sahara was unplugging my emotions. I think my emotions are coming alive but I am uncertain."

I paused, searching for words. Professional and personal— are they linked or separated? I pushed out some more words. I felt their meaning. They were important.

"There was a lady in the Swiss Alps. She revived my emotions the first time since I lost my family almost 20 years ago. That lady in the Swiss Alps... that is where I must go. That is where I can test if I have regained my life. I hope you can understand."

JeanClaude sat quietly, obviously thinking.

Then he said, "We might be able to take advantage of your 'death/disappearance'."

As we finished our drinks, JeanClaude said, "I've got to summarize to Will Clendenon. If he is happy, he will contact you shortly. If not, I will call you."

***

Real Life

The next morning I got a call from Will, he was in the lobby and asked me to meet him there. Before Will said anything, we found a quiet place, ordered two coffees and sat down. Will began.

"JeanClaude said you are good to go, is that right?"

"Almost."

"Almost?! What are we doing here?"

"Will, it's been two years. A lot of things have changed. The desert has screwed me up. I want to get back into my profession; but I've got to get straight first."

"What do you mean 'get straight'?"

"Two things; first, you and JeanClaude are giving me a fresh start, right? Then second, I'll go see Bree, the lady I left behind in Switzerland. If all goes well, I will live with her."

"How the hell do you think that will work? You have no valid ID and in your own words you are 'skint'. And your career? What about your career? You did well for us during your six years in Yenbo. You will become a farmer? I don't believe it; and what if your lady friend has become impatient over the last two years—what if she has another man? And you have no money?"

"All good questions, Will. The more I think about it... I don't want to live 'off the grid' and if Bree still has eyes for me, I need to take care of her. If she doesn't, I have to take care of myself."

"CJ, if you have a plan, we have a plan. We can work together if you are interested and committed."

This discussion reminded me so much of the first time I met Will eight years ago at the Trump Golf Club in Rancho Palos Verdes California. Wheels were clicking in my head. It was easy for me to say, "I'm in."

Will explained, "We have something going on in Istanbul. It's simple but it's real. It's funded and happening. Not as complex as Yenbo but—international motorway 200 kilometres connecting Asia and Europe through Istanbul on a new bridge over the Bosphorus. The motorway and bridge were designed in the UK. Italian, Turkish and Japanese contractors are already on board."

What I heard was Asia Minor landscape connecting to European landscape over the Bosphorus in Istanbul. That perked me up. I needed to get into something real—something I could build.

"Does that interest you?"

I sat up straight and said, "Yes, but I have so many questions and there must be a catch..."

"Catch? You're damn right!"

I sat back a bit.

He continued, "Despite your well-stated understanding of the Cairo new town project, you still left me out in the cold. That was bullshit! That won't happen again. If you work for us in Istanbul, you must commit until the project is turned over to the Turkish Highway Department. And if you don't, your paid salary will be owed back to us and any new established ID and professional credentials will be invalidated. That is my insurance to get a dependable performance. Are we clear? There is no bartering here."

He was right. He had been straightforward with me in Yenbo. I screwed him in Cairo and he was offering me a fresh chance. I liked the sound of it.

"You have a plan for my identity, my income and my return to the landscape architecture profession?"

"JeanClaude will take care of that. The Istanbul job is already underway and has 24 months remaining duration, the landscaping design and installation is a single line item in the construction contract. You will oversee the repair of the earth

48

surface where the highway and bridge have been built."

"That does interest me; but I have to see that lady in Switzerland first. Can we do that?"

"Okay, listen CJ, you sign this contract for 24 months in Istanbul and I will arrange flight for you, via JeanClaude's office in Vienna, to Switzerland where you can have two weeks. Then you must return to Vienna where JeanClaude will finalize your set up for the Istanbul job."

Will put a single page Memorandum of Agreement (MOA) on the table in front of me. Salary good, living arrangements in Istanbul good—if I sign my life to them for 24 months. Ticked a lot of boxes. Job details seemed to be clearing my head. What a relief to feel clarity, logical thought. I had a question.

"Who am I working for and who is paying me?"

"Analysis Corporation Philadelphia, but you will be assigned to their branch office in Vienna. For this Istanbul project, you will be seconded to an American engineering group. But the real commitment is a man-to-man agreement between you and me. Organize your things the next two days here at the hotel. The day after tomorrow, JeanClaude will meet you and together you will fly to Vienna."

He handed me a pen and I signed the MOA. We stood up and shook hands. I was out of the Sahara now. Thank God.

2-Start Me Up

Flight to Vienna

According to plan, JeanClaude picked me up and we drove to the private jet hangars at the airport. As we took off from Cairo, I looked one more time on the Giza plateau pyramids before they disappeared in the polluted grey haze of the Cairo urban megalopolis. I was finished with that. Finished with the pyramids. Finished with Cairo. Finished with the Disneyland remake—the Middle East edition. Finished with the Sahara and the Pharaonic landscape. But... I had a mental hangover that kept coming and going like drifting sands across my head, my mind, my thoughts. I thought I was clear... but not yet.

Then JeanClaude started. "Did you understand that your Executor closed out your life and published your obituary in Los Angeles? Do you know all that that entails?"

"What?"

"The entire administrative process of your death has been activated and completed about six months ago. Dust in the wind. Your life became dust in the wind."

It hadn't truly settled in. Only last week the realities started to reveal themselves when I tried to use a cancelled credit card. Then Bree...

"Did anyone contact Bree about my 'death'?"

"*Mon ami*, your Executor never contacted her or anyone else in Switzerland; but your obituary was placed in the International Herald Tribune."

I swallowed hard; but I recalled Bree did not read media from the newsstand—and online, she was a real off-the-grid person. That was a relief but overall, I felt cloudy with patchy blue skies. I needed total clarity.

We were over the Med before we reached cruising altitude. Dead and on my way to Vienna? Before I could form the question out loud, JeanClaude pushed me.

"CJ, you have to decide who you are." Then he started chuckling.

"Listen, JeanClaude, I already told you I am moving in the right direction—my interest in design and landscape architecture. After all, I am sitting on this plane with you. And the existential questions? Well, they always exist."

JeanClaude was still smiling.

I said, "But I am troubled about this identity thing, the death thing... how do you suggest we handle it?"

"We need to look at it in detail. We can do that when we get to Vienna. I have plenty of resources in Vienna. Resources aside, you and I have to agree the outline and details of the story so that your re-entry can answer any question."

"Wait a minute, why are we going to Vienna? Istanbul project I know, but why Vienna?"

"I thought you'd never ask. *Mon ami*, you are becoming a MENA (Middle East and North Africa) landscape specialist—Morocco, Saudi Arabia, Egypt—and now if it all works out, Turkey. My friend, the Muslim world has become your second home. In Vienna it is time you learn about other efforts the soldiers of Islam have taken to conquer the Christian West. Have you never heard of the gates of Vienna, the siege of Vienna, the Winged Hussar... and the Ottoman Empire. After all, they all did frequent the landscape of your six-year Saudi Arabian home Yenbo."

I was still having trouble fitting all the puzzle pieces together. But one part was absolutely clear. I no longer had financial resources. I hadn't ever been like that. I was raised to be responsible and work to earn what I needed to live on. That was the price I paid—off the grid for a year. My failed search for the Pharaonic landscape. What did I get? Sand in my shoes. The penny dropped—I must work. I shared this with JeanClaude.

He said, "Now you are making sense."

JeanClaude, looking at me with relief, then continued, "I have people in Vienna who have decades of experience in witness protection schemes. They'll take care of you. But we need to work out quite a few details. I think you probably remember Eileen—she has been tracking your Executor and his efforts with your Amsterdam bank accounts, which are empty and closed now. She has also monitored his communications regarding your 'death' and obituary with your parents and the public at large..."

The death details finally started sinking in. I was shocked. Didn't know what to say.

JeanClaude filled the gap, saying, "We'll be in Vienna in 15 minutes. We'll set up and then sit, have something to eat and drink then we can go over those personal details. Rest assured, *mon ami*, I will make sure your professional career can move forward without hiccough."

***

New ID

As our flight descended, I looked at Austria for the first time. Coming from the Egyptian desert and the Cairo megalopolis, I saw, as far as the eye could see, what I had subconsciously been yearning for, the fresh greens of spring. That was a simple comfort to my soul. I really needed it. And lower over Vienna from the sky I was struck by the incredible varieties of green textures in the landscape, the Danube River and the orderliness of the city, its clearly hierarchical system of freeways, highways, roads.

We touched down north of Vienna. According to the name on the control tower, we landed at Brumowski Air Base. The plane pulled right into a hangar which had about six other small private jets parked. Just outside of the airplane hangar, we were met by a driver and his black Suburban —like a private taxi, smooth and orderly.

Our half-hour drive into the heart of town was just as smooth and orderly. We were dropped off at the Hotel Steigenberger. Six stories tall. JeanClaude booked us into two single rooms on the third floor.

My smallish room had an old-fashioned double bed and, I was happy to see, its own private balcony. I walked out on it and looked up and down the street. Every building had beautiful architectural detailing, the sign of successful business and long-term commitment. I felt myself clearing.

This urban setting was free from that Cairene hallmark— vehicular horn noise. And there was no Saharan dust, no Saharan aura. With every breath, I felt the presence of moisture, water and plants. Freedom was re-birthing from somewhere inside me.

JeanClaude called my room to suggest we take a walk while the afternoon sun glorified the setting. As we stepped out on the street, he said, "I know a nice coffee house five minutes from here. This is Vienna—one of my favourite European towns, only behind Istanbul—but that's for later. We're going to the Café Central."

At the hotel, I had picked up a map of the *Innere Stadt*. The entire area looked to be about two square kilometres. Service vehicular access only throughout most of it but it had a core structure of pedestrian-only streets. This place was clean and, from what I could see, without graffiti and without donkeys, camels or cats. Lots of people walking but no pushing or shoving.

Slowly but surely the Vienna urban scene revitalized my memories of Zurich. I said to myself I needed to find some free time to try out the tram and subway system. My thinking... my professional observations had returned. A healthy sign.

JeanClaude and I walked about two blocks until he pointed to the main entry to the Café Central. As we entered I sensed a businesslike atmosphere and also a quietness.

I saw directly in front of us a display case of pastries the likes of which I had not seen ever, not Cairo, not Zurich. These were mini cakes, fancy "cup cakes", but each formed and decorated as individual works of art. I was hungry but these looked all too rich for me.

My time in the Pharaonic landscape had encouraged austerity. And that may have been the only positive. Austerity had given me strength, discipline. Although the café was busy, there were plenty of free tables for two. JeanClaude chose one that had a modicum of privacy and a good perspective over the entire scene.

The café interior had a very high ceiling and multiple arches that made me recall two rich architectural memories. Interior arches reminded me of pictures I had seen of the beautifully proportioned structural arches by the Turkish architect, Sinan. And the light quality inside this café was reminiscent of the light quality inside Egyptian *hamams*, bath houses I had visited. The feeling was solid, stable and uplifting. A great social node and I hadn't even sampled their coffee yet.

JeanClaude asked me what I would like. I asked for something simple without sugar.

Mid-morning in the café and I heard background music that was both powerful and soothing. When I mentioned it to JeanClaude, he said, with a look of surprise, "Don't you recognize Mahler? That's his second symphony—kismet if there ever was. You know it? He called it 'Resurrection'. And that is what we are here to do. Resurrect your ID and make your future."

I said nothing; but the music had emotional intensity that struck chords deep inside me. I felt it in my heart. It was cleansing me. Cleansing... more like an emotional revitalization in progress.

After we sat down, JeanClaude ordered espresso and a croissant and I, too, ordered a croissant but with coffee. At which point he began, "Croissants and Vienna? Have you been wondering why here is important?"

I didn't say anything. The background music was strong.

After pausing for a moment, JeanClaude began, "CJ, we have to get down to business. You want to work again. Let's look carefully at where you are and where you must go. I'm talking about your identity and the people who think you are dead."

I shook myself free from the music and just listened to JeanClaude's description of how I could recover.

"Here's what we know. Your Amsterdam bank people notified your parents and US tax offices. All of your Social Security has been zeroed out. Your passport name and number, driver's license, Social Security Number, birth certificate et al need to be redone. Your Executor thinks you're dead—but he's not convinced—he thinks you may be on walkabout or gone deep undercover. That reminds me—deep undercover—that's an option that can work in your and our, Analysis Corporation's favour on upcoming work. Are you following?"

I still listened—this was all unknown territory for me; but I had confidence in JeanClaude when he said I could continue my professional career without hiccough. But I wondered... and I asked, "What about my name and Bree? Can I still be CJ?"

"You can be called CJ but you will not be Christopher Janus. Maybe we can do something like Mr. Charles Jacobs? That's our starting point. What do you think?"

"I have no objection now. Keeping my nickname and relating it to my legal name make sense. Will your people set up my state and national professional credentials?"

"They'll take care of it all—birth certificate, social security, passport, driver's license, voter registration, banking accounts, credit cards. Don't worry, CJ. If you agree to Charles Jacobs..." he wrote it out, "...then we can get started right now. It will take a couple days, but everything will be in place before you go to Switzerland."

"I'm in. Let's do it." I let my confidence in JeanClaude guide my decision. Honestly, I had spent too much time in the Sahara. My brain was still as slow as shifting dunes.

"Listen, CJ, it is up to you how to tell Bree and your Executor, Kurt. There is no hurry. Are you good with that, *mon ami?*"

I answered JeanClaude's question. "Yeah, sure, I can work that out." I may have sounded confident, but... I wasn't at all sure how I would talk to them—Bree very soon (if she and I are still on), Kurt in a longer timeframe.

"Wait here at our table while I step outside to get my people started. I'll be back in five minutes. On my return, we'll talk more and have another espresso."

***

New Job

When JeanClaude returned, he immediately continued.

"You wondered about Vienna? Like the Bosphorus is a classic Europe vs Asia geography, Vienna is a classic Islam vs Christendom city. The Ottomans lusted after it but could never take it. And one of the many stories about why croissants did not originate in France but here in Vienna references the 16th century Ottoman siege of Vienna. The story has an ironic twist—each time a Viennese takes a bite of that croissant, that crescent moon shape, they relish once again their victory over Islam."

"Ironic?"

"Oh, there are many croissant stories but that one always pleases when I tell it. Now, let's work on your legal and professional details. Before I finalize details on your new identity papers as MENA Senior International Analyst on landscape infrastructure, I should tell you more details about the job upcoming in Istanbul. As Will probably briefed you, it is an intriguing opportunity, but not for every landscape architect."

I was interested. Slowly but surely escaping from the Sahara, I felt I was being drawn into the real world again. It felt good.

JeanClaude said, "You will be landscape construction manager on this huge international construction project, already let. Along with the new bridge over the Bosphorus, 100km of motorway is in Asia and 100km is in Europe. The construction is complex, covering many different ecotypes, bridges, viaducts, tunnels, interchanges, rest areas, etc. It is a massive joint venture. What do you think so far?"

"Connecting Asia and Europe over the Bosphorus—sounds a landscape challenge. I'm in. I need work."

"Good. But here is the unusual bit. The highway design is complete and the construction contract is let, like I said. But the planting was not designed. All the engineering was completed, but not the planting. What you will see in the measurement and payment clauses are four planting items. Makes for interesting run-on paragraphs. Design, provide and plant coniferous trees, deciduous trees, shrubs, and grasses. Additionally in each description is a thick paragraph which includes maintenance and everything but the kitchen sink."

JeanClaude chuckled. He said, "There is your real-world challenge. *As tu faim*? Are you hungry for that kind of challenge?"

Big job with only four paragraphs of specs. I could feel my game face coming on.

I said, "That is a world class site covering two continents. I do have hunger."

"Glad to hear that! Any questions?"

"Timeframe?"

"Your work starts in six weeks, runs for 24 months."

"JeanClaude, what about salary? I have nothing in the bank or anywhere."

"So, you are 'on board'?"

"Yeah, you can say that... half of my uncertainties are clear. And you know I already have signed an MOA with Will. I like that Istanbul set up... but... I am not whole yet."

"What are you saying?"

"Like I told you and Will before—I still feel emotionally crashed... disconnected... I only have one choice. I need to go see my lady friend in Grindelwald. And I don't even know if she is still there."

"Can you call or email?"

"No, she was always off-the-grid... besides I have to see her... eye to eye... it is a big unknown... something happened in the Western Desert, the Great Sand Sea, in the Pharaonic landscape... like I was dissected emotionally and had parts removed."

"In the game? *Mon ami,* I thought you were..."

"I'm healing. When I saw you first last week in Cairo, I didn't think I any longer had professional legs; but this time with you and here in Vienna, plus the Istanbul project discussions, have given me hope. I feel my professional legs coming back; but like I said, my emotions also need to recover."

We spent the rest of the afternoon at our table in the Café Central, going over details. Before leaving, we ate dinner, wiener schnitzel and potatoes followed by apfelstrudel. JeanClaude covered the bill and gave me 500 Euros for my pin money while in Vienna.

Walking back, the evening urban scene was dramatic. Every building had lights highlighting the well-crafted Baroque and Rococo details. I was enthralled with the beauty. And it was quiet. Arriving back at the hotel, we agreed to meet the next morning in the hotel rooftop breakfast room at 8AM.

We shared breakfast the next day on the roof overlooking the Viennese skyline. Grit, human urban texture, such a rich reality. I was reaching for the grit to get back my life from what was taken away in Egypt.

***

Priorities

At breakfast I ate light—only orange juice, coffee and croissant. JeanClaude briefed me about the project timeline. I looked out over the Vienna skyline. This landscape had a history that I could access and measure, that I could understand. It had texture, grit and a communicable visual history.

What I was looking at was diametrically opposed to the Pharaonic landscape. That desert landscape had its own history. But its history didn't let me in. I tried. Its history demanded surrender of thoughts, minds... in exchange for... what? Existential peace? Eternal happiness? That never happened. I was starting to feel that the time I spent on that Pharaonic landscape quest was... wasted.

JeanClaude interrupted my thoughts. He said, "I heard from my people about your new documents. They are moving ahead. This morning you and I should go to the Apple store and get you back in the digital world again."

We went back to our rooms for a half hour to get ready. While there, I grabbed my hotel-supplied tourist map of Vienna. I found an Alpine Garden in the Belvedere district. Alpine Garden? On the Danube? I thought of Bree. She had her own Alpine garden—in the Alps. I wondered if this Vienna Alpine Garden would feel at all like Bree's garden.

I needed to get a *tageskarte* to use the subways and trams to get me to the Alpine Garden. And the Apple store? I needed to make a list of things to do.

The modern world—so much to do—so much to think about.

MacBook Pro and iPhone in tow, we went back to the hotel. JeanClaude was going to set them up with project-specific software, an international business connectivity plan and return them to me when the ID documents were completed. I had the afternoon free. I sighed. Needed quiet time—it was all moving too fast. Off to the Alpine Garden. I expected quiet and peaceful inspiration. The garden was toward the edge of town.

When I arrived at the Belvedere stop, I saw my first graffiti tags and small groups of MENA guys—reminded me of modern Morocco and Egypt— hanging around here and there outside small storefront bakal-type stores. Young men with nothing to do? Vagrants? Graffiti tags? Unsettling it was.

The Alpine Garden was close. Entry fee. Few people inside. Interpretive signage everywhere. Quiet. No vagrants. No tags. But when I sat down on a bench to try to absorb the plants, it didn't happen.

Not even a hint of Bree's Alpine garden. I thought the only true Alpine garden can only be in the Alps. This transplant thing did not speak. Like reading a dictionary. Something was missing. I had to go back to Grindelwald. But I wondered what was missing. Plants? Topography? The Alps themselves? Bree?

Bree. Bree was missing. I left her two years ago. Her haybarn, her garden, her intimacy with plants. She offered herself to me and I walked away on my Pharaonic landscape quest. I hoped that I had not made the largest mistake of my life. Yeah, I needed to go back to Grindelwald, to Bree and her Alpine garden.

My thoughts of Bree? Missing her? My feelings for her, real or imagined? And where was she? Where were her feelings? I was dreaming about two-year-old memories. They felt real, but...

A couple days later, JeanClaude asked me into his room. He gave me my new ID documents and my digital connectivity tools. I was still CJ but now Charles Jacobs. I felt like nothing had changed. Inside I was the same. And my documents? Paper. Bureaucracy. Control. My mind was running on about freedom and loss of freedom. JeanClaude's voice interrupted.

He was serious. He said, "Now, *mon ami*, what are you to do? We have about five weeks till you begin in Istanbul."

I said, "I've got to return to Grindelwald. I have something still missing. I am not yet whole. My time with you here in Vienna has been a boot-camp for my previously atrophied professional interests. That was important. The Sahara had drained my professional nous. I was empty and I didn't care. That professional emptiness has been refilled."

JeanClaude said, "Grindelwald for that girl? There are lots of girls here in Vienna. And I could use your support. I do wonder if you are trying to square a circle."

I said, "I've had my fill of 'bought girls'. They do not fill my void. Grindelwald is about plants and people... and the girl, she may or may not still be there; but she and I had a thing... ethnobotany and sex. She gave me an emotional fullness and satisfaction that I had for too long been without... since New Mexico..."

JeanClaude said, "You have to do what you must, *mon ami.*"

I felt relief from those words. But I had questions. "Will these documents give me access to funds?"

"Not fully. Not until the Istanbul project begins. In the meantime, you will be on retainer. The retainer will be 2,500CHF per month. I'm sure you will use it wisely. You can withdraw that from the Raiffeisen cash machines. They are all over Switzerland. Do not accumulate debt. And do not charge anything. I will contact you a week or ten days before you are due in Istanbul. Now, get out of here. You are on your own."

I felt freedom. We smiled, shook hands and hugged.

Back in my room I tried to get into my new digital kit— not a problem. I did research on Istanbul—had to—needed to strengthen my professional roots. After a couple hours online, I figured it was time to go to the emotional roots that felt so damaged by my time in the Sahara. Emotions unclear—mirage or real? I had to find out.

I arranged to take the Railjet from Vienna to Zurich the next morning. There was free Wi-Fi on the train, so I made a reservation for one night in Zurich at the Seidenhof, across the street from the Hiltl Veg restaurant. Yeah, my memory was returning and I needed a good veg meal. Hiltl was the place.

Train arrived around 13:00 in Zurich Hauptbahnhof. Five-minute walk to the Seidenhof. Checked in, stowed my stuff and crossed the street for *mittagessen*.

When I got back to the hotel I was bushed. Showered and took rest. With the anxiety of my upcoming search for Bree, I tossed and turned all night.

At 6AM, after not enough sleep, I thought I might as well get up. Checked out and got the train via Bern and Interlaken to Grindelwald. Sat in the snack car. Ate a simple muesli and coffee breakfast and watched the show.

The show? My procession from the flatlands of Bern into the Berner Overland, past the 15km long Thunersee, narrow and bordered by forested mountains and small lakeside villages. Then finally into the Jungfrau Region. And a show of beauty it was. I recalled the first time I rode this train how this landscape had inspired, fired up my design thoughts. I could feel my insides coming alive. This landscape was still special.

It had been more than two years since I departed this region for my job in Cairo. And this time, I really felt like I was coming home—the landscape was that strong in me.

At Interlaken I could see the snowcapped Jungfrau looming overall and beautifully smiling at the head of the Lauterbrunnen Valley. I changed trains at Interlaken Ost. Then the train from Interlaken to Grindelwald twisted and turned going uphill. It took me first through dense dark mountain forests, then along a river roiling with rapids, and finally to open on the broad Grindelwald bowl, filled with grassy pastures at the foot of Eiger. Such a water-rich landscape. Oh, that made me feel good.

But I had worries. Bree. Was she still in Grindelwald, in her haybarn? Would she feel for me as she did two years ago? I wasn't sure. I was nervous. I didn't want to think about it. I held on tightly to a simple hope for a good result.

And might I find the answer to the emptiness that overtook me in the Pharaonic landscape? I had hoped for so much—music, desert, ancient history, minimalist components—I had been sure I would find a result. Such a disappointment it was. I shielded my thoughts from further potential disappointments, but... questions and uncertainties.

***

Blumisalp Stubbe

On the ground in Switzerland—year-round land of water, fertile soil and robust vegetation. My train to Zurich and connecting trains to Grindelwald told me that same story of richesse over and over—healthy green, rich soil and plentiful water.

When the train reached its terminus at the Grindelwald bahnhof, I was at the centre of the Grindelwald valley. I found myself once again in the court of the kings, the three mountains, Eiger, Shreckhorn and Wetterhorn. They dominated the foreground. They dominated the town.

They were kings in the landscape. Regal—not an overstatement. Viewing them from the Grindelwald bahnhof, I felt their majesty. I took a deep breath, once, twice, three times. Their energy enlivened me.

Now I had to confront my uncertainties. Not just uncertainties but my unsteady, fragile emotions. The Sahara had ripped me apart. It dislodged all my professional and personal roots.

My professional recovery was well underway... but my personal, my emotional... a void, not even a hint of recovery. In my valuable, eye-opening time with Bree before Egypt, I, for the first time in decades, had felt an emotional rejuvenation—a healing. But the Sahara desiccated those fresh shoots of hope.

Now it has been two years since Bree showed me cause for emotional hope. Is she still here? Does she remember me? Has she kept me in her heart? Or has she followed her own way, the way of the wind, the way of nature? These thoughts, worries,

68

unknowns, anxieties swirled through my head as I walked from the train station into the shopping and tourist centre of Grindelwald. Dizzy. I was dizzy with both fear and hope.

It was early afternoon. I had a 15-minute walk up Grindelwald main street. With each step I felt an increase in uncertainty and dread. Every step was more difficult than the last. My feet were heavy and my legs were stiff. My breathing was shallow. And my thoughts? Bree had to be there. I was glad to feel the strength of my emotional ties to her; but they were also the source of my most anxious thought. 15 minutes? Felt like two hours to reach what I had learned a couple years ago was the unofficial centre of local information, the Blumisalp Stubbe.

The stubbe had a terrace opening onto the Gletscherschlucht— the gap between the Eiger and the Shreckhorn where glaciers regularly advance and recede every couple hundred years. I paused on the terrace.

As I looked across the valley, I saw it was a steep-walled rock canyon with a raging river of glacial and snow melt. The glaciers are in their recessive mode—that is where I hiked a couple years ago with the Scottish guy. I couldn't stop myself from examining the high alpine forests, cliffs, snow, and glaciers beneath a dark blue sky. Such an impressive—imposing landscape. Finally I turned around.

I turned around and saw a couple groups of people eating lunch on the terrace. Made me hungry. Anything to distract from the emotional worry that was still bubbling inside me.

I went indoors. The place was quietly busy. Lunch time. One lady was serving and bussing tables. Maybe 8 tables and another 8-10 seats in the back at a bar. I looked hard back in toward the bar... and yes... the barkeep was the same French lady who had been so helpful to me the first time I visited two years ago.

I walked up to the bar. She was busy. She hardly looked up when she asked me if she could help.

I asked, "Do you have that local fresh mountain cheese... what is it called?"

She heard my English and looked at my face carefully. She said, "*Muetschli?* Is that what you want... wait a minute... you look too familiar... I know you... CJ! Where have you been? It's been years!"

I remembered her name. "Suzie, such a pleasure to see you again. You are looking fit and happy. Yeah, I'd like a *muetschli* sandwich and a half litre of the unfiltered beer... Zwickel, if I remember... you still have it on tap?"

"*Bien sur*! Just opened a fresh keg yesterday. Sit in that seat at the end of the bar and as soon as the crowd goes back to work, I'll come over. I'd love to hear what you've been doing."

She brought my sandwich and beer. The Zwickel and *muetschli* were local landscape products. Simple. I dug in. Filling my stomach pushed aside the emotional uncertainties of Bree and her haybarn. But not for long.

***

Hope and Fear

Shortly after 14:00 hours, the Stubbe became very quiet. The lunch crowd had finished and returned to work. Suzie came over and sat next to me.

"I've got some time now, my help is cleaning up. Tell me, how are you?" she said.

For me, during lunch, fully absorbed in local cheese and local beer, I had begun feeling I was in a refreshing dreamland—that Egypt, that fruitless search for the Pharaonic landscape never happened. Then she asked that question.

"What have you been doing?"

Shook me out of dreamland. I thought before I answered. Memories returned.

"Suzie, I've just had a massive, a big-time adventure."

"Tell me."

"I've been on a quest in Egypt. It began when you lent me a book—that collection of short stories by Algernon Blackwood..."

"I still have that book."

"Okay, Blackwood wrote one story that fascinated me more than the others—*Descent into Egypt*. Okay, stories are stories and fiction is fiction; but hardly had I read it when I was offered a job in Egypt, remember?"

"Definitely. I was sad the day you left."

"Well, I've been down in Egypt ever since I left here. For two years I have been in the Sahara, looking for something in the landscape..."

"Looking for something in the landscape? Artifacts? Gold?

What?"

"No, no, no... nothing quite so material—it's actually quite complicated... so let me try to summarize."

"I'm listening."

"Remember when I first came here two years ago, how mesmerized I was with the Eiger, Shreckhorn, Wetterhorn, the entire Jungfrau Region landscape?"

"How could I forget?"

"Then you went out of your way to introduce me to local people who also had been entranced by the Jungfrau Region landscape."

"*Bien sur*, how could I forget. Those were exciting days."

"Well, as I got to know the music and the country people of Egypt, I thought I was discovering something timeless about the landscape there... but the longer I looked... the more the landscape asked me to give up my past. It got horrible. If I say I was becoming 'zombie' you will laugh."

"Tell me more."

"Here is the difference that is important. The Jungfrau Region landscape enlivened me. It made me want to work, to explore, to grow... we were on that same page, weren't we?"

"*Sans doute.*"

"Well, the Egyptian landscape, I call it the Pharaonic landscape, was extinguishing that fire. But the worst was that it was magnetizing me. It was pulling me to someplace that... meaninglessness... eternity..."

I couldn't find more words. I went silent. Then I remembered the bells.

"Then I started to hear from the back of my mind the softest tinkling of bells—something like the goats wear here but softer still. That sound reminded me of the very things that meant the most to me. The things that the Pharaonic landscape was trying to erase. So, here I am. And am I glad to be back in Grindelwald. Can you refill my Zwickel? How was it that you guys say, *Noch ein mal?*"

"Sure thing, CJ. Glad you made it back alive. That is a tourist story like I've never heard. Let me get your beer."

She brought my beer over with a mystified look on her face.

She asked, "So what might you be doing here, now?"

"I'm filling my lungs with mountain air." And now the emotions started welling up inside, I couldn't restrain myself any longer. I had to ask, "Is Bree still around?"

"Bree? That wild redhead?"

"Yeah, that one. She still stopping in once a month?"

"No."

For a moment that seemed like an eternity, my heart stopped. Then Suzie continued, "About a year ago she stopped visiting here. Haven't seen her since. But now that you ask, a gardener from the church cemetery told me that a red-haired lady had been regularly hanging around the cemetery. He comes in here every afternoon about 15:30. If you wait, I'll introduce you when he comes in."

I was relieved and excited to hear that Bree was likely still around. I turned down the offer, finished my beer, and told Suzie I'd be back. I headed up to the church. My heart was beating fast. My thoughts were a blur of heightened anticipation. I felt like running. But, as I got closer to the church, worries started. What if this? What if that? What if it's not Bree? And if it is, what if she has changed?

My enthusiasm was washed away by a flood of worries. I slowed down for a moment. Then I brushed them, those strange mental hurdles, aside and kept moving.

The cemetery was a place I liked the first time I visited Grindelwald. Right next to the church, it was a place that tourists bypassed. It was a place that gave spectacular views of the Shreckhorn and the Wetterhorn. It had gravestones respecting people of the mountains.

After the 10-minute uphill walk I arrived at the church. The cemetery was on the downhill side away from main street. I entered the gate. Looked around and found no one sitting on the wood benches in the sun along the edge of the church. I came to the central path leading down to the lower section. Nobody at all down there.

I went into the church—nobody there. Disappointment hitting me like an avalanche, a rockfall.

Then I walked around the outer far side of the church past

the mountain climber death gravestones. Just past them, I saw on a secluded bench, one person with a knitted Rastafarian hat. My heart started beating fast. It was pumping. Would the words come out? No more thinking.

I called out, "Bree??"

She stood up and looked my way. We moved toward each other.

***

Bree

Bree's first words, "I've been waiting for you."

"What?"

"I've been waiting for you. I knew you'd come back."

I was speechless.

She continued, "All the flowers you planted in the garden died after you went away—only deep magic and ancient wisdom survived."

I looked at her for the longest moment. I saw truth in her eyes. Was this the answer to my uncertainties? What to do? I finally got some words out. I motioned to the bench and said, "Please sit."

"I knew you were in trouble. About a year ago I felt it. You know me. My life with plants has had little to do with the Christian church; but my feelings of your danger brought me here. I meditated and surrendered to God, a second baptism of sorts. That was logical.

"How else could I communicate with you? And it has worked. Here you are. And if my eyes are true, you are alright. You are healthy. I've been waiting for you. I've been saving myself for you. Where are you staying? I don't care, you're coming with me back to my haybarn. We have lots to catch up on."

Her words and her emotions communicated so deeply in me. I heard in her the—oh it is so mundane but it is so deep... I felt the emotion of Puccini's enchanting Italian soprano aria, "One fine day we'll see" from Madame Butterfly but with a happy ending. Breathless, I was breathless. My heart was alive.

I felt it all. I was happy. She took my hand and we began walking toward *Grosse Scheidegg* and her haybarn.

She said, "As we walk, tell me where you have been. How did you get back? And why? Though I think I know why."

If I remembered correctly, we had a 45-minute walk ahead of us. The afternoon sun was beginning to set. The fullness and greenness of all plants, grasses, trees and shrubs overwhelmed me. Fullness. Richesse of water. Far from the Sahara, I felt... heaven. And I was walking with Bree who wanted to be with me. I felt full, refreshed. This was everything my good thoughts hoped it would be.

She set a good pace as we walked single file up a narrow stoney path. We stopped two or three times to catch our breaths and take in the sunset all around us. Each time we stopped she took my hand and pulled me close to kiss me on the cheek. Her hair reminded me of a warm safe place. That is where I was. My emotional comfort? Alive—softness beyond words.

Her kisses? Her kisses on my cheek were bouncy and light but packed with energy. Hard-wired energy transfers. They felt so full of her energy. And me, I was hungry for that energy. It was what I had been missing. My emotions were beaming, dancing.

By the time we reached her haybarn, we were both heavily sweating. So, we showered and I will leave the rest of the details of that night to imagination.

We didn't talk much that night. But the next morning we were relaxed and comfortable wrapped up next to each other. I gave her a kiss. She was awake. Then a strange memory arrived. I had to share it with her.

I whispered, "On Christmas Eves, when I was a kid I used to lie ever so still hoping to hear the bells of Santa's sleigh—never heard them—always a disappointment. But as we walked up here last night, around all the different pastures, cows, sheep and goats, I heard those bells... and I felt a childlike pleasure, a childlike happiness that resonated deeper than my childhood dreams. I felt a fulfilment I had been missing. And that is how I feel this morning."

I kissed her again. She hugged me, held me tight and returned the kiss. In our shared warmth, without words, we bonded.

***

Talking Design

A man of words and not of deeds
Is like a garden full of weeds...
-Percy Green

The sun was already brightening the eastern horizon. Both of us were spent. But sunrise in these mountains energized the new day for us. I felt I was in a new world. A new world with things to see and do together with Bree. The sexual and emotional excitement of the night before gave way to clear-headed talks.

So much went on between us in the following days. We were growing our relationship. I felt good that I still had emotional bonds. More than growing our relationship, I felt my emotional bonds to Bree strengthening. That they were strengthening? All the better. The Sahara had not obliterated them. We easily grew closer. But not without a lot of to-ing and fro-ing. Some of the incidents of importance I recall.

She asked, "What the hell were you doing?"

I had told that story so many different ways depending on my audience the last few weeks. But now... I let everything out. I let it flow—the logic, the lack of logic, the emotions. Everything flowed, not from my head, but without restraint from my heart.

We sat outdoors, in the shade of one of her apple trees. The sky was clear. The sun was warm, not hot. And the whole broad bowl of the expansive Grindelwald Valley opened in front of us. I was at ease. I began.

"It was always about design."

She looked surprised but understanding as a close friend and lover would. "Tell me the whole story."

"As a landscape architect, design has been my life. Morocco, Los Angeles, Saudi Arabia, Egypt, here. Here in this Jungfrau Region, I felt the first time there was something essential to be learned from this landscape. Some essence of design.

"Here the landscape was beautiful, entrancing. Here it had been managed for centuries by humans. Here the humans sang to it. They treated it with common sense and reverence. So..." I paused for a minute and looked deeply into her eyes. I saw reflected back at me a deep affection, love so strong that I almost lost track of my story.

"Keep talking," she said.

"So, Egypt. There too was a unique ancient landscape that supported a population of humans over millennia—music and power. I had to look—the Nile, the Sahara. I had to find if the same essence that I found here was in that Pharaonic landscape. I went with hope, with excitement. But everything I explored disappointed me. I never experienced the deep pleasure that this Jungfrau Region landscape gives me. Here I don't have to try to find it. This landscape exudes it. And the Pharaonic landscape? Exudes nothing but the void of emptiness and the pulse-beat of commercial tourism. I have been so pleased to return here and to find you."

"But what is this design quest you always talk about? Is that over now?"

She sounded interested. I continued.

"Design is the conceptual core of my landscape architecture profession. Every landscape architect deals with it—has an approach to it. I found landscapes to be so innately powerful—a drug of good feeling for humans—that I wanted to understand how I could build that into my design work. Thus the quest. And thus the impact of the Jungfrau Region as well as my approach to planting design—rooms and sequences of rooms with a goal to bring the garden visitor to the effulgent bliss accessible through sensual interaction with plants.

"Plant design aside, I was psyched to get to Egypt to see if there was a common thread shared by the Pharaonic landscape with the Jungfrau Region landscape."

Then Bree added, "If I understand, tell me if I'm wrong. You have had effulgent, or transcendental experiences with plants and the Jungfrau Region landscape; and you want to design to provide the same experiences for others? Am I right?"

"Yes, that's a pretty good summary."

"Well, you and I have both shared these types of experiences. And to me that is such an important thing to have in common. Downright unusual. I love that we share those experiences." She took my hand in hers to emphasize what she said. I loved the look in her eyes. It stimulated me so very deeply. But then she went on.

"I think those feelings are so much dependent on the individual. Just like some people who come to the Jungfrau Region as tourists just to visit Jungfraujoch or just to base-jump the Lauterbrunnen Valley. They are here for material things. Not for transcendent effulgent glories.

"I work with plants every day in my garden and a day does not go by without effulgent experiences with those plants. That is personal. I think that you're trying to find a way to design, to arrange things in the landscape to bring effulgent experiences to visitors... tilting at windmills... you, in less kind words... are taking the role of the almighty—saying you can arrange for effulgent glories—might that be hubris? Stop searching for the 'snark' and stay here with me in this little garden, in this glorious landscape. Let us live, work and enjoy together what we are blessed with. There is one more saying that crosses my mind—you can lead a horse to water but you can't make him drink."

As her words settled in, some clouds that had just billowed up, as they do in these mountains, generated a few drops of rain and a clap of thunder. More were on the horizon. We moved to a bench under the one-metre-wide overhanging roof of her haybarn. My thoughts were occupied with what she had just said. Chasing the snark? Had I been chasing that snark since Tangier, for more than two decades?

***

What's Next

A room without books,

is like a body without a soul.

-Cicero

I could see, further down the valley, heavier rain coming our way; but for now the wide overhang easily protected us. It was one of the features of traditional Berner Oberland house and barn building—substantial roof overhang on all four sides, providing sheltered work/storage area.

The weather was changing. The wind chased away all heat. Cool breezes filled the air. Bree was working with some recently picked flowers. I went inside the haybarn to look around.

For the moment I put aside my design thoughts. It had been two years since I was last here. I wondered about our future. I wondered about Bree's last two years and before. And as I crossed the haybarn threshold, I wondered what the inside of her haybarn in the light of day—last night we had only one thing on our minds—might tell me about her. I slowly looked around.

Most noticeable were large jars, some clay, many transparent glass, everywhere, on the table, on the floor, on the broad windowsills—everywhere. Then I saw plants drying, hanging from the ceiling. And every spare space on her table was covered with parts of plants. I had entered her plant world— never before had it been so obvious. It looked like fun. It was my pleasure. She was doing things with plants that I had never heard about in university landscape architecture classes. Her outdoors and her indoors—all plants.

I shook myself and forced myself to see beyond the plants. She had a variety of bookshelves around the perimeter of her place. On one shelf, I discovered a couple Carl Gustav Jung books. I recalled Jung—I had some history. I liked his ideas of archetypes and the landscape. And Vrndadevi in Ban Muang (*Yenbo Palms*) told me about how Jung looked at both Eastern and Western approaches to spiritual life, the outer vs the inner landscape, the lower vs the higher self and the purpose of life. As I was holding one of Jung's books, recalling my past encounters with Jung, Bree stuck her head in and asked, "You've read Jung?"

"Not in depth but..."

"How so?"

"Well, he gets into the inner/outer of spirituality and I'm always stuck on what to call my landscape portal experiences—paranormal, effulgent glories or the answers to existential unknowns... all inputs coming from nature, its landscapes and plants..."

"I have listened a lot to your talk on portals and their inner/outer linkage. On that subject and Jung, I think it just might be the world of emotions, dreams and imagination. Don't you find it our invisible world? Do not each of us as we carry blood throughout our bodies, we also carry emotions, dreams and imagination—but these? Invisible yet powerful. Perhaps instead of a ride on hubris or megalomania, you could be riding on imagination or some unknown mix of emotions and dreams?"

"Interesting take, Bree. But I can't dream up in my imagination the feelings I have gotten from certain plants and this landscape. And what about those feelings you get from your plants? And those feelings you had, long ago, on the edge of the Sahara?"

"We should spend some time exploring that together; but now before the heavy rains begin I have a couple chores to finish outside."

She ducked back out. I put up the Jung book and continued

exploring her bookshelves. I saw something strange. Something I'd never read or even heard of. There were a number of issues of *Fullmetal Alchemist*. They were comic books. But alchemy always interested me and definitely was part of her life.

As I was flipping through one, she came back in and said, "It's too windy and rainy to work outside. I see you paging through one of my *Fullmetal Alchemist*, do you see anything that interests you? What do you think about them?"

I said, "They look in style like Manga; but I have never gotten into Manga—what about you—you like these stories—what interests you? The alchemy or the fullmetal?"

"I am intrigued by a modern society where alchemy is respected and revered."

"But is there a story line in that series?"

"Young protagonist brothers have lost their mother—she died... and they are trying to bring her back."

"Does it have any special meaning for you?"

Bree paused for the longest while... before saying, "I lost my mom when I was young."

"And..."

"I don't usually talk about it, but it does rest inside me. The story, *Fullmetal Alchemist* does involve a quest for the 'philosopher's stone'."

I quickly said, "Philosopher's stone? That came up in some talks I had in Saudi Arabia..." I paused thinking the loss of her mother was more important than any chat about the philosopher's stone.

I was surprised and understanding about Bree's loss of her mother. Because of the loss of my wife and kids in New Mexico I could understand the long-term internal lingering. Out of respect I did not ask any further question at the time. But over the next days the subject returned and she told the whole story—absentee dad, an Army Ranger from Viet Nam war era, never been in the picture and mom so broken up that she just shrivelled up inside and outside—shrivelled away—that's how Bree described it. But Bree was not going to shrivel, she was attacking life on her own terms. That's what she said and I liked it.

Bree and I had so many interests in common. "Alchemy and deities..." I said.

"What do humans search for that they can't obviously find in their day-to-day material life—their dream life—their imagined life?"

"A special fullness..." said Bree. She paused looking into my eyes.

Then she continued, "A special fullness that comes from following one's own internal path. We can take instruction from other people, other books, other religions... but inside is where the truth, the fullness is found. And that brings me back to you, CJ. You have felt that internal fullness, haven't you? Plants and landscape? Yes? Well, why continue searching? Continue running? God has been kind to you. Maybe it is time to simplify your life."

I had to chew on that. Then I said, "I have to work. I have to earn money to live—to come here..."

"I'm glad you brought that up—I need to clear some of the air on that. Landscape architects? I think they, and maybe you, are like dogs chasing their own tails. Narcissistic. Too focussed on design for design's sake. They don't have a grasp on the multi-generational nature of plants, especially trees!"

That felt like a blow—after all we had already shared about plants, landscape and nature. Worse still, her words reminded me of Tolly and Fyodor's diatribes back in Tangier against landscape architects. I paused, holding back my passion that verged on anger.

"Bree, perhaps your search for perfection springs from the same human well as my design quest. Human life is without perfection, is it not? We each make the best out of the life we have been given—the cards we have been dealt... don't we?"

She was quiet—not quite crestfallen but quiet, maybe humbled, obviously thinking about what I just said. She reached out for me and took me in her arms.

Holding me softly, closely she said, "You are the best I have in my life. I don't want to hurt you. We can agree to work through the rough spots together?"

She looked at me with a tear in her eye. I kissed her and said, "We will work through everything."

***

Next Step

The next day dawned bright and clear. We had gotten through yesterday's emotional clash. Today would be about the hard facts of keeping a roof over our heads.

"What do you do for money? Are you still living off that bequeath or..." I asked.

"Good question. The bequeath is exhausted. I am bartering to live—my plants, my muscles in return for food. It makes sense in the short term as long as there is no political, social or weather disruption. It is kind of old-fashioned."

"Well, I make good money on my international work. I've got a job lined up—maybe we can make a deal? Lots of questions, lots of hurdles... marriage, kids, legal stuff like visas, passports..."

"Marriage? We've already had two of the greatest honeymoons together I could ever dream of... and I could use more of that," she said.

Our eyes met—in the deepest way. All of our chakras were flaming.

"Kids?" I asked.

"Those days are passed. I'm in it only for the pleasures now."

"And the legal stuff... property, accounts, powers of attorney, will?" I asked.

"We should keep everything separate. I'll continue with my local plant alchemy and you with your international landscape architecture—and what is that job you have lined up? Not so important... but what I offer to you, besides our pleasures, is my home here in the haybarn. Make it yours. Are you in?"

"I've been in since we first met here in Grindelwald two years ago. I'm all in; but what about my being here full time—I only have a three-month tourist visa?"

"We can get around that by getting legally married here. I already have my Swiss passport."

"Jobs, what about my jobs? I have to be online. You don't do digital and I live or I should say my jobs live on it. Can I get a connection here?"

"SwissCom is everyone's dependable—that is what they say—but no cable."

"No trouble there."

We worked out the marriage details, including admin difficulties that would require months to solve. Nevertheless, these problems didn't stop us from continuing to consummate our "marriage".

In the next weeks we worked on plants in her garden, discussed the various alchemy books on her shelves and opened a Raiffeisen bank account for me to make monthly wire transfers (only about 10% of my monthly pay), from my job in Istanbul to her. I bought her a used iPhone and set up a SwissCom account so we could either talk or message each other. Setting that up was a bit of a challenge—even though it was an Apple product—it had been more than a year since I dumped my own digital kit into the Nile—but the SwissCom people helped me out. This was also a new world for Bree—she had always been off-the-grid.

On the third week, checking my inbox, I found an email from JeanClaude. He wrote:

Well my friend have your emotions revived? Are they shared by your lady friend? Are we on for Istanbul?

I sat in front of the keyboard for a minute before I wrote:

Yes to all. We are on! What's next?

JeanClaude must have been online because his answer came immediately.

His answer included details regarding my return to Vienna. He had set me up with a US gov't approved G5 flight out of Bern to Vienna. I explained to Bree that I now had details for my 24-month job in Istanbul and had to leave. I explained to her that I would earn vacation time every nine months and she could visit me or I could return to the haybarn for my vacations.

She showed no interest in Istanbul. She reminded me, "My time in Morocco was all I needed—no more. Besides, I have plants to look after."

I agreed to send her a monthly bank draft. We kissed and off I went.

***

Back to Work

I took the train from Grindelwald, changing in Interlaken and Thun, to Belp where Bern located its international airport. To facilitate my passage through passport control and check-in, JeanClaude had given me detailed instructions to arrive at a private hangar away from the main terminal. Like he had in Cairo, he had arranged a flight for me on a G-5 direct to Vienna Austria.

The G-5 touched down outside of Vienna, like before, at Brumowski Air Base where JeanClaude met me. A government driver drove us into downtown Vienna and dropped us at the Hotel Steigenberger.

Along the 20 kilometres to downtown, JeanClaude expanded on the technical scope of the Istanbul job.

"This is a great professional opportunity for you, CJ; but before I start, what happened in Grindelwald?"

I smiled as I told him, "Better than I ever expected. I wasn't sure because two years had passed; but... we are together. My emotions are in place. The Sahara has gone. The Pharaonic landscape has gone. I'm back. The game is on. Oh, there is one thing, if you could help..."

"What do you need *mon ami?*"

"In order to get married, I need a Swiss residence permit for my next entry. Is that doable?"

"I'll look into it. But please remember, your information gathering is not to be shared in the matrimonial. It is the best way to protect loved ones. *Compris?*"

"I follow."

"And I'll look into the residence permit after we get started. Let me elaborate on the project details first. We've got work to do today."

I was confident that JeanClaude would do everything possible to help me get that residence permit.

"Okay, CJ, let's review once more what we have. Two hundred kilometres of international-standard motorway connecting Asia with Europe including a new bridge over the Bosphorus. This motorway will ultimately connect, via Syria, to the Arabian Peninsula through Saudi Arabia, along the Gulf all the way to Qatar and the United Arab Emirates. And, please note, relations between the Turks and the Arabs have long been an open wound, could be problematic, but not likely on this project.

"The job. The planning is complete and all the right of way has been purchased by the Turkish Highway Department. The design and engineering are complete. A Turkish engineering firm, appointed by the Turkish Government and funded by UN International Development Bank grants, joint-ventured with British and American firms to fast track the design and engineering.

"Now for the construction, the construction contractors are Turkish and Italian. They are managed by the joint-venture design team members. You are the sole representative from the American transportation engineering group. Analysis Corp has seconded you to that American company. You will be responsible for design/build pay items for repairing the landscape along the entire two hundred kilometres. You will also manage the American company's books—money in/money out.

"The Turkish engineering company has a landscape specialist with whom you will work day in/day out. Your colleague is older and experienced, an Anatolian original, Seljuk roots, Ataturk sympathies—a modern but traditional married Turkish family man. He has a wife and two sons, though one has died young in an earthquake. He's a good dependable guy. You can get information from him but never tell him about your information gathering."

"Tell me about the information gathering."

"I'm not on the ground. It'll be you and two guys from the Brit firm who we'll meet later today. The issue? Funnelling money from this billion-dollar contract to contentious forces trying to further upset the powers-that-be in the Muslim world.

"One of the guys is a Quantity Surveyor and all funds approvals go through him. Even though the landscape is only 3% of the full contract value, the owner of the landscaping construction firm is a person of interest. Recommended by the main contractor, he is known as 'Pasha'. Your work is to get, through your contacts in the landscape, whether there is any talk of 'out-of-the-ordinary' use of funds. Contact me and we'll take it from there. One more thing, the Brit Quantity Surveyor works for the other Brit who's in on this. He will be the Deputy Project Director so he will see all the personnel files of everyone involved. The Quantity Surveyor feeds the Deputy Project Director and you feed me. You never exchange information with the Brits. You just work with them to get the landscape restoration done. Clear?"

I nodded.

"And one more thing that Will wanted me to emphasize, you must remain on this job, not like Cairo—you must remain until the Turkish Highway Department (THD) accepts the work. No maybes, no walkabouts. Your professional future and your financial well-being are in the balance. I have assured him, *mon ami*, that he can depend on you."

"I'm in, JeanClaude. Fear not."

"I'm glad to hear that.

"We'll meet the Brits later today at the Café Central. This way you all get face-to-face familiarity before full on-the-job engagement. They will present you some of the technical basics of the landscape part of the project."

We arrived at Hotel Steigenberger and JeanClaude said, "Grab your stuff. I'll take you to your room."

When we got there, he gave me a small packet of information from the US government about Turkey, its history and culture. After putting my stuff away, I met JeanClaude in the lobby and we walked over to the Café Central.

"The job sounds direct enough. I'm looking forward to the challenge," I said.

"Glad to hear that. Give me your passport and I'll arrange work/residence permits and visas for Turkey. Then we can carry on. My people will have you ready to go in 24 hours.

"The Brits are having lunch now. We'll join them for an espresso to wrap everything up. Oh, by the way, here's a card with the address of the head construction field office in Istanbul—any taxi driver can get you there. Hold onto this card."

I put it in my wallet. Up ahead I saw the Café Central— got my game face ready. Vienna made me feel like I was in the heart of Western businessman world. Everybody dressed sharp. Everybody dressed conservative—tie/suit/shoes—neat proper—clean, no dust, no scuffs and well-coiffed.

We entered the café and JeanClaude led me to a table that already had two well-dressed professional men finishing their lunch.

***

Café Central

The two Brits had just ordered dessert and coffee. Our timing was spot on. JeanClaude shook hands with a greying, portly older man, introducing me to him, Clayton Carmichael, the Thracia/Anatolia Motorway Deputy Project Director. I shook hands, a firm handshake, with him. He, in turn, introduced a middle-aged man, looking a fit 6', Derek Ashcroft-Scott, Quantity Surveyor to us both. He had an equally firm handshake.

Clayton added, "Derek is a Chartered Member of the Royal Institute of Chartered Surveyors (MRICS), and for the benefit of you Yanks, he is responsible for life cycle costing, cost planning, procurement and tendering, contract administration and commercial management. He will be evaluating all materials, processes and costs on this project."

I have heard the 'almighty professional Brit' palaver before in Yenbo—didn't take offence. Glad to know Derek was well experienced.

After all four of us settled down in our chairs, the waiter came by. JeanClaude ordered an espresso. I took that to mean he figured this meeting would not last too long. I ordered the same.

Derek said, "Landscaping—that's your bailiwick. I've never seen a set of documents that so underplayed the landscape as these. There are four pay items and nothing in the specifications. It will be up to you to build out the management details, define the work, inspect the work, define the payments and partial payments."

I nodded my understanding. Derek continued, "The four

pay items are:

Grass-6 million square metres

Coniferous trees-31,000 units

Deciduous trees-85,000 units

Shrubs-2,600,000 units

The agreement has a thick paragraph describing each, which essentially describes that the contractor is responsible for every cost. I've got a dossier of the contract documents for you with the original English and Turkish. I'll hand it over after lunch."

"What about design? I heard no landscaping design has been done," I asked.

Derek laughed. "Correct. But in the thick paragraph on grass, someone tacked on a sentence that reads 'preparation of landscaping designs under the approval of the Supervising Engineer'. That will be you and your Turkish colleague."

"So I will organize, oversee the landscaping design as well as the landscaping construction and maintenance?"

"Correct."

"And that will be one contract for all two hundred kilometres?"

"Yes and no. The two hundred kilometres is divided into four sections. One section, Section 2 for the Bosphorus bridge only—Japanese contractor—not under our control. We control Sections 1, 3 and 4. They cover 100km in Europe and another 100km in Asia. Sections 1 and 4 are being built by Turkish contractors. Section 3 is being built by an Italian contractor.

"Three sections, a Turkish construction management engineer for each, two main contractors and a single landscaping subcontractor for all three. A bit of a hash but you'll get the hang of it. Lots of front-end management work for you. First task is the landscaping subcontractor must prove to you that he has the experience, skills and personnel for this project."

"Okay—can you tell me more?"

"Next week you will meet your Turkish colleague and the main office staff on the shores of the Bosphorus just north of Bebek. You and he will examine the entire right of way—

already staked out with cuts and fills underway. Then week two, the landscaping contractor will meet you and your Turkish colleague to make his case."

"Is this a 'done-deal' or what?"

"Yes and no. Nobody in Turkey has ever landscaped a project even 1/10 this size; but this contractor has worked successfully for the THD before—so you might say it is a 'done-deal'. You are the Supervising Engineer and it needs your approval."

I sat back and took more than a sip—half of my espresso, without sugar, in one swallow. This job is interesting and challenging, I thought. I finished my espresso and looked at JeanClaude. He had already started to stand up from his chair. End of meeting.

As we walked back to the hotel, I asked JeanClaude, "What about payments? Nothing was said about how I, we, get paid."

"No big deal, *mon ami*. You will have access to our corporate account as you settle in—hotel, finding and securing an apartment, daily expenses. That will cover your first two months. On the project, monthly payments will be one month in arrears and they will be paid to you by Clayton—all in cash—80% in US dollars and 20% in Turkish lira. Your salary is 25% of that total monthly corporate payment. Follow?"

"Yeah but Turkish lira?"

"You have the choice to take some of your salary in Turkish lira—for day-to-day expenses, or exchange it all into dollars. Clayton knows a jeweller in the *Kapila Çarsi*, Covered Bazaar, who exchanges Lira for Dollars or British Pounds at a very good rate. And if you do that don't delay because the Turkish lira has been regularly losing value—if you wait a week the lira will buy substantially less dollars. Bottom line, each month you must make a dollar deposit in the corporate account minus your salary. I'll give you all the details, letters of authorization etc., that will enable your full access to that account."

"I follow."

I was back in the game for sure.

3-Istanbul

Eymen Bey

My new Istanbul job? I had been thinking about landmarks and culture beyond measure. I was dreaming about Agatha Christie, the Pera Palas Hotel, the Orient Express—Pierre Loti and his Eyup tea house... Byzantium, Constantinople, Ottoman history, Mimar Sinan. And, by the end of the week I was in Istanbul. Finally in real life

I had checked in at the Dedeman Hotel. Soon I would be on my way to my new job where I understood that my weekly work schedule would be 8-5, one hour for lunch Monday through Friday, Saturdays and Sundays off. That was a huge workday difference from my Yenbo job in Saudi Arabia where the work week was Saturday through Thursday, with the daily hours 7-5:30, Fridays our only day off. And my job in Cairo, hell, that was like a university job, get in, take lunch and take off when you feel like it. Though each of these three countries was dominated by Muslims, daily life was so different. This is the fun of a new international job—never know in advance what it will be like in real life. I was excited.

I put my things away and went downstairs to find a taxi. I showed the doorman the office address and he marked up my map. I looked carefully at the map. We were in *Zincirlikuyu* and my new office was next to *Boğaziçi Üniversitesi* just above *Rumeli Hisari*, a famous 15th century Ottoman fortress used to control Bosphorus water traffic. It was tough getting my eyes accustomed to the Turkish alphabet.

At the turn of the 20th century Mustapha Kemal Ataturk, founder and first president of the Turkish Republic, enforced the historical change from the Arabic to the Latin alphabet. Easier said than done. But now well established. Lots of diacritical marks: ç, ı, İ, ğ, ö, ş, ü.

Gave the driver my new office address and off we went. Crazy busy. All the roads chock-full of cars, busses and trucks. More disciplined than Cairo or Bangkok but... crowded with impatient, impassioned drivers. We had only 5 kilometres as the crow flies but the twists and turns of the hills made it, by my estimation, closer to 10km.

He dropped me off at the guarded entry to a complex of single storey, obviously temporary, four doublewide interconnected construction trailers. I had a 9AM appointment with the Head Engineer/Project Director, a senior Turk, Mr. Safetin Çelik.

When I found his office his secretary ushered me right in. He stood up, welcomed me with a firm handshake, very much American style. Six feet tall, a three-piece grey suit and tie, in his 60s, fit with silver hair, wire-rimmed glasses and nattily trimmed moustache, he oozed respectability. From his greeting I figured he was a polyglot man who both sounded and looked like he had the experience to manage a billion-dollars-worth of contracts—a new bridge over the Bosphorus plus 200km of international quality motorway connecting Europe and Asia. There was another older man, in a tie and sweater, already sitting with him in the private office.

We had a short meeting. Mr. Çelik spoke English to me.

"Welcome to Turkey, Mr. Jacobs and to our project." That was the first and last time any Turk used my last name; immediately I became known among my Turkish colleagues as Mr. Charles—a cultural aspect I often found throughout the Eastern Med, Levent and the Gulf.

Mr. Çelik continued, "Please let me introduce you to your colleague, Eymen Bey (in Turkey, Bey, like mister, is a traditional title of respect). Together you both will oversee the landscaping of our project. Eymen Bey will show you to your desk. We look forward to success on the Thracia/Anatolia Motorway."

As we stood to leave, Mr. Çelik shook my hand again. Then Eymen Bey led me to the desk we would share for the next two years—shared desk, not private individual desks. Eymen Bey in his 60s, 5'7" medium build, retired from Turkish Forestry Department where as a Forester—you want old-school? In every forest he worked, he had travelled by horse. He went to Galatasaray Lycée, and was a lifelong Galatasaray football fan. He didn't speak English. I didn't speak Turkish. But because of his Galatasaray high school, he spoke French as a second language, as did I. French became our workplace language.

And our office? Construction engineer spec—no interior designers here. Minimal maintenance requiring finishes, rough-trowelled concrete floors. Eight desks arranged around the perimeter of the room, twice the number of desks that would be comfortable. Low light level via two small windows and two bare fluorescent tubes on the ceiling. It really felt like a temporary site construction office—space heaters, no fans, no AC. The entire room already had a heavily used aura, everything had a faded grey colour.

Aura? Yeah, everyone was smoking unfiltered Turkish tobacco cigarettes; clouds of yellowish brown-grey smoke hung in the room. And everyone was drinking dark brown Turkish tea (they told me proper tea comes only from Turkey—Rize region on the Black Sea), everyone drank from identical tea glasses—small, clear Turkish tulip-shaped tea glasses. The tea glasses, small size and delicate shape—simple elegance. But the rest of the office? For a huge billion-dollar intercontinental project, our construction management office felt crude, functional but crude. I thought—no pretensions here.

First thing, the office tea boy offered me a tulip-shaped glass of tea on a coaster. The coaster? The only way to serve that small glass of tea that was so hot, I could barely touch it. I came to learn that hot tea service and drinking was a test of Turkish manhood, drink it hot or you are not a Turk. I always had to hold the glass by the rim and sip, slurp the tea. Me? Not a Turk.

The only guy who could speak English in our office was the *terjuman*, the translator. He was always helpful, translating everything from social politeness to contract documents. Eymen Bey introduced me, one by one, to every one of our office colleagues as Mr. Charles. Everyone was courteous.

But the office building itself and its internal setting, so far below the modern standard of my job in Yenbo. The office and its furnishings, though we were the engineers-in-charge, were less than contractors' offices in Yenbo. Even my office in Cairo, which felt like a university classroom, felt more modern. Here, there were no frills.

Eymen Bey did not have a driver's license. A few years ago, in the earthquake that killed one of his two sons, he suffered a broken hip and was infirmed. So I was the official driver—he was my navigator. He lived in *Uskudar*, the Anatolian side of the Bosphorus, the Anatolian side of Istanbul.

Many times he made it clear to me there was a difference between the two sides of Istanbul. European, modern, flash. Anatolian, traditional, of the earth. Eymen Bey was definitely Anatolian.

***

Feet on the Ground

I liked my 2-day weekends. I used the first one, and every one, to look around—Istanbul. Constantinople. Byzantium. Stamboul. This place was everything Cairo was—an aged world-class city sitting in a spectacular landscape.

Big landscape picture. Cairo: the Nile, a half-kilometre-wide river lazily snaking through the city, the majestic date palms, the Sahara and the great Pyramids. A culture rooted deeply in the sands of time with an uncertain future.

And Istanbul: the Bosphorus, a two-kilometre-wide body of water powerfully keeping two continents apart; a thoroughfare of international shipping (providing Russia's only ice-free port with access to the world), its coastal hillsides covered with the sentry-like, tall, dark, upright Italian cypress (*Cupressus sempervirens*) watching, protecting all. And the architectural highlight? Old Istanbul's spectacular skyline featuring Mimar Sinan's breathtaking mosques. Mature artifacts, mature culture, at least on the surface.

I crossed the Bosphorus—Europe to Asia, Asia to Europe—again and again on the Scottish-built 1950s heavy-duty ferries (1,000-2,000 passenger capacities)—they were the most economical way for workers to travel between the continents and as plentiful as New York taxis. I regularly took their 20-minute ride across the Bosphorus—the best way to appreciate Istanbul's world-class landscape setting. That Bosphorus setting—bustling waterway, skyline mosques, waterside residences (*yalis*), adjacent landforms both urban and vegetated—overwhelmed me the first time and throughout my 24 months in Istanbul.

Unfortunately, in the big picture these magnificent historical cities Cairo and Istanbul were both boiling with residents and overrun with tourists. Each had a blended historical and landscape setting—magnetic and so complex. There was plenty to keep me busy in this town of two continents, separated by the beautiful Bosphorus, but I still had no idea what cultural mysteries I might encounter. They would reveal themselves in their own time.

It wasn't long before I found at heavily touristed places like Topkapi, Hagia Sophia and the Blue Mosque—you guessed it. Tangier had its teeps. Cairo had its dragomen. And the Istanbul variety? Men—same age, young and aggressive—just like Tangier and Cairo. I just kept away from them.

Cultural issues aside, for me, a job is a job. I was glad to be back in my professional world, back into landscape architecture. I was anxious to get my teeth into 200 kilometres of European (Thracia) and Asian (Anatolian) landscaping.

***

Settling In

I spent most of the first morning drinking lots of tea, meeting Turkish colleagues, civil and structural engineers, and getting to know Eymen Bey. Also in week one, Derek, the Brit QS, issued me the Renault 12, a small Renault badged in the name of the Turkish consultant, which would be the work car for Eymen Bey and me for the duration of the project. I got to know Eymen Bey even better over the next days as he guided me on a tour of the entire 200-kilometers right of way.

This trip was of massive importance as my introduction to the varied ecosystems, future viaducts, tunnels and our key personnel over sections 1, 3 and 4. We visited the construction offices at each section, meeting the Turkish engineers managing construction who arranged to drive us in a 4x4 along the entire right of way. We followed the haul roads, the construction roads along the centres and edges of the right of way. Most of the route was countryside. It took us two days—one day for the Thracian 100 kilometres and one day for the Anatolian 100 kilometres.

That same week Derek took me to a small apartment north of Istanbul, in *Istinye*, which he had arranged—furnished, built in the 60s and with an excellent view south down the Bosphorus. My new home. It had an "almost-modern" European feel. This, I came to learn, was the design essence of the European side of Istanbul, a reflection of the vision of Mustafa Kemal Ataturk, the 20th century post-Ottoman, father of modern Turkey.

***

The Pasha

On Monday morning the second week on the job, we were supposed to meet the owner of the Landscape Contractor company (*Istanbul Peyzaj Proje Burosu,* IPPB) that wanted to do the landscaping for 200km of international standard motorway (quality like US interstates).

At 10AM the front gate guard let pass a convoy of three cars led by a large, late model, black S-Class Mercedes.

Eymen Bey and I waited at the front door of the office. The black Mercedes pulled up right in front of us. The driver got out first. He was the size of Jabba the Hutt in Star Wars. The driver was the boss. Three more men exited the black S-Class Mercedes and lined up behind him. Multiple occupants from each of the following two convoy cars also lined up behind him. He smiled, shook my hand, handed me his business card. Then he shook Eymen Bey's hand and began speaking in Turkish.

Eymen Bey translated in French to me. Namik Bey, I already nicknamed him "the Pasha", had brought his three proposed site managers and their field superintendents along with the man responsible for design—must have been near a dozen people. The plan for the day was that the Pasha would drive us out to a 10-year-old highway project he had done. And that was the only similar project.

Earlier that morning I had asked, in French, of Eymen Bey, a slew of questions. I learned that the landscape design and construction situation in the country was nascent at best. No projects the size of ours had ever been done. No private-sector nurseries of adequate size existed. There were no landscape

106

architecture offices of the size this project required.

I was introduced to and shook hands with each of the Pasha's team. We did not invite them inside for tea, instead we immediately prepared for the site visit.

The Pasha indicated I should ride shotgun, with Eymen Bey in the back seat. I deferred to my elder, Eymen Bey, offering him shotgun. No, no, no, he said. I must ride shotgun. I asked him who was sitting next to him in the back seat. He said it was the Pasha's main man, Erhan Bey, who would be our contact point should the Pasha be awarded the work. And that was our job that day, to decide yes or no would the Pasha get the work.

Off we went, over the Bosphorus, from Europe to Asia. Along the way I asked a couple questions which Eymen Bey translated into Turkish. How would they design the landscaping? Answer: we have a landscape architect—you met him earlier—he will do whatever you want. And the plants—what about the plants? Answer: we will start our own nursery in each lot collecting and propagating local plants. I couldn't find fault with that. The contract specified quantities. I'd have to build out a schedule with the quantity surveyor to assure that this work could be achieved in a timely manner.

We drove about 45 minutes east to see a verge on a stretch of an earlier motorway. The three cars in the convoy all stopped on the asphalt shoulder. We got out and walked on a 10-metre-high cut slope 100 metres long. Nothing but grass. I asked Eymen Bey. He told me this slope was all that the Pasha had to show us. How long could we look at a well-covered grass slope—planted 10 years earlier. I said, looks good, what's next. The Pasha said he was taking us to lunch at a seaside restaurant in Tuzla on the Marmara Sea. After only an additional 20-minute ride, Eymen Bey and I along with the Pasha and six others sat at one large table in the seaside restaurant and ate lunch for about two hours.

Then Eymen told me that if I would like, Pasha would take us on his boat back to Istanbul. I hiccoughed. Looked at Eymen Bey. I'd already been surprised when I learned that, when they were just out of university, the four key men and the Pasha had worked with Eymen Bey in the Turkish Forestry Department.

Well, I was a bit dizzy, never having been so blatantly favoured prior to awarding a contract.

I remembered what JeanClaude had said, the Pasha should get the contract and I should observe how funds are allocated—money laundering was the issue here. Along the way I asked Eymen Bey if, according to his experience, accepting these favours would compromise us—was it in any way unusual? He told me not to worry.

And before I knew it, we were at a pier getting onto the Pasha's boat.

To make a long story short, I asked Eymen Bey what was going on and he told me we were going fishing. Well, the boat was no Miami Beach "cigar boat" and it was no billionaire's "floating five-star". But it wasn't a commercial fishing boat by any means either. More like a fishing yacht, a simple 40' inboard fishing yacht—not flash, not fast. It did have good all-round fishing access and a fair size galley below deck.

I'd never been a real boat guy or fisherman even though my dad, when we still lived in Michigan, took me ice fishing a couple times and in the summer perch and trout fishing on smaller freshwater lakes in Michigan. I was still on the alert for nefariousness. I didn't see any fishing rods. But Eymen Bey told me it was all about *balık* and *ekmek* (fish and bread). The guys hung fishing lines over the edge and relaxed as the boat and the day slowly moved toward sunset.

I wondered about the galley. Was there entertainment down there? So I asked Eymen Bey to go down there with me. What did we find? There was a team of young men serving. Eymen Bey told me they were sons of a couple of the landscape contractor's men. The servers oversaw trays of fresh fruits (peaches, apples, pears, raisins, figs, oranges, melons), nuts (hazelnuts, walnuts, pistachios, almonds), and sweets (baklava, bird's nest, revani, cookies, lokma) on a central table. On the side was a counter with bottles of Raki (an anise liqueur), and a small stove for preparations of Turkish coffee and tea.

No women, no girls, no young boys. This really was a fishing trip with a bunch of guys who were in their 50s now and were in their 20s when they studied forestry together at university.

Boys' day out. Their plan was to catch some bluefish (in season), then clean them and pan fry them for fish sandwiches.

I gave in. We all just lazed about as daytime eased into sunset. I let the Marmara-to-Bosphorus ride take me into landscape mode. The islands, Princes' Islands, the hills, the mosques and then the sunset. South of the Golden Horn, on the historical peninsula, Mimar Sinan's 16th century Ottoman mosques took my breath away... or was it too much Raki? I read the architecture as patterns—to the glorious—connections to worlds beyond. I wondered if Sinan spoke like this about his work. It was such a pleasure for my eyes, his works topping the seven hills of Istanbul without anything modern disturbing their skyline.

But north of the Galata Bridge, north of the Golden Horn— might as well have been Century City in Los Angeles—modern skyscrapers everywhere, choc-a-block. An hour later, after fresh fish sandwiches, they dropped me off at a dock in Istinye, where I had a 5-minute walk to the small rooftop apartment I had just moved into.

Right, approving this landscaping subcontractor—a mere formality.

***

The Program

The four landscaping unit price descriptions needed some elaborating. I prepared partial payment formats for each. Then I prepared request and approval forms for the work. All of these were essential for the smooth execution of the work over the next 18 months so that the motorways landscaping would be 100% complete on the day the motorway opened.

The contractor had at the most 15 months to get 2,600,000 cuttings rooted and ready to plant. This was a big number in an unbelievably short time. The Pasha knew it and made an alternative proposal—delete all shrubs and replace with pine tree seedlings which he could get quite easily from the Turkish Forestry Department. He offered this with no cost savings to the project.

I argued against it because our intent was to reinstate the ecosystem components that existed prior to excavation for the motorway. Thus we needed the uniquely eco-consistent plants appropriate for each individual section.

Ultimately, the young landscape architect for the Pasha was an environmentalist and he, along with a senior experienced forester on the Pasha's team, selected local shrubs for cuttings that rooted easily. The trees they procured from Forestry nurseries. For the shrubs, they set up three local ecotype-based nurseries, one each for Sections 1, 3 and 4. And they met the schedule. The schedule?

Year One:
A. Design-spring;
B. Establish nursery, take cuttings, grow inventory-early summer;

Year Two:
A. Commence plantation-spring;
B. Plantation complete-late fall

Most of the work went smoothly. Eymen Bey and I were on the road every day inspecting ongoing work. Both of us had a preference to be in Section 3 for lunchtime as often as possible. Why? The Italian contractor ran that section and their site restaurant was a proper Italian restaurant. We took full advantage of *il pranzo Italiano—aperativo, antipasti, contorni, insalata* followed by fruit and cheese. No wine on the job. There was always a sweet to have before closing with strong espresso. Beside the restaurant was a room with a pool table—the contractor's men were always playing pool after lunch—a full two-hour break. That was a contractor's lunchroom the likes of which I had never seen and probably won't see ever again.

As it became clear that the work was progressing and on schedule, Eymen Bey invited me to his Uskudar apartment to watch afternoon matches when the Turkish national football team was playing. While we watched football on television his wive made cheese borek with walnut *salça* (spiced tomato paste with crushed walnuts) for us to munch on. I felt at home in his house.

That was only part of Eymen Bey's hospitality. After the match his wife always served Turkish sweets. Eymen Bey showed me how to prepare Turkish coffee. It started with the coffee supplier, a two-minute walk from his apartment. He never bought more than 250 grams and he had it ground very fine right there. At home he put the finely ground coffee into a pan already containing the water. Then he brought it almost to a boil, once, twice, three times. Never let it boil, he told me. He always made it himself. His home Turkish coffee was better than any coffee house.

I told Eymen Bey that I was curious about Mevlana and the whirling dervishes—one of my music and landscape quests. He knew Istanbul like the back of his hand. Eymen Bey was a helpful gentleman during my entire stay in Istanbul. If I could say, Eymen Bey was a secular Muslim. He always had his prayer beads but he was a classic objective professional dedicated to achieving a successful project.

So this was a pleasant job as far as international projects go. One morning we were running down Section 3. The general contractor had already placed the topsoil on the cut and fill slopes. The Pasha had a team working to prepare the topsoil for seeding—removal of oversize and unwanted material and fine grading—a lot of rake work.

When we found the slope that was being worked… it was all Gypsies—young boys and girls, some women and one man in charge of a crew of at least 30. When Eymen Bey and I got out of our car, they all stopped working. They waved and called greetings to us. I'd never seen such enthusiastic greetings or greetings at all from landscape labourers. Eymen Bey told me each Gypsy worker was likely earning, at the very most, the equivalent of one dollar a day.

It was a fun experience but after doing the math, extrapolating how many square metres of topsoil preparation over 200 kilometres, I shared my cost savings calcs with the QS. Derek said the costs involved, compared to the overall landscaping budget, were insignificant. I contacted JeanClaude and told him I saw nothing unusual that might link to money laundering. In the end, I thought the Pasha was more interested in getting a gold-star recommendation from this huge project.

***

Istinye

A landscape architect, a person who is convinced that urban residents need green in their lives. That's me. So here I am in Turkey after two years in Egypt. Istanbul feels like it is years ahead of Cairo—the modern part anyhow—though neither have much in the way of urban green.

Here I don't see any half-finished apartment buildings fully occupied. But I have seen edge-of-town neighbourhoods where, if you are on government land and you can build your own home (*geçecondos*) overnight, including the required planting a tree, the government will put that property in your name. They are not slums. They are rudimentary single-family homes that many improve over time. Many of the men work in Germany and improve their homes and family condition with their wages. The city builds the streets and installs utilities. I visited these areas and saw BMWs and MBs—usually signs that at least one of the family was working in Germany. Hey, it's not Hollywood but it's people improving the quality of their lives.

I got to know my walkable local Istinye neighbourhood. Just a few kilometres north of my office, Istinye had recently undergone a significant transformation on its waterfront, now called Istinye Park—a huge mall and mixed-use centre. Everything a modern and aspirational Turk could ever want. It is fast, aggressive and in-your-face, high-pressure marketing of over-the-top material consumption. But this is the way of life that Bree and I, in the haybarn, have turned away from. I wonder if, in time, the Turks will reject this or, like many in the Western world, be overcome by it.

My apartment, a less-than-ten-minute walk away from the mall, was a small footprint on the top of a five-storey building, with a spectacular view of Europe meeting Asia on the Bosphorus—I said that already—but the view was so captivating—rusty merchant ships from Romania and Bulgaria, Russian naval vessels, water taxis of all sorts, and the remarkable huge modern yachts of successful Turkish entrepreneurs. Something about the time-immemorial flow of a water body like the Bosphorus. Its riverine mood of steadiness and dependability is contrary to the mood of Istinye Park. I heard the owner of my building was trying to sell it to a modern developer. I hoped I could see out my full time here. I also hoped I could talk Bree into visiting me in this active and historical water's-edge setting.

Unfortunately, the quality of the electrical infrastructure did not match the high-quality view. My computer got burnt out by a short or a surge. The QS, Derek, had helped me on connectivity and, about the electrical problem, since it was a job cost it was reimbursable. So, I got back online at my apartment.

But to do it, I had to replace my Macbook—Apple did have an Istanbul store—and then get a truckload of surge protection at a place in Uskudar called the *Elektronic Passagi*. It was in an ancient building with an internal courtyard—small footprint overall. I saw electrical/telephone wires hanging open everywhere, like decades of cobwebs—took stairs, the only way, passing unoccupied spaces falling to decrepitude, to the third floor, the top floor and they had everything to counteract the unpredictable electrical infrastructure. This was the issue of how a centuries-old town evolves with new materials and technologies. Urban change and its timescale is a subject all its own. Visually it is fascinating—old and new, cheek by jowl.

In Istinye at the same dock where the Pasha had dropped me off my first month on the job, I found a nice café down at water level where I could drink tea watching the ships on the Bosphorus anytime, day or night. And if I was a little peckish, I could from that same dock take a small water taxi for 5 TL (Turkish Lira) across the one kilometre to Kanlica for a cup of thick, freshly made yoghurt topped with powdered sugar. This scene, the water's edge of the Bosphorus, documented the best example of human desire to be at the water's edge for relaxation and refreshment. The Turks had it figured out.

And Cairo? Not so much, the edge of the Nile never felt accessible in the city—maybe it was the history of flooding? I had to go to Cairo's south end, Helwan to find easily accessible Nile water's edge. Maybe... Mediterranean climate versus Sahara climate. In Yenbo New Town, we had projected and planned for an accessible waterfront for retail and recreation. I hoped as Yenbo developed, its Red Sea water's edge would have the feel of what the Turks have done in Istanbul on the Bosphorus.

***

Kapalı Çarşı

Being the only representative of the USA consultant on this project, I was the recipient of the monthly payment to our firm. It was as the Brits told me, a wire transfer of dollars into our corporate account and a percentage payment in Turkish Lira cash.

So here's how it worked. Derek handed me the Turkish Lira in cash. Then to take advantage of the current and best exchange rate, I had to go each month with the Turkish Lira to a jeweller in the Kapalı Çarşı (Covered Bazaar). The Covered Bazaar was a jumble of small shops, narrow passageways, lots of people, easy to get lost. It was just like Moroccan medinas.

The routine had been long established. The jeweller welcomed me and showed me behind a curtain into a small back room—out of public sight. There, monthly from a briefcase I gave him 250,000 Turkish Lira. He put them in a paper bag and made a phone call. In 5 minutes a young boy, maybe 12-13 years old, came into the shop. The jeweller handed him the bag and the kid took off. Then we had tea.

Before we finished, the kid was back with the paper bag filled with Benjamins, US one-hundred-dollar bills with Benjamin Franklin's picture on them—and, I should add, the currency of international drug runners and money launderers. The jeweller took out a machine to verify their authenticity. Then he put them through a counting machine to confirm the quantity. Then he banded the $20,000 into two packs of 10,000 each, gave them to me and I put them in my briefcase. Said thank you and left to go home for dinner.

That was my monthly visit and that's how I became familiar with the Covered Bazaar and its adjacent landmarks, the Nuruosmaniye Mosque and the Column of Constantine. Some people fall in love with Istanbul—for me it was my work; but its history was magnetic and oh so deep.

***

Bree Marriage

Bree was stubborn. She had a mind of her own. I couldn't talk her into visiting the Bosphorus. Yeah, we got the iMessaging going—but it was minimal communication. Like:

Me: Did you get the wire transfer?

Bree: Yes, no problem.

Me: Come and visit, they have great yoghurt.

Bree: I'm not going to spend a couple thousand to travel for yoghurt.

I could understand her logic. Made sense. After 9 months I took my vacation to Switzerland via Vienna. I passed the night in Vienna, met with JeanClaude and he had arranged to have my approved Swiss visa papers and a passport stamp. That was necessary for Bree and me to be officially married in Switzerland. I was stoked.

When I arrived in Grindelwald, it was early winter, all deciduous leaves gone, no snow or ice yet. Bree and I made all the necessary arrangements. After the civil registry office approved our application we had a small ceremony in Grindelwald's Reformed church. We were married—civilly and in the local church.

My heart overflowed with happiness. I was on top of the world. We had a joyful three weeks walking the hills, forests and pastures around the Grosse Scheidegg, the Schwarzhorn and the Schwarzwald—our landscape backyard. Down in the bottom of the Grindelwald bowl the pastures were still green. Up around our haybarn and higher, the pastures and alpine grasslands were golden. Rising just above the golden were autumnal red masses of alpine blueberries. Glorious days we had in these mountains.

Honeymoon days are golden. Together, we worked in her garden. She gathered this season's hardwood from her herbaceous plants and cuttings from her shrubs. I helped her as she prepared stock for maceration.

We talked about everything. She had heard so many landscape stories over the years from the wildings, who walk the Alps on paths unknown to tourists. She had explained that these wilding types were people, mostly men, who wanted nothing to do with modern society, family life, science, academe, media, politics. They kept their distance and lived on the land—real outsiders—not on the edge but off the edge. One story intrigued Bree, and caught my interest.

It was in our neighbourhood between Grindelwald and Interlaken. It was, I'd call it a tale, a legend, about the days of the Crusades. That would make it over a thousand years ago. The times when the Alps were indeed impenetrable for strangers; and the mountain people—with their Celtic roots—would, for a fee, guide them. She said the fees were gold that had been looted from the Middle East by the Crusaders and that gold had been stored in deep caves not far from here.

Tale? Legend? Truth? I didn't know; but she put credence in a lot of what she learned over campfires with the wilding visitors. And she always, even back in Morocco, had a bent for adventure. And local adventure? She was into it.

***

Effulgent Glories

After my Swiss vacation and marriage to Bree, returning to Istanbul brought a huge environmental shock. I discovered their winter. The Istanbul winter arrived sooner than I had figured. I was surprised because I thought of Istanbul as a city on the Med but the reality was that the Adriatic Sea, the Dardanelles, the Marmara Sea and the Bosphorus separated Istanbul from the Med and we were truly further north.

After the first couple cold winter days, the Istanbul air changed. Home heating everywhere had to be soft coal, because after a week of the cold weather the city air became brownish in colour and incredibly harsh on my throat.

I asked Eymen Bey and the people in our office. And the answer? Soft brown coal was a plentiful Turkish resource. And it was cheap. Everybody used it. And everybody tolerated the bad air during the winter.

My first Istanbul winter experience shocked me. For the entire winter season the Istanbul city soft-coal-smoke air choked my throat and burned my eyes. I never got used to it but it made all the more enjoyable, spring's arrival along the Bosphorus.

The beautiful Mediterranean red buds, *Cercis siliquastrum*, brought their full bloom spring joy to the Bosphorus coastline. They looked like electric pink balloons nestled amongst the plentiful tall dark green upright columnar Mediterranean cypress, *Cupressus sempervirens*. By then the residents' winter heating had long been off and the air was clean, crisp and warming. But I'm getting ahead of myself.

The job, however, went so smoothly, it was almost boring—but covering 200 kilometres of motorway in Asia and Europe? Geographically, I was always on the road. Eymen Bey and I talked a lot. First of all in the winter, we were both glad to get out of Istanbul. Most of the new motorway was in the agricultural countryside—that meant clean air. And that pleasure for both of us transcended inborn cultural differences. We both lived our daily lives in our secular professional world, putting aside cultural, religious and political differences. That, too, was a pleasure.

Even though both of us spoke in a second language, French, I gleaned Anatolian culture insight from Eymen Bey. And cultures have always fascinated me. Fascinated?

If I look back, I see that the street culture in Morocco forced me to seek shelter—a cocoon to protect me from their culture. And in Saudi Arabia, I had no access to their culture—Muslim entry only. Again in KSA, I used cocoons to live my life. In Cairo I had access and examined the landscape and culture. The Pharaonic landscape and modern Egyptian culture chased me away.

Here in Turkey, I was free to access local culture and the landscape. And there was more to Turkey than Islam. There were dervishes; and dervishes had music and landscape components in their searches for effulgent glories. Eymen Bey showed me their centre in Beyoglu.

Thus the dervishes... the sufis re-entered my life. The sufi I met in the Zerhoun mountains outside of Meknes actually gave me insight on how to restructure my term abroad design study there. It was a positive outside-of-Tangier cross-cultural experience. But dervishes?

I first read about dervishes in Arthur Conan Doyle's end-of-the-19th-century novel written about the Nile in Egypt, *The Tragedy of the Korosko*, where they were feared brigands from the Sudan. Here in Turkey, it was Mevlana Celaleddin Rumi and his whirling dervishes. Sufis, I was in the world of sufis again.

What interested me? I was interested because of the

Mevlana sufi entry into the glory and grace of God via music and artistic endeavours—something that had its parallels in Western cultures. Mevlana is known as an Anatolian mystic. The soil of Anatolia, with roots in ancient sources and beliefs, was the perfect place for Mevlana's sufism to germinate.

His whirling dervishes combine music and dance to enter a trance that they say is a channel of connection to the "Supreme". That interested me—that was chum for my design sense of old. Which was interesting in a couple ways.

First of all, on the highway project my "design" ideas had to be put aside because the movement of people through the landscape was actually the movement of high-speed vehicles through the landscape. These highways had become infrastructure like the railways and earlier in England like the canals. We were not building gardens for humans to casually walk through. Here it was about safety of high-speed travel and repair of disturbed existing ecosystems.

Second, it was logical to treat the landscape as skin that was cut open to install a "temporary" line of infrastructure. Then repair the skin to its original condition. But even after my talks with Bree and the logic of this job, my blended design and culture ruminations were still active. So I had to look into Mevlana's whirling dervish music and dance while in Istanbul. It was just my fun in my free time.

The whirling dervish ceremony, *sema*, is credited to Mevlana and has become a part of Turkish customs, history, beliefs, and culture. The *sema* ceremony represents the mystical journey of man's spiritual ascent through mind and love to perfection. My old friend Bo was seeking the location of Jacob's Ladder for the same end: the mystical journey of man's spiritual ascent through mind and love to perfection.

I read lots about it, visited lots of websites, listened to 10's of YouTube videos and visited their lodge. Long story short— dancing was graceful but the music never captured me. I never got close to the feeling of the Jungfrau Region yodellers or even the magic melodies of the *felaheen* sung by Umm Khaltum.

My reading showed me that today's tourism hype is nowhere near Mevlana's austere mysticism. The lodge tour and show are just a list of things. And Mevlana said people had to become devoid of things to begin the journey. Didn't add up for me.

Turkey, actually Anatolia, is a land that, when searching at its deepest, is part of the greatest empires in the history of the world. It is a land that has connected Europe with the Orient, the Aryans with the Vedics. Those are deep landscape roots. I read that but couldn't feel it.

In Istanbul, even though Mevlana's beliefs, famous writings, peaceful and tolerant teachings have reached people of all sects and creeds, I couldn't break through. The live performances felt like tourist side shows. I'll leave it there.

***

The Turkish Landscape Architect

There weren't many landscape architecture practices and the ones around were doing residential gardens and the odd local park here and there. Few universities offered landscape architecture. The contractor's landscape architect was a young Turk.

He was an environmentally based landscape architect. He had studied ecosystems across Turkey from Thracia to Mt. Ararat, from the Black Sea to the Mediterranean. He was enamoured with Turkey's forests but ironically found himself working in the Istanbul region where, as he described, aside from areas directly adjacent to the Bosphorus, the landscape had been totally deforested. He was eager to understand the processes and workings of landscape architecture in the real world. Perfect he was for this project.

Along with the young landscape architect doing the design, the contractor had another young person coordinating the procurement, installation and maintenance for all three sections. Those two key people were both named Kemal. They called the designer *Kuçuk* Kemal (little Kemal) and the field construction coordinator *Buyuk* Kemal (big Kemal). Often the reality of landscape architecture in the field—construction bigger, more important than design, the smaller.

Kuçuk Kemal was a classic right plant—right place guy. The two Kemals walked the hills surrounding Sections 1, 3 and 4 of the motorway to identify the local plants growing in similar conditions to the motorway verges. Then they reviewed their lists with their team of senior foresters. At the end they had a

124

short list of shrubs easily propagated by cuttings. Then *Kuçuk* Kemal began the planting design. At the same time *Buyuk* Kemal gathered the cuttings, and the foresters at each section began preparing the nurseries to receive the cuttings.

The schedule was tight. We needed what some in LA had called "cast iron plants". Easily rooted and tolerant of adverse weather. Foresters kept book on the number of strong-rooted cuttings. *Kuçuk* Kemal used those numbers for design. He walked every cut and fill slope identifying shrub and tree planting areas. Then he drafted the design accordingly.

I set up the scale and sheet numbering protocols. Then I reviewed his design for vehicular safety. One review and the design was finished. And 98% of the final design went directly, without changes, to as-builts.

Buyuk Kemal organized the planting and *Kuçuk* Kemal verified it was according to the approved design. Then there was maintenance. We had good fortune with weather. Grass seeding was done by hand and watering by natural rain. Excellent germination. Excellent establishment—no land slips. The contractor had 12-month maintenance responsibility following pre-final inspection/approval. I had one visit back to the project in the coming year to verify the establishment and health of all trees and shrubs. Both Kemals walked with me to confirm for final inspection of all the sections.

This project was so different from my work in SoCal. How? Plant selection—in SoCal we selected from a catalogue, almost like shopping for cold cereal in a supermarket. Here we selected from plants successfully growing nearby in the same ecotype. And irrigation. Every SoCal project had automatic irrigation systems installed. Here, we said our prayers for the rainy season to arrive when it habitually did. We were fortunate this time.

This wasn't commercial work like SoCal was. We would never have been able to count on natural rainfall for an opening day result. No way we could do a commercial project in SoCal without an automated irrigation system—the expectation was always an "established" look on opening day. Here the expectation was that young plants would gradually grow and mature under natural conditions. Plus we didn't have enough lead time to grow larger plants in the nurseries. And that last point is excellent for discussion in early/long-lead project programming—final expectations vs. project schedule.

I always wondered who and how did those huge original contract tree and shrub quantities get set... nobody knew. We just worked with them. At the final result those quantities made sense—they worked.

***

End of Project? Almost

This was my third international project. Each one has been uniquely different. I had years of multi-disciplinary design/build in New Mexico. And years of high-quality design in LA. After those jobs in the US, I started my international work—Saudi Arabia, Egypt, now Turkey. Each of the three international projects required me to adapt my US-based professional skillset to local and regional international on-the-ground realities.

My US experience had dependable, high quality and competitive nurseries, contractors and material suppliers. In the Saudi Arabia Yenbo New Town we had none of those. And more, we had a climate and water situation that was truly unfavourable to horticulture.

Simple things like plant specifications, spacings, and hard landscape material procurement required massive rethinking in order to be successful, on schedule and budget. To stock our contractor nurseries, all the plants had to be imported from other countries. And the contractors were not local. They had to import their labourers from other countries. It was not their country. A different mood from when you work in your own country.

Skin in the game or no skin in the game. Everything was a bit off-balance in Saudi Arabia Yenbo New Town—climate, social. Getting a good, successful product was a continuous struggle under strict schedule deadlines.

Egypt? Cairo? Different animal altogether. It did not include construction or maintenance. It was more like a planning project with about 10% design. And in the end it was more like a college classroom assignment. I managed students; and the project was cancelled before it was finished. If there ever was a project that needed auditing, this was it. Supposed to have licensed professionals but instead we were given fresh-out-of-school graduates.

And this project in Turkey, Istanbul where Asia meets Europe, we had climate and soils amenable to horticulture. But our project was so large and had such a tight timeframe that we had to adjust all planting specifications. This was workable because the landscaping contractor had staff fully experienced in forestry and environmental issues. They were all Turks. This was their country. They had skin in the game.

The scope of work was 100% plants. No hardscape at all. They had to set up three nurseries, collect cuttings from the field and root them before planting on the project. Every plant was young and we planted them at spacings 80-100% based on their full growth. They looked scant on plantation.

The complete opposite of my US experience where most clients demanded that everything on opening day looked, as I have mentioned, not only fully established but mature—no bare earth. I always thought this was a hangover from the movie and TV industry in LA—stuff had to look like it had always been there. Here, on this project, expectations have been environmentally realistic.

Our success in this intercontinental 200km motorway project was essentially repair the skin of the landscape that had been cut open to install the highway. It was a very practical, straightforward bit of healing landscape. We had none of that overhead of design this, design that. But on my own in a strange culture, and with weekend free time, my old issues of "best" design resurfaced.

I had an internal drive to discover—something—it wouldn't quit. And my work, my profession drove my thoughts into a larger picture. How could I best serve those who walked through the landscaping, the gardens I designed?

Made me think about my professional future and how it would relate to my wife, Bree. Bree had told me that I was trying to replace God, be omnipotent, be omniscient in my attempts to provide transcendental portals for others. She had said—keep it personal, keep it local—stop the megalomania—the changing of the world. I agreed. There was too much hubris in my design efforts.

I enjoyed working in Bree's gardens and the garden's plant treasures... and Bree herself. I couldn't wait to get home to our haybarn on the Grosse Scheidegg, Jungfrau Region, Switzerland. But my job wasn't finished yet. I had one more month of inspections on this highway job late next spring before THD acceptance and sign-off.

Besides technical and cultural adjustments on international projects, there is a lesson I've learned on international contract jobs. I have to be on the lookout for the next job all the time because when my current job is finished—so are the pay checks.

My next job? Search online? Foreign? International? Switzerland? Or maybe I will wait for contact from JeanClaude or Will—would Yenbo New Town come alive again for me? Professional uncertainty was baked into international contract work. But Bree gave me emotional security. That gave me certainty and confidence—big time.

4-Mannlichen Plans

Haybarn in the Bowl

After 23 months with the Istanbul project plantation completed, I returned to Grindelwald and our haybarn. It was just past peak summer season. I missed Bree the most; but when I saw the forests of the Jungfrau Region, I was rebirthed. Overstatement? No way. The pastures, the forests, the cliff faces, the Alpine glories—they refreshed me beyond words. Bree asked me about the differences between the Jungfrau Region landscape and the Istanbul landscape.

"I've learned that the native forests around Istanbul had been decimated for I don't know how many years. And any street trees or park trees have been subject to either bad pruning or midnight 'vultures'."

"Vultures?"

"Wintertime in Istanbul requires home heating—just like here. But there is a big difference between this haybarn in the sparsely populated rural countryside and Istanbul's 10-million-person high density. As many here have done for centuries, you get your wood for heating from carefully managed nearby forests. But there, most people used the plentiful soft coal—but the problem with soft coal burning on a massive scale is air pollution—I used to choke every morning when I stepped outside in the winter. And some people would do anything to save money—such as bastardising trees—'vultures' carrying away anything they could burn for heat.

"That meant there were rarely any trees that grew to their naturally well-balanced maturity without being hacked over by 'vultures' at night. Here in the Jungfrau Region, maybe we get too accustomed to it—but all the trees have a beautifully mature balance to them—even the ones hit by lightning or rock falls regrow to a beautifully rebalanced configuration. Seeing that mature, healthy landscape gives our hearts peace and pleasure."

"That description of tree vultures convinces me even more that I made the right decision not to visit you in Istanbul—tortured trees? It hurts me to even think about it!"

Then Bree quickly changed the subject. She said, "I have two summer passes for the Jungfrau Region trains—I'd like to take you on a round trip of the Grindelwald and Lauterbrunnen valleys via Kleine Scheidegg—a welcome home landscape treat. Let's look at the healthy forests, the trees."

"When do we go?"

"Tomorrow morning—it's about a 4-hour round trip. We can be back home for lunch."

That night she welcomed me the "old-fashioned" way married people "renew their vows". Me? I felt strong the next morning as we walked down into Grindelwald to catch the first train up to Kleine Scheidegg. I had never taken this train before.

Still in the glow of last night's marital pleasure, we sat close to each other on this narrow gauge, cogwheel, electrified mountain train. Very few people were riding this first-in-the-morning train—a couple workers for the mountain resort cafés and that was all. We pretty much had the train car to ourselves.

We slowly rode uphill at the base of the Eiger. The train, three cars—all second class—carried us along one of the top edges of the huge Grindelwald Valley bowl. The bowl was noteworthy because of its many large green pastures. It stretched broadly, close to 10 kilometres across to our right.

We could see the higher elevation solid forests extending their thick fingers down into the pastures. The forest fingers were clues to steep topography, usually the edges of a ravine with mountain stream—terrain too steep for pastures. I could see so many pastures—very low density of farmhouses, definitely farm country.

But much lower and closer to Grindelwald *dorf,* the village centre, the density dramatically increased. In the Grindelwald Valley bowl 3,500 people lived. But that "urbanization" was swallowed up in this huge mountainous landscape. The village scale looked minuscule, as if ants lived there.

Bree told me the bowl was divided into seven different alps—farmer holdings. Since 1900, some might call it sprawl; but in the 21st century, the mountains and forests still ruled. A spectacular sight.

Then as we continued along the base of the Eiger, the cogwheel train began passing through three separate tunnels (protection from Eiger rock fall and avalanches), moving through the Swiss stone mountain pine forests. Amazing trees—tall, elongated ovals, such fresh green. Some had been damaged years ago by natural events (lightning, Eiger rock fall) but they were all majestically healthy, recovered and visually well balanced. I said to Bree, "We'll have to hike up here and get closer to these trees."

"Definitely."

To reach the Kleine Scheidegg the train had to climb above the treeline. And as we got off the train we saw nothing around us but towering granite cliffs, bulging glaciers and bright white snow. The ground around us was summer green with wildflowers but rising up out that green, the mountain's grey granite peaks touched the powder blue sky. Air was light, crisp and clean—maybe about 50F. We had a 30-minute wait until the next train to descend into the Lauterbrunnen Valley.

We sat in the sun at the foot of the Eiger, on the steps of the hotel made famous in the Clint Eastwood movie *Eiger Sanction*. I tried to take it all in. Then Bree said, "What will we do for income after you finish this Turkey project?"

At first the question took me by surprise. I was fully immersed in the Eiger landscape. Then I recovered.

"Fair question—need to carefully manage expenses because... I am like a mercenary, a white-collar mercenary. I work on a contract-to-contract basis. And in between contracts I have no income. But because of where I work, the Middle East and North Africa, the contracts are fat—few American landscape architects want to give up life in the US for what

I do—supervise construction of large projects—so we have to mind expenses and not live a flash lifestyle... do you follow?"

"Do you think my haybarn lifestyle is flash?"

"Hell no! It's sweet. We shouldn't have any trouble if I have to go 12-18 months between contracts—but we need to be cautious with expenses."

Just then there was a deep, crashing sound, somewhere between thunder and a low jet flying by—it was a small avalanche down one of the Jungfrau faces. Clouds of white snow puffed out as the thundering avalanche continued down the steep slope until all the snow was used up. After about 30 seconds, quiet returned.

"What time does the Wengen/Lauterbrunnen train leave?" I asked.

"About five minutes—let's get on."

***

Walk in the Woods

Grindelwald was 1000msl (metres above sea level), Kleine Scheidegg is at 2300msl and Lauterbrunnen, where we were headed, is at 800msl. As we began our descent we were above a partly cloudy covering of the Lauterbrunnen Valley. I could see across the narrow (not more than one kilometre wide) valley to the stone cliffs opposite—the realm of BASE jumpers. Then white-out as the train descended through the clouds.

Just as we got out of the clouds the train arrived at a small pedestrian-only mountain village, Wengen (1275msl). While the train took on more passengers, the clouds drifted. I could see everywhere tumbling down the valley's steep and high cliff faces—long waterfall tails. I could see all the way (east about six kilometres as the crow flies) to another small, pedestrian-only mountain village, on the other side of the Lauterbrunnen valley, Murren (1650msl).

Bree suggested we get off at the next stop, Wengwald, and take a little walk—we could catch another train down—they come every 30 minutes. Wengwald? One of those "on request only" stops because so few people get on or off there. It wasn't a proper station, just a shelter for extreme weather. After we got off and the train disappeared into a tunnel—quiet. Quiet in the mountains. I felt reverence in this landscape.

"What do you want to do?" I asked.

"Look up there—that's the Mannlichen *gipfel*, not much of anything, a minor peak covered with alpine pasture and forest. Below that, in fairly steep terrain, a couple houses, a few haybarns, more alpine pasture and forest. Off the beaten track. Let's go into the woods and look at trees."

"I like the sound of that. Is there something special you want to show me?"

"Show? Not exactly." She paused, like she was looking for the right words.

"Wildings. You know that over the years, I have had wilding guests at my haybarn. They never come in. I give them natural ointments, honey and dried foodstuffs. We sit around a campfire out back and talk. Legends. They share legends, some might call them tales, from a landscape tourists never see—never dream about. Fiction or fact? Hard to know when listening—but often interesting. Adventures always." She paused again. She was looking up at the landscape between us and the Mannlichen *gipfel.*

"Tell me."

"This is an old and long tale—begins over a thousand years ago—during the Crusades—and as the story goes, continues through WW2 up to modern day."

"You may have mentioned this once before, but I don't recall any details."

"Believe it or not... the Swiss have ancient gold stores that they began filling during the Crusades with their takings for services rendered to the French, the Germans, the Norse, the English crusaders who struggled to get across the Alps on their return home after re-conquering and looting the Muslim riches around the Holy Land. Are you with me? This is an adventure."

I nodded.

She continued "You have to ask yourself, where did the Swiss get the skills to build all those railroad tunnels 150 years ago? Rhetorical question. They had been tunnelling the Alps for centuries."

She paused. Respecting her rhetorical question, I said nothing

"And where did Tolkien get the idea of *zwergs* storing gold in the mountains? Another rhetorical question. As a teenager, Tolkien visited this very Lauterbrunnen Valley with friends— walking and talking." She paused again.

We continued walking along a well-worn path—not paved but well used. We chanced upon a bench and sat down.

"The wildings said this mountain on which we are sitting now has one of the original repositories of gold. Tunnels and caves almost 1000 years old."

"And you believe these... wildings?"

"I doubted at first... good stories around a fire... but I've done some field research and it is clear that there is a very large network of ventilation shafts that reach the surface, and they are not visible along existing paths, the *wanderwegs* tourists frequent. Adventure?"

When she paused, I showed my growing interest, "Tell me more."

"I figure those shafts are modern—modern—the last 100 years. You'll see as we take the train down there is a huge complex of military buildings and service vehicles near an entrance to the mountain down at 600msl. I heard that is a huge cavern made to hold most of the residents of this region should there be a catastrophic event. It is an upgrade from the 1950s and 60s when every new building had to have a nuclear shelter in the basement."

"Now that is a story. Why are you telling me?"

"I like adventures—adventures in my backyard. Listen to this. One wilding in particular told me about how just before chough mating season when there is a particular lunar condition, certain choughs gather in the location of the original access tunnel to the oldest repositories."

"And..."

"And I thought you and I might check it out—the chough part—and see if there really was an access tunnel up there below the Mannlichen *gipfel*—doesn't that sound like an interesting local adventure?"

My head was spinning from her strange wilding story, but it did make sense. We were definitely off the beaten track, away from the tourist activity nodes... and we were on a sparsely populated small-scale agricultural mountainside. It did sound like fun.

"Might need careful planning," I said.

"Yeah, damn straight! I'm all into that! And you, are you with me?"

"Perfect local recreation in between contracts. Let's talk about it back at the haybarn." As I thought about it I asked myself—what if it was access to gold? My head got flooded with questions—safety, security. It might be a rather complicated adventure. I wasn't convinced.

She leaned over, gave me a passionate kiss as only Bree could and whispered in my ear, "There's more where that came from. Let's catch the next train to Lauterbrunnen. And back to the haybarn."

The walk in the woods could happen another time; she had me thinking about something else. And I was all for that— Lauterbrunnen, Zweilutschinen, Grindelwald and a walk to our haybarn. The best part of the day was coming. We washed. We did what marrieds do. Then we showered, ate, sat outside in her garden and cuddled.

***

THD Sign-off

I enjoyed my gardening with Bree in what I came to privately call a "Faeryland" garden. It was a happy place, a friendly garden like I'd never seen or heard about. Faeryland? Well, you know, it was not just Bree who felt the effulgent glories (bliss accessible through sensual interaction with plants) in Faeryland. There were days of hard work. Days of cold. Days of sweat. And times when a flower would let my eyes taste those effulgent glories—so special they were.

It was everything—a cottage garden, an allotment garden. It was a garden of fragrant, aromatic and medicinal plants. I was in seventh heaven—watering, weeding, "holding hands" with the plants. And Bree was busy making jellies, jams and unguents for sale/barter in the small local village summer markets. On her days at the market she made sure to take bouquets to the church of our wedding—the church where she found comfort during my 2-year Egyptian walkabout.

I was surprised to not have heard from JeanClaude. He had set me up originally for the Istanbul job. Months went by. Autumn to winter to spring. And it was time for my contractual four-week follow-up visit to Istanbul to assess the establishment status along the 200 km motorway in Europe and Asia.

When I arrived the same engineers were there. Eymen Bey and I drove back and forth the new motorway with *Buyuk* and *Kuçuk* Kemal. The spring weather around the Bosphorus had been mild and wet. All the plants had established. I signed off on the project as 100% complete. And the THD accepted it. That meant I had been 100% true to my agreement with Will.

My professional career was back on track.

The third week though I got a rare email from Bree. She told me:

> ...someone has walked up to the haybarn asking for you—said his name was Garrett Howe. I told him you'd be back next week. He told me he is staying in Grindelwald at a place near the Blumisalp Stubbe. He said you can ask Suzie. Do you know him?

That was a shock. An email from Bree was unusual. And the message? Garrett Howe? I thought and thought. Howe? Howe... Garrett... and Gordie? From years ago? Back in Yenbo New Town, Gordie, my contract administrator? The guy who committed suicide and got me started on the quest to Thailand and my first visit to Switzerland? Gordie's brother? Gordie told me he had a twin brother, an Army Ranger, who, after multiple tours of duty, fell out of touch with Gordie. Off the grid, that was how Gordie had described him—an intelligence operative, a soldier for hire, Gordie had said. What does Garrett want with me?

When I finished my month of final inspections in Istanbul, I returned to Grindelwald and our haybarn. Bree was expecting me and had a nice *mittagessen* prepared—mead and all. She had her own special blend of herbs in the mead. It seemed to give me a peaceful eagerness. And naturally, we spent the entire afternoon renewing our marriage vows. I felt good. I felt at home. We both showered and went outside to dry in the sun, then sat under the apple tree for a glass of tea.

It was then that Bree launched into what she had learned when I was away. Apparently the old-timer wilding had passed by her haybarn again. The same one who had told her about the ancient gold stores under the Mannlichen.

Almost breathless with excitement, she said, "You've seen the crows around, haven't you? Well, they're not all crows. There are crows and choughs but at first glance they all look alike. The crows are called carrion crows and they have black bills. The choughs look like crows but they normally have yellow bills in this area. You with me? Well in the spring, during mating season—choughs are, by the way monogamous. Up under the Mannlichen *gipfel*, on the Wengen side, there have been a pair of red bill choughs, normally seen only in the neighbouring canton Valais—I don't know if this makes sense when put on a time scale over centuries—but the story is if you find them flying around in a pre-mating frenzy—they will lead you to the updrafts from the ventilation shaft leading to the ancient gold storage cavern beneath... what do you think?"

She was still breathless. I didn't know what to think. Bree was Bree, always into the landscape, in the deepest way. But, as I saw it, this was an adventure into the landscape of the Swiss government—much more than her haybarn garden. I just listened. I had to let it sink in. I really didn't know where it was headed.

I asked her for more details about her most recent wilding talks. "I asked him if anyone had ever tried to find the shaft," she said. This interested me.

"He said something like 'nobody messes with it'. I asked him why. He gave a bunch of reasons: it's a legend—a thousand years old—forests grow and change—birds come and go—and there are too many tourists around—and then he repeated it's a story."

I could see his point. This was just what I thought. We should drop it. But Bree still had the fire. I didn't say more. I hoped it would not become a front burner issue.

***

143

Garrett

The next day as I was walking into Grindelwald, I wondered about Garrett Howe who out of nowhere had found his way recently to our haybarn. I stopped at the Blumisalp Stubbe. Suzie and her help were busy with service for a full house *mittagessen*; even the terrace was full.

Gordie's twin brother Garrett? Gordie never said they were or weren't identical twins. I looked around for someone who was most likely alone, a Westerner and at least 6 feet tall.

Then I saw Suzie pausing with her hands on her hips looking straight at me.

"Look what the *foehn* (an usually strong wind that blows from time to time without warning) blew in! *Comment ça va?*" she asked.

I walked over and greeted her as a good friend.

"How have you been?" she asked.

"All's well, just got back from a landscape project in Istanbul..."

"You've got the life—all the world-famous places plus your home and wife in Grindelwald!"

"Can't complain—speaking of my wife, Bree told me an American has been looking for me—what do you know about that?"

"Look, I'm busy with *mittagessen* service now. No time for talking but there was a guy, he's been by a couple times. He usually stops in after *mittagessen*—nice guy—straightforward— speaks directly and confidently—seems a trustworthy type... can I get you anything?"

There was an empty stool at the bar. I sat and asked, "Zwickel *stang* please."

"Right away!" And off she went.

I hung around till 2PM when the entire *mittagessen* crowd had left. Suzie and her help were cleaning up when I saw a guy come in. Had to be Garrett. Similar build as Gordie but with a full beard. He dressed like a tourist who was into hiking, big-time—his clothes, well-worn from continuous outdoor activity. He carried a medium-sized backpack. He fit right in as a regular outdoors person. Wouldn't attract attention.

He sat down in the shade of an umbrella on the terrace. I walked over and introduced myself, "CJ's my name, and you?"

"Garrett, I've been looking for you."

His voice was deep, gravelly and slow. A serious presence.

"Mind if I sit down?" I asked.

"Help yourself."

"Looking for me? What's up?" We talked a while about our roots, Michigan, sports... the more he talked the more I felt I could get on with him.

Then he got to the point, "Gordie, my brother—you guys worked together on Yenbo, right?"

I nodded.

"What happened?"

That was an open-ended question. I launched into the whole story—Gordie was my most dependable friend, right-hand man and colleague. He had been blown away by the deaths of his wife and newborn and was trying to get right. He met a Malaysian girl in a Bangkok bar and was starting to feel better. He wanted to marry her... and then something happened... I don't know what. He took his life. And it being Saudi Arabia, there was never access to details—I don't know if ever there was an autopsy. Our company took care of it all with Saudi authorities.

"Did you put him under pressure on the job?"

"Never, he was always, on his own, ahead of things. I was shocked. I had to clean out his desk. But the company took his computer and cleaned out his flat. Have you ever been to Saudi Arabia? Strict—their country, their rules—argue or dispute and you get expelled."

"Anything else?"

"I found a map and a note in his desk—the only personal things in the office—he was disciplined that way."

"The map and note?"

"Name of his girlfriend and the bar where she worked in Bangkok. I went there when I learned she was his fiancée."

"What did you find?"

"Well, that's not a good story and I had to draw a conclusion... she had left Bangkok, accepting an offer worth a lot of money to work in Geneva. I tracked her down and all she could say was 'Life is short. I am sorry about Gordie.' I concluded that the hope Gordie had for getting his life right was based on the warmth he got when with this girl—but she was in business— Gordie wasn't. I figured he must have learned that she took off with another guy to earn the big bucks in Switzerland and it was too much for him."

Garrett was quiet. He was analyzing what I had just explained. He and I both took long drinks of beer, then, looking me square in the eyes, he said, "I thought you may have pushed him over the edge. I knew he was struggling with his loss of wife and newborn but I couldn't get free from my work. He made the wrong choice in Bangkok and paid the price. Sad, but that book I can close now."

"What are you planning? You still in the Army or what?"

"I was 20 and out. Now, out of Belgrade, I do contract training for them wherever they need me."

"So what're you doing now? Taking off or...?"

"I've got some free time. I think I'll explore this area—has a good feel and I need a bit of that."

"You staying in a hotel?"

"Nah, I like to sleep rough."

"That's a small backpack for sleeping rough."

"I'm used to it."

"That's real landscape experience, no?"

He smiled.

I stood up shook hands with him, and before leaving said, "Maybe we'll run into each other, I do a fair amount of hiking around here myself."

He stood up, shook my hand, smiled and said, "Thank you for the truth. Be seeing you."

***

CJ in the Garden

As I walked uphill back to our haybarn, I wondered about the meeting I just had—it was like an epilogue to the years I had worked with Gordie in Yenbo, in Saudi Arabia. But as soon as I saw our haybarn in the distance and Bree outside in the garden, my emotions warmed. My heart swelled. I was home.

Bree told me about her plant notebooks and her personal library from used bookstores and personal interview research she had done. She, like me, habitually kept notes about her garden observations. She said it also included the wilding stories she gathered over the years.

Summer was slowly moving into autumn as we sat in her garden, watching the sun move across the Grindelwald bowl valley below us. Watching small puffy white clouds form and drift against the mountains only to dissolve and disappear. The afternoon warmth healed, then the summer temperature broke, as it does in the mountains, and sunset commenced. The cool didn't chill, it refreshed and as the sunset turned into the crepuscule, Bree brought out some of her mead for us.

I felt comfortable emotionally—a strange feeling for me—I thought it was something I had missed ever so long. I had finally overcome my worst memories. I watched the para-gliders release as a group from First, each to then slowly find its own way to Grund at the bottom of the Grindelwald bowl. Watching their slow descent was peaceful. I loved watching them. I was in the right place.

My eyes returned to the garden around us, around the

haybarn. It was full of plants landscape architects never use and rarely knew—poppy, clary sage, yarrow, rue, hyssop, vervain, mugwort, wormwood, datura, henbane, belladonna, mandrake, plantain, calendula, camomile—more than I could name. Bree was deep into the processes for making soaps and oils, not to speak of her healthy teas.

With respect and love, I looked at Bree. She could read my mind. Without a prompt she said, "Faeries are the guardians of nature. And I have been working with them based upon the 13 months of the lunar calendar."

On a small arbour arching over the central path, I relished the climbing white roses over beds of fragrant pinks.

"You get into the fragrances, don't you? Come with me..."

She showed me stocks, phlox, honeysuckle, regale lily, wisteria, petunia, tobacco plants. I did not know what to expect next. It was as if I had never seen her garden before, even though I had worked in it for months before my last trip to Turkey.

"You might enjoy digging into some of the books I keep— that would help you see the landscape journey I have taken to get here."

"Tell me more."

"I look at alchemy as a rainbow bridging the chasm between the earthly and heavenly planes, between matter and spirit... alchemy, the means of penetrating the very secrets of nature, life, and death, of unity, eternity and infinity."

"That sounds a lot like my hopes for transcendent design— might I be talking about alchemical landscape design— something that transmits the alchemical nature of landscape through design?"

"Well, like I've said, as long as you can keep hubris and megalomania out of it. Paracelsus, a heretic in the opinion of Swiss Christians, but a great 17th century alchemist deeply into plants and health, wrote something that I think applies to you. It goes something like this: 'nature in itself was raw and unfinished, and man had the God-given task to evolve things to a higher level'."

I wondered again—am I trying to make alchemical design?

Her research was deep, she had a way with languages—in Morocco, she picked up Arabic like a breeze. She had gone into alchemical roots—Arabs and Hellenistic Egypt, Hermes, Descartes.

I've always wondered... what's behind, beyond the door? And it was clear that Bree, herself, was opening doors. As sympathetic, as understanding as I was about the roots of Bree's beliefs, it was her day in/day out work here in Switzerland that convinced me the most.

The third mug of mead had me looking inward. I thought about domains, certain cultural domains in the Swiss landscape:

1. The big city-Bern;
2. The intermediate city-Thun;
3. The tourist town-Interlaken, Grindelwald;
4. The village-Bonigen, Habkern, Saxeten;
5. The farmers; and,
6. The *trychlers*, the bell-ringers.

And just beyond the outer edge of the *trychlers*—absinthe and the not quite legal old way...

7. The wildings.

There are stories of the mountain landscape that exist outside of day-to-day civilization. The wildings live those stories. And the conviction of the reality of those stories diminishes the closer one comes to the big cities. In the big cities the majority call those stories fiction, lore.

But the big cities have their own domain of unbelievable stuff. Stories, urban legends, often generated by trafficked people uprooted from poorly developed countries, that require one to live in the city to believe. Urban legends—not for me.

At both ends of that domain spectrum are dangers to human life. I shook myself, looked over at Bree—she still had her hands and thoughts with the plants. It is all landscape.

***

JeanClaude Visits Interlaken

And then I got an email, from JeanClaude.

Arriving this week Friday 3PM Interlaken West, *mon ami.* We should talk. Meet me at the station. Please confirm.

I was glad to hear from him but I had no idea what he wished to talk about... a new project, perhaps? Was he on his way to or from Papua New Guinea—his favourite ethnobotanical research landscape?

On Friday, I arrived early because the train from Bern was due about 10 minutes to 3. And that was his train. He had no suitcase, only a briefcase he carried on a shoulder strap— traveling light. We warmly greeted each other and shook hands.

"Have you eaten?" I asked.

"In Bern. Let's walk, what's the shortest way to the countryside?"

"Follow me, in 10 minutes we'll be in the forests of the *Kleiner Rugen.*"

And we set off.

"I like this path because the local *gemeinde* (government office) has added signage to tell the story of a family that supported Interlaken as a health town."

"Do you ever ask yourself what it means, a 'health town'? Probably a rhetorical question for you, because you understand, eh *mon ami?*"

"Of course—something in this landscape region causes improvement in people's health. It is about the landscape, exactly as I felt my first time here."

"And that is how I know you. You have that refined sensitivity to appreciate what the landscape emits."

Before long we had entered the *Kleiner Rugen*. We paused, after walking a bit uphill in the *Kleiner Rugen* forest, to appreciate a view.

"This *Kleiner Rugen* is the landscape of Clara von Rappard who lived here in the 19th Century. This view of the Jungfrau was the source of her inspiration. She never said it but knowledgeable art critics talk about her representations of the Jungfrau through delicate veils of clouds and mist—lit-up fields of snow and the gorges and valleys sinking into deep shadows. She did this with tones of white, blue and grey. She had to feel it. And her dad was instrumental in bringing tourists to this region to appreciate its curative properties."

"CJ, that is the way you've been looking at landscape ever since your term-abroad design study experiences in Morocco. Me, I have my ethnobotany—that is my canvas—that is where I search for that depth, or is it breadth, that leads to the connection between material and spiritual. You, especially since that yodeller experience in Grindelwald, seek the same through the landscape. *Mon ami*, we are both searching, maybe for the same thing."

As we continued our walk around the *Kleiner Rugen* we came within view of some kind of recreation centre named SeilPark. We were in the midst of a well-established mixed evergreen/ deciduous forest filled with mature trees and understory. "Do you hear that?" JeanClaude asked.

"Yeah, it's the sound of people having fun, a lot of people."

We headed in the direction of the fun. SeilPark—a rope park—wooden and rope bridges for walks, swings and zip lines through the forest at various levels (from 2 metres to 20 metres) above the ground. These were a huge variety of connected skill challenges having varying levels of difficulty for muscles and balance. We saw kids and families. Groups of middle schoolers, high schoolers all having fun.

"What were you saying about health and the landscape?"

"I don't see any electronics, I don't hear any motors at all—just people having fun in and amongst the forest trees."

"Well, *mon ami*, you have Tangier, Istanbul, Cairo and Saudi Arabia under your belt—have you ever seen anything like this?"

"That question is too deep. I'll call it rhetorical, but now you can see why I like living here. Looks like lots of local people, only a couple from the Far East and Sub-continent."

We paused. Too much thinking—I got hungry.

"JeanClaude, I need something to eat and I know a brewery stubbe about a 10-minute walk from here. The brewery is over a century old, called Rugenbrau. And the stubbe is small, local, not a tourist stop—are you up for it?"

"I would enjoy a beer, let's go."

In the stubbe, late afternoon, not crowded—we sat outside under a chestnut tree surrounded by flowering geraniums and scores of small gnomes looking busy in the garden.

"What is the attraction? Why aren't these found in other parts of the world? Is it a cultural thing? Is it a climatic thing?"

JeanClaude said, "That's your bailiwick—outdoor recreation—landscape architecture—making your own dinner or ordering it out and having it delivered..."

"What!?"

"Outdoor recreation—doing it yourself or have someone else do it for you."

I thought for a while. Do it yourself—isn't that homesteading? Then I thought the desire to play in the trees in a civilized country in the early 21st century—isn't that an indication of some deep roots coming to the surface—new growth—maybe all is not lost in electronics, engines and digital social life.

As I was "busy" thinking, JeanClaude said, "What is intriguing about these questions is that they lead into grey areas... and these grey areas are just what the best of the alchemists were exploring. I am not talking about the grifters trying to make gold out of lead, I'm talking about the Flamels—alchemists who achieved enlightenment from the landscape like Nicolas Flamel on the road to Santiago de Compostela..."

"Like my friend Bo who a long time ago walked that Santiago

de Compostela landscape looking for Jacob's Ladder in real life."

"And Paracelsus right here in Switzerland who sought his answers from the plants..."

JeanClaude's conversation was making me think of Bree and her commitments to plants, gardens and the landscape. And what about myself... landscaping, landscape architecture... design? I must have said design out loud because JeanClaude said, "Design? You mean liminality."

I thought and recalled that liminality was about the limit below which a given stimulus ceases to be perceptible—in other words a threshold—movement from one to another—matter to spirit and vice-a-versa.

"Liminality, liminal space, liminal realm—it is that place that you have described as a portal, a threshold. Your friend Bo called it a stairway—Jacob's Ladder. It is a strange term of description for something no one can see but some people of heightened sensitivity are keenly aware of. Are you still chasing that ladder?"

"I suppose I am—it always seems to pop up—Morocco, Egypt, Turkey—Sufis, music—I am fated to make design sense out of it. But here with Bree, I have brought my interest into the foreground of my daily life activities—hands-on stuff with the plants in her garden... and the landscape? It sits in the background as an always-available source of refreshment."

"So what are you really into these days, *mon ami*, design, gardening, your wife?"

***

Go-bag

The late summer day had been partly cloudy, no wind, temperature in the low 20s centigrade—peaceful. We were relaxed, sitting at a two-seat garden table with no one else nearby. I had a good opportunity to respond to JeanClaude's question and quietly run Bree's wilding legend by him, so I began.

"Bree is my focus now. But I always question/explore landscape, cultures, music, design... There is one curious thing that is linked to our earlier discussions on the clashes between Islam and Christianity in Vienna. I'm talking about the earliest, the Crusades when a lot of northern European Christians travelled back and forth through these mountains to find the shortest route to Jerusalem and back home..."

"And?"

"The people living here in the Alps worked as guides and also mercenaries during those ancient times, leaving behind legends. Legends of gold hoards stored in deep caves in these very mountains. Bree has kept notes of stories she has heard over the years and has a plan to find a long-hidden access to those ancient stores."

"What? You are going to go after the gold? The Swiss gold? Well, I know a bit about Swiss military traditions and can only warn you not to mess with any so-called 'ancient gold' stores—they will be well protected, and the Swiss protect, at all costs, their heritage."

"She doesn't talk about finding or taking the gold—rather about verifying if the legends about the access point are real,"

I clarified.

I had finished my sandwich and we had dawdled long enough with our beers in this garden overlooking Interlaken, Matten, Wilderswil and the Brienzersee. I had listened to JeanClaude's warning and it was part of his mood today which was altogether different from his normal jokey self. I wondered.

"Did you say you were leaving tonight?"

"I have a flight out of Zurich first thing in the morning—must spend the night in Zurich."

"We're only a ten-minute walk to Wilderswil and a bus stop that will take you back to the train station."

We paid our bill and off we went. It was another walk through forests and pastures with the Jungfrau, and all its snow-capped glory, up ahead of us. Along the way JeanClaude paused at a bench and suggested we sit for a bit to enjoy the view. That is when he broke the news.

"CJ, I am retiring—getting out of the game—the liminal spaces are calling me. I've got to get back into the deep ethnobotany. I'm headed off the grid—Papua New Guinea—for as long as it takes."

"Analysis Corp and all that finished?"

"*Bien sur*, it is time to put a lid on that."

It started sinking in, I had been subconsciously figuring that as long as JeanClaude was providing services to Analysis Corp, I would have interesting landscape architecture jobs through him... but... now?

I asked, "I had expected we would be working together for a while? I'm not sure what this means."

"Will Clendenon is still there and he keeps tabs on you. So I figure when the right opportunity arises, he will contact you. But CJ, I worry about Bree's 'adventure'. I think it could be dangerous. I understand how close you are to Bree so I have an idea—a form of insurance should trouble arise. Actually, I have some things I was going to give you anyway—documents and a useful piece of kit to remember me by—but now, after you revealed Bree's ancient gold adventure plans, it has become a lot more."

I was mystified. I didn't know what he was talking about.

Retiring? Out of the game? He seemed preoccupied with something important. I watched.

He reached into his briefcase, pulled out a mobile phone and started messing with it. When he finished, he said, "Let's get that bus."

We took the bus back to Interlaken West. At the train station JeanClaude studied the schedule then said, "I've got some time, the train I'll take leaves in two hours. Do you have a place where I can sample some of that famous Swiss hot chocolate?"

"I know a place, just up the street—Schuh Chocolateria—they have a nice outdoor terrace opening on an historic open space in the centre of town."

It was early evening and not many on the terrace. After the waitress delivered the two hot chocolates—hot milk with a chunk of "*haus gemacht*" (homemade) dark chocolate at the bottom that we were supposed to stir in, JeanClaude pulled out his briefcase again.

As we were sipping the hot chocolates, he began, "*Mon ami,* your ideas about nosing into the Swiss ancient gold are much more dangerous than your information-gathering efforts for the Analysis Corp. Let me suggest you prepare should things go pear-shape on the day. Have a go-bag ready."

"Go-bag?"

"Yes, go-bag is what you need to take care of yourself if you have to leave in an emergency. You need details?"

"Help me out."

"For one person a lightweight backpack would be fine like the one you are wearing now but packed in advance with only the essentials for escape, for being on the run for 10 days-two weeks—ready to go. With money for international travel (a lot, 10 grand with at least half in small bills should get you to your destination), ID, the basics for survival on the road for two weeks or so. Here." He gave me my old Christopher Janus ID documents.

"Why my old ID?" I asked.

"If you really have to run from the Swiss military intelligence, you must ditch all IDs, plus your digital kit, that have you registered here in Switzerland—all your Charles

Jacobs documents. Use your old Christopher Janus docs after you exit from Europe. I'll show you a route how to get out of Switzerland and Austria without passport control." Then he gave me the mobile he had been fussing with.

"Take this, tuck it in a safe place deep into your backpack now and your go-bag when you set it up."

"What is it?"

"It's what they call a pre-paid burner phone—don't use it for anything other than way-finding. Nobody can track you. Leave your own phone and computer at home. The pre-paid, once you activate it, is good for one year anywhere in Europe. Everything I'm about to tell you is clearly shown and explained on that phone, should you need it.

"On the phone, I have set up a gpx file and software that is a route out of Switzerland without crossing a border check point into Austria and similarly from Austria to Slovenia. I know this route well. When you get to Slovenia, dump your old passport and all the rest of your Charles Jacobs documents. Then make your way to Port Koper where you should find a freighter, a cargo vessel to Fujairah in the UAE. Stay on the ship the whole way.

"Before you dock in the UAE recheck all my notes on the gpx file, then dump your burner phone into the sea. Upon UAE entry use your Christopher Janus passport—I can assure you that your entry there will be safe and unquestioned."

"You really think I'll need this? And what about Bree?"

"You are messing with the Swiss army, and they take care of their own, *mon ami*—best be safe. And Bree? That's between you and her. Be careful what you say. You could be in two danger zones—the gold with the Swiss military and your info-gathering identity with Bree. If you do that wilding gold adventure, it could be much more than a walk in the forest."

"What?"

"Keep your info-gathering work to yourself; and if you make that adventure—stay alert."

I was nervous—JeanClaude was going off the grid and he warned me of dangers... I didn't know what to think. But I had an inkling early on that this adventure of Bree's might have a downside. JeanClaude made the downside clear.

He said, "Time to go, got to catch my train. *Au revoir, mon ami.*"

And that was the last I saw and heard from JeanClaude.

***

Jobs Is on the Way

The months turned into fall, winter and then spring. Together, Bree and I put the garden to sleep for the winter. Working with her in the garden, I realized there is no such thing as low maintenance, which is as much a fallacy as cast iron plants.

Plants are alive and taking care of them is the same as small pets—dogs, cats. Love and care? For all yields excellent results. Short of love and care—weak and untrustworthy results. Plants—always something to do—four seasons—every year.

Indoors Bree was busy with her tinctures, elixirs, essences and fermentations. I helped where I could. Other times, I just read from the books on her bookshelf, her arcane collections—reprints of *The Hermetic Corpus*, Jung's *Man and His Symbols*, Paracelsus' *First Do No Harm* and many others. She was happy to see me paging through them. Every once in a while, while working over pots of plant parts, she would just start a monologue.

Bree said, "I've got to share this so we have no misunderstandings on this subject. If I mention alchemy to someone—what do they usually think of? The Middle Ages with old men in some forgotten attic, tinkering over bubbling flasks filled with some unknown fluid; or in front of an oven, trying to turn molten lead into gold. These are the images of the alchemist that time, mythology, and prejudicial history have handed down to us. Now, I know you are more broadminded than that; but when you talk about witches... you are part of that group."

She continued, "Alchemy, occult, esoteric—words that have carried for centuries negative overtones because they are 'outside' the major religions—but actually they are a part of every religion—they are about the purpose of life, why we are here, where we have come from, and where are we going."

She kept on, "For the alchemist, the universe is perceived as a reflection of the imagination of the Godhead. Its laws are consistent and logical, and if we are created in the image of the Creator, then we can also create as the Creator has—through the power of imagination. Intense imagination creates a stress on the 'fabric' of the universe, drawing to it magnetic power, thus bringing our images to fruition."

I wasn't following this bit but I was listening as she reached her conclusion, "I have no conflicts between my belief in God and Christianity in relation to how I work with plants. The Supreme Lord is the Supreme Lord and daily life is daily life. Working with God's creation is lovely, enthusing, refreshing— yes, and hard work. It all makes a physical and emotional balance. You feel that too, don't you?"

"Yes, definitely—of course." It was getting deeper than I could follow but I agreed with the basics.

She went quiet—deeply absorbed in her work. I, too, stayed quiet and remembered what JeanClaude had said about go-bags. I asked Bree, "What do you think might happen when we search for that access to ancient gold?"

"Never thought too much about it—an adventure..."

"But what if we get into a store of gold?"

"Well, I did think it would be nice if we could get some of it..."

"What if the wilding legend is true—wouldn't it be protected by the Swiss military?"

"Never thought about that..."

"I'm into the adventure. I'm into the search but... I think we should be prepared for some kind of surprise—some kind of danger... don't you think that would be practical?"

I had my computer open while we were talking and just then I got an email from Will Clendenon; he was in Vienna. He had a job for me in The Gulf—Bahrain. He left his telephone number and said to call him if I was interested

It was timely. I told Bree about it, saying, "This is how I get work—from people who have been satisfied by my past projects."

I stepped outside and called Will.

Here's the bottom line: take charge of (manage) an already established design/build/maintain team of eight (Yanks, Brits and some others) on a one-square-kilometre private island recreation project for a Bahraini haut personality. The offer was 7,000pounds/month, one month home leave after 12 months and an annually renewable contract until the project was finished. Will was in Vienna for two weeks and would arrange a return flight (Bern-Vienna-Bern) for me to discuss the Bahrain particulars and sign an MOA (Memorandum of Agreement—same as a contract).

I shared the details with Bree. "Okay, this is how it works. The money is good but I will be away for twelve months before I can see you again. But I must act quickly and efficiently to make this work, so tomorrow AM I will take the train to Bern-Belp where I will fly to Vienna to close the deal. I'll return before I go to Bahrain but only for a couple days."

She looked sad at first but then I could see her strength and understanding. I said, "I will wire transfer the same amount as I did in Turkey—that worked out okay, didn't it?"

"Yes... but... twelve months?"

"I don't want to talk too much about details until I return from Vienna."

I still saw disappointment in Bree's eyes but she was practical. I tried to ease her concern. "I'm sure we can work out my visits and our communication details. It is the core of our long-term financial stability—must do."

***

Bahrain Details

Ifollowed Will's instructions and had no complications arriving and taking off from Bern-Belp. A driver met me at Brumowski and drove me to Vienna central city. Will met me in the same office JeanClaude had used. We shook hands and he got right down to business. He thanked me for a job well done in Istanbul.

Then he began to introduce the Bahrain island project to me.

"Bahrain is not just a one-island country. Bahrain has 30 islands in addition to the main island everyone sees on maps. Like I told you on the phone, this is a fast-moving planning/design/construction/maintenance set on the one-square-kilometre island. The island belongs to one of the highest governmental officials.

"For security, we are not allowed to use his name, so we call him haut personality, HP for short. He is hands-on and visits that project every day when he drives around the island reviewing on-going projects on site with you. For all other issues you will interface with the HP's right-hand man, a Singaporean Chinese, who functions as his Facilities Manager (FM)."

I listened intently. Lots of potential personality pitfalls. Will continued. "On site and ready to go, there are two construction companies on call 24/7/365 so when the HP gives the go-ahead on design or doesn't like what he sees being built, they take immediate action.

"Your title will be Project Manager. Your team is linked to

a Kuwaiti office for architecture, engineering and quantity surveying. The previous project manager was a Scot who rubbed people the wrong way and would not associate with our information gathering.

"In addition to your base salary, you will have both a furnished apartment and a 4-wheel drive vehicle as part of your package.

"Now, our purpose is to observe the FM, the Singaporean Chinese. We believe he may be laying the groundwork for major Chinese influence into the Gulf Region via Bahrain.

"All visa details and staff salary distribution come through me. You have only to manage day-to-day activities on site."

I asked, "Now that JeanClaude is no longer with us, who do I report to?"

"Alan, you know him, is handling the Gulf Region for me. You'll have to report directly to him. He passes through Manama once a month. I know you don't have a good relation with Alan, so if you think things are off-balance you can call me. I am in Kuwait on an oil project and Eileen, you know her, handles all my incoming."

I squirmed but said nothing. The project was interesting and the pay packet was excellent.

Will continued, "There's a construction trailer on site. There is no internet connectivity on the island, but you will have broadband connectivity in your apartment. Your work week is 7AM-5PM Sa-Th. You will be on call from HP or his FM 24/7.

"HP wants first-class international hospitality standard and his FM makes efforts to get that with Chinese suppliers and prices. Everything is here in the Memorandum of Agreement, MOA, and here is a dossier with complete backgrounds of all your employees on the island."

As he handed them to me, he said, "We need you now. There is no one in the Project Manager position—a planner, seconded from Kuwait, is acting now and he will fill you in all island politics and activities. If you want the job, sign the MOA and I will fly you back to Switzerland for one week with your wife. I will give you a business-class round-trip flight from Zurich to

Manama, departing in one week with the return open."

I skimmed my employee dossier (the people who would be working for me), signed the MOA and was back in Switzerland before sunset.

***

Brambles

I sat down with Bree and gave her the Bahrain job details. That was all straightforward. I didn't have much to pack so I had some free time.

"Bree, might it be a good time to explore just below the Mannlichen—that area you told me about—the access shaft to the ancient gold? Just explore for the entry shaft—look for the red-billed chough mates and the like?"

I saw her eyes light up; but she said, "Weren't you all worried about a go-bag and some-such?"

"No, no, no—that's just if we find the entry, then if we try to enter. The entering, that's the serious part."

We spent the night working out the plan. The next morning, the weather was in our favour—clear and no wind. We packed our lunch, took a couple bottles of water and headed to Grindelwald to take the first trains that would get us to Wengwald.

At Wengwald, we walked and walked on unpaved roads then along a narrow wanderweg, always uphill. We continued walking uphill through tall, thick spruce and fir forests. The path curved down slightly as we crossed a dry brook. Something told us to follow the dry brook uphill. We did.

We suddenly found ourselves on the edge of a Swiss stone pine grove at just under 2,000 metres above sea level. The brook bottom was stoney, difficult to walk. We forged our way uphill till we came to a grassy opening with Swiss stone pines all around the edge. We put down a cloth and sat for sandwiches and water. Bree pointed out a scattering of cowslips, the

Primula vera, around the clearing. Their clear yellow flowers stood proudly. They were obviously at home. It was a quiet, peaceful setting. The sun warmed us.

We observed. There was shady forest around us but I could see another opening about 30 metres uphill. After sandwiches, we headed further uphill to the next patch of sun—larger than the last. We stood on the shady edge of the Swiss stone pine forest and listened. It always takes some minutes of human quiet before the birds return to normal behaviour and their calling to one another. We stood, then we sat on a partially exposed boulder.

We heard choughs in the distance. We didn't move, we didn't speak. We waited. Then we saw them in a treetop, a middle-aged Swiss stone pine. We waited as they called to each other. They took to the air and frolicked as they descended. They were red billed. I held my breath, watching intently.

They descended on the uphill far side of this open space, about 50 metres away, and alighted on a pile of rocks that seemed to be overgrown with brambles, wild blackberries. The choughs were eating them. We didn't move. We watched.

After a couple short minutes of feasting on the blackberries, the choughs lifted off. Bree absolutely danced without restraint. She figured her wilding legend was confirmed. She danced across the meadow over to the wild bramble clump. I stood and absorbed the joy she was giving off.

Then I walked over and together we examined the huge bramble clump. The clump was a good two metres high and six metres across. Like any wild bramble it was thickly covered with thorns. We couldn't just grab branches. We couldn't untangle anything.

We could only use our eyes to inspect and even the tangled branches were covered with early summer leaves. So we circumambulated—maybe 20 metres of circumference. Could not see the ground underneath the brambles anywhere. So, I dropped a pin on my maps program and we headed home.

The next day we returned with leather gloves and pruning shears. We selectively pruned out one by one the arching bramble branches in part of one of the plant's quadrants—

working toward the centre. We didn't know what we would find. I told Bree we should be careful because if we found something, we wouldn't want to leave a trail to the doorstep. She agreed.

We did a minimum amount of cutting and bending of long bramble branches. There we uncovered stonework, rough stonework—the kind you see when farmers clear a field for the first time. We cleared more of the bramble suckers and found a hole—a vertical tunnel leading down. A shaft? The sides were rough stone, like on the surface. The inner diameter was just a bit wider than one person. Bree and I looked at each other. Didn't say anything. I dropped a small stone down the entry. I didn't know the math but it must have bounced two or three times off the sides before it hit bottom—three or four seconds.

Then some sense returned. I said, "We better stop. That clattering stone? That was an entry. We better call it quits, go back home and carefully plan our next move."

We tried to put everything back so it looked like the usual undisturbed bramble thicket. All the while, Bree said nothing. I think she was in shock.

We didn't say anything walking or on the train. We didn't talk until we were back in our haybarn. Bree got something together to eat and drink. We sat down, looked at each other and laughed. I said, "What just happened?"

"I don't know. It's still sinking in."

"It's no longer a legend. We have to get serious."

"We had a fun adventure but now... what's next?"

"Let's not be hasty. I have to go to Bahrain and will be away for 12 months. That will give us plenty of time to carefully think it through."

Bree said, "We do have to go down that tunnel, don't we... don't we?"

"We should ask why and how... very carefully. We need to figure out possible consequences—getting caught, finding something, getting trapped. Neither of us are climbers."

"And I don't know about you but I've never explored caves... what do they call that... spelunking?"

"Me neither. We'll need equipment lots of it—safety, lights

and all that. The more I think about it, it's good I am going to a good paying job now. That gives us time to work through all of this, evaluate alternatives and move forward with the best course. It's not like going on a *wanderweg* hike, is it?"

"You're right."

"I think we should keep this to ourselves—nothing to locals, nothing to wildings—do you agree?

"Agree, let's promise."

"Agreed."

5-The Gulf

Bahrain: On the Ground

The Arabian Peninsula is a geographic reality; but beyond its geography, its definition becomes difficult. It is politically divided into seven countries. Even though dominated by the most arid of deserts, the peninsula and its people have historically been influenced by a number of significant, nearby human cultures.

On my way to Bahrain, I couldn't help thinking about my previous six years working on the Red Sea coast in the Western Region of the Kingdom of Saudi Arabia (KSA) Yenbo. Beginning the descent, I was 1,300 kilometres east of Yenbo and the Red Sea. I was arriving to the Gulf Region on the eastern side of the Arabian Peninsula. And the sea surrounding Bahrain is known as... what is it known as? Depends on whom you talk with.

People on the Arabian Peninsula side call it the Arabian Gulf. People on the Iranian side call it the Persian Gulf. Culturally, if, like I experienced back then, Africa influenced the Western Region of Saudi Arabia, then Persia and maybe the Indian sub-continent might have exerted cultural influences here.

Hell, I didn't really know what to expect. I had learned that among Muslims there is dramatic variety... Sunni, Shia, Sufi and hundreds of variations in between...

But the unknown? This had become my game.

Everyone knows the anxiety of day one on a new job, right? But Bahrain? This was a new job in a country I'd never visited. I'd have to figure out bureaucracies, interpret driving habits, find my way around, learn where to shop and establish daily routines in a place I'd never been. Not to speak of getting on with the people, scope and priorities of my new job!

Expatriate life. If you get triggered by change, never leave your home country. I had grown to like the challenges of foreign cultures. New and strange—anxiety and excitement. A heady mix.

As my flight into the capital city Manama descended I could see the entire main island of Bahrain—a small island, only 50 kilometres long by 15 kilometres wide, less than 1,000 square kilometres. Part, the northern third of Bahrain, was green—lots of plants. That surprised me but the balance, the southern part, was 100% barren desert, not a plant to be seen, as I had known in KSA.

Jeffrey Tennant met me as I arrived at Bahrain International Airport in Muharraq just next to Manama. He told me to call him Jeff. That surprised me. His shortened name sounded American. I was not accustomed to the way Brits shortened Christian names. But Jeff? I could live with that.

He was the senior representative from the Kuwaiti Architecture/Engineering (AE) firm that held the contract for my new project. He was a senior planner from the UK with all professional credentials, a Charter Member of the Royal Town Planning Institute. He grew up in Hertfordshire, Letchworth Garden City, and earned his credentials after a decade with a major international AE based in London. Interesting background.

He suggested we go nearby to have a drink at the Oak Lounge in the Gulf Hotel where we would go over the critical details of the island project and its people. Getting right into it, good start, I was encouraged. From the airport, the highway drive was smooth flowing, quite crowded but disciplined. Jeff led me away from the lobby to a quiet lounge. It was a place that had the warm aura of private conversations. I liked it. He got right down to business.

"This is your first time in Bahrain?" Jeff asked.

"Yeah, but I spent 6 years in the Western Region of Saudi."

"Not the same. Bahrain and the Eastern Region of Saudi Arabia? It started maturing during the Gulf Wars—Manama became like Bangkok—alcohol, R'n'R bars and night clubs in all the big hotels. And carloads of Saudis crossing the causeway every weekend to get a 'taste' of Western culture."

"Still a thing?"

"SE Asia dancing girls in miniskirts and playing in R'n'R bands—every weekend. That doesn't affect our project but—it is the cultural envelope of booze and sex—I'm sure you never saw that in the Western Region."

"No kidding."

His description of the Bahrain social envelope surprised me. Istanbul had all those sex and bar attractions—but here in the Islamic heartland? Jeff had described Bahrain like it was Bangkok. Started with the Gulf Wars? Maybe. That's what they said about that prostitute bar The Creed in Bangkok—started with the Vietnam War. I couldn't stand Bangkok when, after his death, I was searching there for Gordie's fiancée. Bahrain the same? I'd have to see it to believe it.

***

Mr. Wong

Jeff interrupted my thoughts with context about my new job. "Okay, here's some good news, our production team on site is limited in size and scope but they are steady and dependable—except one, the senior American LA—always sick—I think he's not accustomed to being out of the US. He does good work but—too many sick days..."

I interrupted, "What is his contractual situation? Should we bring on someone else?"

"He signed an annual contract that automatically renews every 12 months—if we want to change we need to give him 3 months' notice and the same goes for him. If he wants out he needs to give us 3 months' notice. Talk with him. Decide yourself; but I think he'll stick it out and like I said he does good work."

"I'll keep an eye on him. Tell me how the engineering and architecture work is done."

"Our architecture and engineering support is from Kuwait. It is solid but their support needs appropriate lead time—don't expect overnight turnarounds."

"So, we're not in any serious trouble there, eh? And I don't hear any serious weaknesses on the team." As I said this I was thinking that Jeff could be the Project Manager, so I asked, "You've been acting Project Manager, why haven't they made you permanent PM?"

"The requirement for PM is that he must be a landscape architect. Welcome on board. And here's where you come in. You are the interface with two very important people—the

HP, who we don't name for security reasons—he is the Prime Minister and that's the last time you'll hear that from me. The other key person you will interface with is Mr. Wong, a Singaporean-Chinese, who is the HP's right-hand man, his Facilities Manager (FM)."

"You have some background on them for me?"

"I'm getting to that. The FM, Mr. Wong, talks like an aggressive WW2 character still fighting the Japanese. He speaks good English but with a heavy Chinese accent; and his every sentence is filled with four-letter-words. The HP, on the other hand, is a gentleman, speaks English like an academic; but he is distant in his own way. You must listen to him if you want to work here. But the foul-mouthed FM? You really have to use a hard filter. The rest is up to you—you will meet them both tomorrow."

"Thanks for the profiles. How does a typical day go?"

"We work six days a week, Saturday-Thursday, from 7AM to 5PM. Mr. Wong has his own construction trailer office and meeting room right next to ours. He gets in every day at 6AM to meet with the two active construction contractors on site where they share their daily work program and update their project status—procurement, time and budget. He expects to meet you tomorrow morning at 6:30 in his office."

"And the HP?"

"The HP usually arrives, driving himself, MB G-wagon v12 biturbo, all black, around 2PM, and drives around the island for a half hour. When he is on site, you drive behind him. When he stops you stop, get out and go to his window to take instructions. Listen carefully. Take notes and initiate our team action. Mr. Wong has a big white Land Rover Defender and he rides behind you. At the end of the daily drive through, you will meet with Mr. Wong to review your notes and actions."

"Doesn't the HP have security with him?"

"His security team waits at the island entry for him. The island has only one land entry point, a narrow causeway. It is well protected—no public—only the authorized with ID, like us and our team, and of course, the contractors. And the island waterfront is regularly patrolled by their coast guard— a couple guys on a Defender-class, a small 25-footer.

"As well as a copy of the approved master plan, I have a copy of our work program. Every one of our tasks is listed with its current status—under design, in construction, under maintenance—plus responsibilities, due dates and durations."

He handed me an A3 size plastic-cover, ring-bound master plan and a spreadsheet. I looked at the spreadsheet. I could look at the master plan later. The island project had already been active for two years and a number of tasks had already been completed and under maintenance.

I was hungry. Jeff said, "You ought to get something here because there is no food in your apartment."

I ordered a club sandwich—without the bacon—roast beef instead.

Jeff said, "There are a couple headaches."

"Headaches?"

"Yeah, they are both expatriates—long time here in Bahrain. An Egyptian head gardener, has some kind of degree from Cairo—he provides all the fruit and veg to the HP family. Oh, by the way, the HP family is never seen on the island. They do not visit. But the Egyptian head gardener knows how to successfully grow in this climate, with this water and he has been in his position for over a decade."

"Water, tell me more—how come there is so much green in this part of Bahrain?"

"The water table is high here. The entire aquifer from the Arabian Peninsula flows this way. Wells have been successful for a long time. But... and this is a big but! The water from the wells is becoming more and more saline. The time will come where the wells will have to be desalinated—but not yet. We have plenty of water from wells on the island. We use salt tolerant plants. If you have any hort question, the Egyptian is helpful. But, he is careful to keep his position safe—he is cautious—but he has been successful. Ask him to see his nursery."

"So he is a useful resource?"

"Yes, definitely."

"And there is another headache?"

"There is a Scot, named Andrew, a landscape architect working as a consultant for the Bahrain Ministry of Housing. He's been in Bahrain for 6 years and likes to think of himself as the landscape architect for Bahrain. Well, he has been a close friend with another Scot, the guy who you have replaced. That guy disrespected the HP regularly and lost his job. Andrew lost some cred by association. He gets onto the site from time to time to act 'independently' and that is the headache. If you do well with the HP and Mr. Wong then I'm sure that headache will go away. It's getting late, let me show you your apartment and vehicle. The apartment is not far from here and your vehicle, a grey Suzuki 4x4 Jimny, is parked in the basement garage there. The Jimny is air conditioned, like everything including your flat."

"That's one thing that is the same on both sides of the Arabian Peninsula!"

"I'll give you the keys and documents for both when we get to your apartment. Oh, by the way, all the utilities are on and in the rental agreement. You'll not need to interface with those agencies."

At the apartment Jeff offered, after work tomorrow, to show me around town—day to day necessities, shopping, groceries, pharmacies. I was pleased. He was helpful—easy arrival and intro to Bahrain.

I asked, "Any dress code on the job?"

"Hot and humid, 365. Hat, recreation-wear—long sleeve and long pants."

"That works, I have everything I need already with me. How do I get there?"

"Takes about 20 minutes from here—follow the signs that lead to KSA. Our island is the first one on the right after you leave the mainland. You can't miss it. There is an exit and the narrow causeway takes you north about 2 kilometres to the security gate. I'll meet you at 6:15AM at the security checkpoint. I can get you through, the island is small and we will have plenty of time before we meet Mr. Wong at 6:30AM.

"Oh, I almost forgot." Jeff took a mobile out of his pocket.

"Here is the official Project Manager mobile. Always keep it on. Mr. Wong issued it and he keeps you on speed dial. You'll get used to it. See you in the morning."

***

New Home

My new one-bedroom apartment, top floor of a four-storey building, was clean as a whistle—AC, fully furnished, carpets, curtains, towels, sheets, cutlery, kitchen appliances and comfortable. I had a small balcony with a view north. I looked forward to a look around town with Jeff for my typical daily needs.

I was tired. I unpacked and showered. Funny thing about showers. They are like a cocoon. Close the curtain, turn on the hot water and I could be anywhere!

I thought of Bree. Hardly 12 hours ago, I was in her arms at the haybarn saying goodbye. So many of our conversations flashed through my head. We talked, seemed like forever, about plants, landscape, design. She warned me about hubris and megalomania. Hmm... and here I was in a new reality. Starting tomorrow, no theory, no dreams, just real-world get the job done. I had no idea what I would find in my meetings with the HP and his FM.

I had my info-gathering to do—seemed like no big deal, except my handler, Alan, had always been a pain in the ass; but the pay was good and I'd be back in the haybarn soon enough.

Haybarn! That adventure Bree has been on about up on the Mannlichen—what to do about it? Sounds like a fun adventure. That's what Bree sees. But my common sense and cautions from JeanClaude flashed warning lights—danger, danger. I've got time to figure something out. I cranked up the hot water higher. I relaxed. The shower water pressure and temperature suited me.

Then my thoughts turned to local culture. That discussion I had with Jeff when he talked about the Bahrain night scene was strange. Sounded like Bangkok but what I saw on the streets of Muharraq and Manama was nothing like I saw in Bangkok. Bangkok street scene was crowded, overcrowded and weird— like it was evil personified.

And here? Even though here and Bangkok were both hot and humid, the streets were orderly. And the sidewalks I saw tonight were not crowded, were not overflowing into the street. It won't be like Bangkok. Anyhow the project is off the main island and will likely be quiet—only active contractors on site—no public admitted. I was looking forward to tomorrow.

***

It Begins

My personal and professional life had stabilized. The negative impact from my yearlong walkabout in Egypt searching for the roots of the Pharaonic landscape had disappeared. I felt good, I felt balanced.

Before I took rest, I looked closely at the master plan and the current program. This project looked like fun—some troublesome personalities—but which projects don't have troublesome personalities?

I dug into my work and reviewed the list of tasks:

1. Villa 1
2. Villa 2
3. Villa Cluster
4. Historic Restaurant
5. Guesthouse/Hotel 50rms
6. Aviary/Fish Pond/Nature Centre
7. Exotic Gardens
8. Date Palm Orchard
9. Health/Exercise Centre
10. Aquatic Park
11. Marina
12. Island Entry
13. Roads
14. Pedestrian/Bikes Network
15. Teahouse
16. Mangroves
17. Swimming Lagoon

18. Maintenance Yards/Irrigation Reservoir
19. Landmarks
20. Planting/Irrigation
21. Electrical/Water/Sewerage/Communication Infrastructure
22. Outdoor Retail/Fast Food Court
23. Street Furnishings
24. Water Features
25. Interpretive Signage
26. Coastal Protection/Development

That's a lot of tasks. Twenty-six. This was a huge project and our on-site team was small and landscape oriented. It looked to me like the project was being slow-walked when I compared it to my years at Yenbo New Town. And the motorway in Turkey with its viaducts, tunnels and associated infrastructure required full-time teams. But our Kuwaiti AE support team was essentially part-time.

I thought about the scope of work, the personalities (HP and FM) and my thin team, and I concluded, "Slo-mo. This project appears to be moving forward in slow motion. Like it or not I'll have to do what I have to. The master plan has a lot of exciting features—looks challenging—but the implementation? Appears to be slow. I'll do my best to assure highest quality. I need to get a good understanding of just exactly where and how I fit in."

I hit the sack.

I left early in the morning and arrived at the island entry security post just after 6AM. While I was waiting I recalled that Will had told me that the FM, Mr. Wong, was my information-gathering assignment. At 6:15 Jeff arrived, signed me in and we headed to our office. He showed me around—secretary, open area where all my staff would work, conference room, tea room, store room, toilet, etc. Then we headed next door to Mr. Wong's office.

Jeff knocked on the door.

"Come in!"

As Jeff and I entered, a thin man behind a construction site work desk began to stand up. He was taller than 5'6", a bit of a slump, but nowhere near 6'. He wore wire-rimmed glasses, had thinning dark black hair and a noticeably yellow cast to his complexion. He was late 40s... maybe late 50s with a wiry build. He spoke loudly, "Mr. Jeff, is this the new man?"

"Mr. Wong, this is Mr. Charles Jacobs, a senior landscape architect, with over a decade of Middle East experience. He starts today as our team Project Manager/Director of Landscape Architecture."

Mr. Wong reached out his hand and briskly shook mine firmly—nothing limp fish about it. He could have been American the way he shook hands.

"Please sit down. Mr. Jeff, you are free to leave, I'll introduce Mr. Charles to his duties." Jeff left the trailer and Mr. Wong did not offer tea or anything else. Mr. Wong's mobile kept buzzing until he shut it off.

He looked at me and started, "Mr. Charles, this job is not complicated. Every time the HP comes to the island, you must be here. This is HP's project. We give him what he wants. You will listen to him, answer his questions, pay attention to his comments and follow his instructions. Keep a journal, write everything. Then after HP leaves the island, you sit with me to review everything. Are you clear?

"I am HP's Facilities Manager—here on the island and at his home. I provide everything he needs. He takes a shit—he wipes his ass with toilet paper I provide. Same here. If HP wants something, your team designs it and I have two contractors on call 24/7/365. They are my bitches. I give orders, they bust their asses, I pay them. Your Construction Manager watches them on site to make sure they build HP's approved design. Are you clear?

"Questions?"

"Do we have a budget?"

"No budget, you design for HP. I review construction documents before giving to my bitches. You no worry about budget. Clear? Is that all?"

"There are 26 tasks in the master plan—who sets the priorities?"

"HP and me. If HP asks you about program priorities, answer

your best professional. Then you and I discuss. Otherwise, HP and me. Clear?"

"What about government approvals? Is there a contact person or procedure to follow?"

"No worry. I make it clear. Only one contact, only one procedure, Mr. Charles. HP. Clear? And if you have question, you see me! Clear?"

I nodded my head. But inside, I was smiling because every time Mr. Wong said clear it sounded like queer. But he was clear about chain of command. I liked that. Then Mr. Wong said, "You got my phone, yes?"

I showed him the mobile Jeff gave me.

Mr. Wong's last words, "Let's work. Get started!"

***

The Island

I reached out to shake Mr. Wong's hand and thank him for the introduction but he had already sat down and begun talking on his phone. I left his office without another word and headed next door looking for Jeff. Found him and he introduced me to our staff.

I asked everyone to meet with me in our conference room in a half hour in order to have each one individually brief me on what task they were working, especially to identify problems impeding their task progress.

At the meeting were my six staff members: Jeff, the Hertfordshire Englishman, my senior planner and right-hand man seconded from his Kuwaiti AE company, and the rest were direct hires specifically for this project: 2 senior landscape architects, a Brit and an American, one junior landscape architect, a Turk, a Turk LA?! In an Arab country? I knew him because he was a guy who worked for me in Istanbul and had been hired to work here. Even though I was not involved, I could guess why. In Istanbul I knew him as *Kuçuk* Kemal—he was experienced in reading micro ecotypes. That's why he was here.

We also had a senior American construction manager with 15 years' experience in Saudi Arabia, and the only female, a Bahraini intern environmental scientist supporting Kemal especially on the mangroves—her thesis project at University of Bahrain. She, though not of his immediate family, was related to the HP.

Additionally, there was an Indian secretary and a Pakistani

teaboy. One senior LA, the Brit, had worked for years in Kuwait. That was my team.

They turned out to be a solid team—experienced, dependable and without drama.

I asked Jeff and Kemal to accompany me on a drive around the island to familiarize me with the real-life environment and task status. From a distance all I had seen was a rocky islet but up close I saw sandy beaches and 10-metre-high limestone cliffs. Jeff explained to me that nobody lived on the island. And at night the island was patrolled by one of HP's Egyptian bodyguards. At the end, Jeff figured, this island would be used for private entertainment for HP's "invitation-only" guests. But, he made clear based upon past experience, these goals can change.

Outside our office was an established date palm orchard— lined up like soldiers—mature, in place for at least a decade. Impressive—a bit raw with undergrowth unkempt—in need of cleanup all around. Maybe 200 date palms overall, roughly 15nos by 15nos and 6 metres on centre. Jeff told me they were the work of the Egyptian head gardener.

That is where we started.

The island loop road was interlocking pavers under which all of the island utilities had been installed. The island's windward north and west sides were limestone out-crops creating cliffs on the water's edge. Along the water's edge pieces of the limestone had fallen off generating a dramatic visual alternative to the leeward side that was sandy and flat.

Near the tallest cliffs, Jeff asked me to stop. He wanted to add some background. "Decades ago, this barren island," he said, "was the site of a political activists' prison—long since torn down and removed. That is the site of the current date palm orchard—a carefully considered replacement, no? The HP does not want that history to be a feature. So we ignore it... but other Bahrainis haven't forgotten. As such the island carries a murky socio/political undertone—just for your information. And because the HP does not want it featured, we won't speak further of it."

We drove on.

Kemal pointed out the subtleties of microclimate on both the windward and leeward sides of the island where there were thin traces of indigenous salt- and drought-tolerant ground covers. He said, "They will be a feature of the site interpretive signage system and along the spine of the pedestrian bike network."

Then he showed me the mangrove establishment program, seedlings already in place, he had developed with the lady from University of Bahrain. He said, "There is a boardwalk planned among them along with interpretive signage." He pointed out that the sand beaches were not natural; rather sand that had been hauled in from the southern desert.

I wasn't too keen on the native plant groundcovers but as long as we could plant the other more heavily used areas with flowering shade trees and fragrant shrubs—the final effect would be of intriguing variety. I'd have to review in detail the plans before I'd take this further. All in all I liked the site, it had drama and can't go wrong with a date palm orchard and mangroves. This project looked like fun.

In summary:

1. Villa 1: *under construction ongoing*
2. Island Entry: *first phase complete, under maintenance*
3. Roads/Utilities main loop, spine: *complete, under maintenance*
4. Electrical/Water/Sewerage/Communication Infrastructure Loop: *infrastructure complete and under maintenance*
5. Pedestrian/Bikes Network: *design and construction ongoing*
6. Teahouse: *planning complete, starting design*
7. Mangroves: *seedings planted, ongoing*
8. Maintenance Yards/Irrigation Reservoir: *pump house operational, ongoing*
9. Landmarks: *design and construction of limestone sculptures, ongoing*
10. Planting/Irrigation: *ongoing*
11. Street Lighting/Furnishings: *procurement and installation*

ongoing–Louis Poulsen, Bellitalia, Lazzari, Cyria, Neri.
12. Interpretive Signage (bilingual like Yenbo–Arabic and
    English): *first stage procurement and installation ongoing*
13. Coastal Protection: *complete under maintenance*

All other master plan components were on hold awaiting
HP's initiation.

***

Teahouse

My meetings with the HP were rather perfunctory. He would stop. Roll down his window and ask a question about the status of an item. I would explain and that was it. Sometimes he would say something like, "I like the Welsh red clay pavers" or "I prefer Italian style for street furnishings". He was educated and a gentleman.

I came to think of this island project as little more than a hobby for him. He wanted to see it happening—to see progress. He visited every day, that is why we were on site and why there were two contractors at his call. Or I should say at Mr. Wong's call. Judging from the approved master plan, the project looked to be a recreation island for local users. It had no international hospitality features suitable for large numbers of foreign tourists.

My team specified products based on comments I received from the HP. Most of the time the manufacturers were German, Italian or British. When Mr. Wong reviewed these construction documents, he instructed the contractors to source similar products from China. When I objected he had the contractors produce specifications and tests from the Chinese manufacturers. The Chinese specs and tests always matched our original European specs. Discussion ended. I shared this with Alan as information regarding Chinese infiltration into the Gulf Region. He didn't seem interested.

During my time on this Bahraini island job, the teahouse became our first major construction project. It took us and the A/E support team in Kuwait four weeks to churn out the construction documents. The day after I delivered them to Mr. Wong, he called me into his office to be present as he distributed them to the two contractors.

Mr. Wong's construction trailer was smaller than ours. Besides tea room, storage and toilet he had only two other rooms—no secretary, only a tea boy. His office, which beside Mr. Wong's desk had chairs for only three other visitors. He did have an adjacent meeting room with seating for 10 or more, but we never met there.

I sat with Mr. Wong in his office while he called the two contractors he wanted to build the teahouse. They had their own construction trailers just outside the security gate. I heard Mr. Wong for the first time in full flow on his mobile.

"Manu, get your fucking ass in my office now or your wife will never see you again!"

Then, "Kapil, if you're not in my office in five minutes, I will fuck your wife in the ass till she can't sit anymore!"

Mr. Wong was always short with me but never with the personal foul-mouthed threats. Before I took two breaths, the two contractor reps were knocking at the door.

"You're late, get your asses in here now!"

They stood as Mr. Wong handed each of them a set of documents. "Kapil infrastructure and structure. Manu fixtures, furnishing and finishes. All finished in three months or you will lose your balls and I will fuck you in the eyes. Clear? Start today. Now get the fuck out of here." They shuffled out of the meeting room.

I was shocked. Somehow I felt like I had just seen the master abuse two slaves. They were treated as no-counts.

Then Mr. Wong turned to me. "Those assholes report to me. They have questions? They see me, they ask me. You have your construction manager observe every day. Make sure design is like HP approved. Clear?"

***

Cultural Discussions

That was the first time I heard Mr. Wong speak with the contractors. And that was mild compared to the way Mr. Wong spoke to them during the construction. That was the job and I was being paid well.

There was no way I was going to stick my nose in because I didn't agree with the way Mr. Wong treated the contractors. I am not a social activist, I am a landscape architect, bringing plants into people's daily lives. I had to keep my focus. After all, every expatriate working here was doing it because they could earn more here for a better life for their family than back in their country of origin, myself and the contractor employees included.

The FM continued to have his contractors supply Chinese alternatives to our European materials, fixtures and furnishings suppliers. The Chinese manufacturers, believe it or not, always 100% matched our original spec. This happened on every item throughout the project.

I continued to advise Alan of these Chinese substitutions. And honestly, I was surprised not to see Mr. Wong arrange to have a Chinese contractor on site to do the work. Like I saw back in Yenbo, a Korean firm had brought an entire team of Korean labourers to build their project. They were soldiers dressed as labourers. They were housed offshore on a ship.

One evening, I was talking to Jeff about Mr. Wong's treatment of the contractors. Jeff said, "One of our Kuwaiti owners went to China to get projects. You know Arabs are tough bargainers... well... when our owner returned he had a story that I can summarize... he said he had met his match in China and wanted no part of business with them."

I thought about the weird cultural differences. I thought business was something people could work out. Then I thought the only way that works is if one is obviously stronger than the other—like the era of Britain dominating the waves—people saying in a gentlemanly way what Mr. Wong says—"do it or we will fuck you up."

Jeff looked over at me and said, "The rules of the game are set by the strongest. Had you not twigged that yet?"

I thought about my earlier Yenbo project—where we had 2,000 people and lots of resources... then Jeff said, "You and I are white-collar slaves out here. We do what we are told and they make the rules. At least we are paid well. In our Kuwaiti office, the mood is more civilized than here. But... in this part of the world there are a lot of strange things we have to accept. Have you heard of Ashura?"

Ashura. I'd heard of it in passing. It was a Shiite religious festival where public self-flagellation is the main feature. I asked, "Does that happen in Bahrain?"

"Oh yeah, big time. It's coming up, I've gone a couple times—it used to be something that the unfaithful would not visit because those involved would attack them—but now the government leaders are trying to turn it into a 'Disneyland' cultural event—sort of civilized—make it palatable to foreigners—want to go? It happens next month."

"Is that an invitation?"

"Yes, because there are two forms—the official public gov't version, and the acolyte version that is located in a limited area away from the official public—it's the 'way it used to be version' for the hardline devoted Shia. I know how to do it—safely."

"It sounds interesting but... I worry because once in Meknes in Morocco, there were guys marching in all black—everyone said keep away from them because they were in a trance and would attack any non-believers... might that have been the same?"

"They all dress in all black—maybe they were Shia but here it is intense, very intense and… well, you'll see and hear if we go."
***

Bahrain Dénouement

Before the next month clicked over, I had my regular visit from Alan—talk about intense. He had a bee in his bonnet, to say the least. Something got under his skin. He wasn't satisfied with the information I shared about Mr. Wong's Chinese connections. He unleashed like never before. He hammered me.

"I need more from you. Who pushes Mr. Wong? Who does he contact? You've got to go deeper. I don't care if you have to suck his little yellow Chinese dick, I don't care if you have to be his bitch—get me more info or else! Next time I expect results." And he took off.

"Or else?" I wondered... what was this guy talking about? I never signed on for this kind of information gathering. This was the third project where Alan was my contact and each time he had gotten worse. I thought about it for a couple days and decided to contact Will Clendenon in Kuwait. I used my own phone. His number was in Al Ahmadi, an oil town south of Kuwait City.

A lady answered the phone. I identified myself and asked for Will. She said, "CJ, is that you? Been years, Eileen here... the nursery in Southern California, the hotel in Casablanca? Remember?"

Yeah, I remembered. She was the one who got me started on this info gathering business—the good and the bad.

"Nice to hear your voice and speak with you again—is Will around?"

"Not now, can you call back in two hours?"

196

"Yeah, no problem, are you okay? How are you doing?"

"Yeah, I'm good but very busy—listen maybe we can get together sometime—talk about old times and new times; but I've got to run now—remember, call Will back in two hours, I'm sure he'd like to talk with you. Take care, talk to you later."

And she hung up before I could say goodbye. I called back two hours later and Will suggested I come to Kuwait to speak personally with him. We set a date just before my next scheduled briefing with Alan.

My Ashura experience in Bahrain with Jeff came—it was weird, intense and more but that's another story. I told Jeff I had to go to Kuwait on business and he suggested we go together so he could show me the office that provided architecture and engineering support to our island project.

I put our island project construction manager in charge and went to Kuwait for three days. I told Mr. Wong that I needed to "shore-up" our support services to reduce the lead time required to move our next tasks forward. I also spoke with HP and explained that our construction manager would walk him through the on-site construction details of the teahouse, which was moving quickly to completion.

Kuwait—the Gulf Wars—the burning oil wells. Those are memories we all share. But before that… a long time ago Kuwait City had a famous American master planning team establish a waterfront master plan which was still being implemented.

I had plenty to look forward to; but first I had to see Will Clendenon in Al Ahmadi. If we drove from Bahrain to Kuwait, the trip would include 300 kilometres plus twice crossing the Saudi border. It would be 100% a gruelling desert drive with unpredictably time-consuming border crossings. We chose to fly.

Jeff had contacts in Kuwait City and set me up with a company car which I drove to Al Ahmadi. I was to meet Will Clendenon at the Al Ahmadi Golf Club to play a round of golf. I hadn't played since I was a kid. Used to go with my father. He used to say the golf course… that's where all the big business deals are made. I heard him back then; but I had other ideas—still do—not into big business management.

Built 1949, Ahmadi Golf Club course was a brown sand course—only the tees had artificial grass. Golfers have to carry a piece of artificial turf in their bag to place under each fairway shot—greens all compacted and rolled brown sand—no grass.

We walked the brown sand golf course and I told my Alan story. "Will, I've had enough of Alan. I'll finish my 12-month contract in Bahrain but I won't meet Alan again."

Will nodded and told me that he understood.

"If it is good with you I'll send my monthly reports direct to you via email. But, the Alan thing is finished."

"Come and talk with me when your contract is up. Text your monthly sit-reps to Eileen. Stay cool, we can work through this."

That was all I needed to hear.

***

Coffee in Kuwait City

After 9 holes on the brown sand course and clearing the air with Will, I left and drove to Jeff's office in Kuwait City. It was a 6-storey building of which his company was the primary occupant. He showed me around the office. It was a proper architecture and engineering group—well established long before the Gulf Wars. There were at least 200 people at work in the office on projects in Kuwait and Africa.

I learned that in the firm Jeff wasn't just a senior planning person; he also supervised the architecture and interior design staff. He showed me the landscape architecture group—small, with a handful of people from India and the Philippines.

Jeff took me downstairs to a café. He wanted some quiet, private time with me. After sitting down and ordering coffee, he said, "Well, CJ, how have you found Q8?"

"I've just gotten my feet on the ground but your office feels very professional compared to our construction trailer setup on Jidda Island in Bahrain. but I don't know... I wonder about behind the scenes."

"Behind the scenes?"

"I was speaking to my colleagues in Al Ahmadi and they told me a story about bidoons, or are they bedouins here in Kuwait—something to do with the distribution of Kuwaiti oil wealth—I couldn't really follow it. Is there an issue here?"

"Well, your colleagues are correct. There is an issue here in Kuwait with bidoons. No they are not the same as Bedouins but ... specifically here in Kuwait they are called bidoons, meaning 'without'. Without citizenship, without nationality. I'll leave it to the human rights researchers to say definitively that bidoons are or are not Bedouin. I've heard plenty of arguments both ways."

"What's the issue and is it really a visible problem in daily life?"

"I need to share some history because it rises up every once in a while—like a social boil."

"How do you mean?"

"This goes back to the time of the First Gulf War. I was working in London then but when I was hired to come to Kuwait there was an American who had been working for us for five years through the entire Iraqi Invasion—he told me the story of the bidoons and the First Gulf War."

"An American?"

"He was from west Texas. He was acclimated to this difficult climate.

"I can summarize his perspective—very conservative, loudmouth American—he said something like 'bidoons and Palestinians one and the same. They are all made up of homeless tribes not unlike Bedouin. But these guys have always chased the rain and they never have built anything. They are envious grifters. Palestinians is a basket built by the UN to include these homeless who are the same troublemaking do-nothings that TE Lawrence encountered in his run into Damascus. So when the Bidoons/Palestinians supported Saddam—they were out of here and not allowed back.' ...very intolerant but more truthful than many would accept. Anyhow, the Egyptians have taken over all the mid-level jobs once held by Palestinians and the problem is more a political one without any day-to-day visibility except by NGOs and the UN."

"Phew, that's why I like to keep my nose to the grindstone on my projects. The politics are so sticky and so prevalent, just under the surface in this region."

"That makes sense. Quagmire. Dry quicksand—whatever you want to call it. But hell, CJ, we can sit here, have coffee, relax and go to work daily without any of that quagmire."

"I hear you."

This conversation got me thinking about foreign cultures

and cocoons. I could do my work in strange foreign places and be completely detached from these boiling local/regional social issues. That didn't bother me one bit. And in Bahrain I didn't even try to partake of the "night scene" that Jeff had described as being like Bangkok. Long days at work, nights keeping my diary and journals—I had my hands full.

***

Cutting Loose

Jeff and I relaxed over our coffees.

"On a more personal note, I've heard that our Jidda Island project may shut down because the funding, from a foreign entity, is drying up and no longer politically sustainable," Jeff continued.

"What?!"

"Yes, and I will be returning to our Kuwait office by year's end."

"No kidding, this is the first I have heard."

On a three-day trip to Kuwait, my future was being restructured. We flew back to Bahrain the next day.

The island project did wind down, just as Jeff had heard. Mr. Wong told me that the Bahrain Ministry of Housing was slated to take over any new tasks on the island; and none were foreseen in the near future. I de-mobilized our team, thanking them all for their hard work.

And Alan? He disappeared like he did in Yenbo, only this time JeanClaude did not take over. I texted my last monthly sit-reps to Eileen—nothing other than continued construction materials from China.

I had one more task before returning to Bree and our haybarn in the Jungfrau Region in Switzerland. One last trip to Kuwait to visit Will Clendenon in Al Ahmadi. Eileen was the first person I saw. She welcomed me to Kuwait and hoped we would be seeing each other. I told her I was on my way back to Switzerland, but had to see Will before going back. She took me into his office.

I shook Will's hand and said, "It's been a long run, Will, since we met in Palos Verdes at Trump's golf club. Done my best to keep you informed as I performed and built my professional career. Thank you for your confidence and assistance; but... and I'm sure you knew this was coming... without JeanClaude handling me, I've been taken advantage of by Alan. I can't do it anymore. I feel like my professional standing is being undermined. That was not part of our initial agreement. Your support has been strong but it is time for me to step out on my own. Do you understand?"

"I understand but I don't want it to end like this. I'm going to be leaving Kuwait soon. We are having an internal re-organization. If you don't mind, I'd like to give you contact details should you wish to assist again. Can we part like that?"

"Sure."

Then Will asked, "Are we good, then?"

"Yes, definitely." I was glad to say goodbye on amicable terms.

With that Will shook my hand, hugged me and thanked me for my service. I was embarrassed because I thought my contributions had been minimal. The information gathering had provided me cultural insights improving my understanding of local context. The result had been a higher standard for the sociological side of my landscape architecture work.

I left Will's office and saw Eileen. I shook hands with her. I said goodbye and she said she hoped we could stay in touch. I wasn't so sure. Personality clashes and obscene demands had gotten in the way of my professional work. While some of the information gathering had been helpful to my career, I was glad to focus solely on my landscape architecture work and especially to be rid of Alan. And about Bree, between my Istanbul and Bahrain projects, I felt I was too long away from Bree. Inside I knew I had to be closer to her—in more ways that one.

***

After 12 Months

It had been a year since I had seen Bree. I was excited. My year in Bahrain around Mr. Wong and Alan had been non-stop tension. Bree was my answer. I emailed her from the Kuwait Airport to let her know my arrival.

In fact, on my flight back to Switzerland all I could think about was being in Bree's arms. When I finally got off the train in Grindelwald, I almost ran to our haybarn. The Grindelwald spring landscape and her garden softened the hard skin of tension; but it wasn't until 48 hours later that she, with her love, removed every last vestige of tension from me.

We had plenty of time to sit and talk. We started off slowly; after all, 12 months had passed since the last time we spoke eyeball to eyeball.

"Tell me, what have you been doing?" I asked.

"More like who and what I have been seeing—all my days are in the garden or at my workstation, cutting, dicing, grinding, boiling, steaming—I've been fully in the plant world. Seasons change and so do I."

"I'm listening."

"I found some old-fashioned comfort—brownies, elves—the elves enjoyed so much the fragrance of my garden flowers... now I doubt if you, from the world of landscape architecture, will believe this. But the elves gifted me a necklace of raindrops. As I was looking at it, I became... absorbed into their world... lost track of time and when I returned, the necklace had already evaporated."

Even though I was simply listening to her story, I, too,

became absorbed. I was so happy to be back with Bree in the haybarn. Brownies? Elves? I was too happy to be with her to say anything but my thoughts did weave a skein. I remembered a conversation years ago at the Blumisalp Stubbe, with Suzie and her Lauterbrunnen friend LN. I had asked about *zwergs* (gnomes), real or a tourist thing. They deflected. And so did I now after listening to Bree's elf story; but she did have form. She had always heard things in the landscape—things not taught or even discussed in schools of landscape architecture.

But then again, on the subject of being absorbed, I, too, did have form from my times in Tangier gardens, the Hibiscus House and the Obelisk Garden in northern Thailand.

So, it was easy for me to sit in silence just looking at her. The professional landscape architecture tension that had been my world in Bahrain these last twelve months... had evaporated.

We did a lot of talking as weeks then months passed. There was no pressure like the short-term vacations and home leaves of my long-term expatriate contracts. One subject worked its way into our talks about plants and landscape. It was about Bree's adventure.

One day we were in her garden. She was bustling with cuttings. I was nosing around. It seemed like I was always discovering something new in her garden. "Hello, what's this?" I had noticed a clump, 2-3 shrubs multi-stemmed, 2.5 meters high and similar spread covered with white flower clusters.

"Are these elderberry shrubs? *Sambucus nigra?*"

She stood up from her work and came over. "Those are. Here we call them *holunder.* Flowers and fruits both are healthy and excellent sellers in the local market—if I process them."

"Not much in the way of fragrance but their vase-shaped form and broad crown make for a very balanced and healthy-looking plant."

"They are happy here and I like to work with them. You know the flower tisane is calming in the evening and berry tisanes, syrups and liqueurs keep the body waste processes active."

I was interested but that was more than I needed to know. But Bree? She had such a broad knowledge of plants. It only convinced me how important plants were to human life and our existential condition—it wasn't just food and drink.

Bree refreshed me in so many ways.

"Bree, have you given any more thought to our Mannlichen adventure?"

"Since we verified the wilding legend?" she asked.

"Yeah—I still find it so weird—the legend to follow birds that can lead to access an ancient store of gold from the Crusades! Quite weird. Have you been thinking about it?" I asked.

"Are you up for it?"

"Me? Am I up for it? Without a job now, I have free time—so I thought we could talk about it, if you want."

"What are you thinking?"

"I have questions if we go there again and try to enter— what if we get caught? What if we find gold? I think we need to answer those questions carefully and completely. And if we decide to enter, how do we enter—it seems like it could be a rappelling exercise—have you ever rock climbed or rappelled?"

"Never. It's all new to me."

"Maybe the attempt to enter is a non-starter. Maybe we should just be happy that we found that shaft by the wilding legend. That was cool. We have our life in the haybarn. No need to jeopardize that. What do you think?"

"Jeopardizing our life in the haybarn?"

"Yeah, if we enter and get caught—we don't have any idea what goes on in that shaft or where it leads to. But we know there is a large and regular military presence at the base of the Mannlichen, between Zweilutschinen and Lauterbrunnen."

"How do government workers say? Above our pay-grade?" Bree showed sympathetic understanding.

"No hurry. Let's put it on a very low boil." In the back of my mind, I was thinking about how to make a couple disparate things link—Bree's interest in an adventure and the danger if someone thinks we are trying to enter a forbidden military zone. The more I thought about it, the more unanswerable questions emerged. For the time being, Bree did not seem to have the fire for that adventure. Maybe the Faeryland raindrop-necklace gift had softened her wilding persuasion for adventure outside our haybarn.

It wasn't long before I got an email from Jeff, the Brit planner who had been my right-hand man on the Island Project in Bahrain.

> CJ, how's it going? Might you be interested in at short term assignment in Ras Al Khaimah (RAK) in the UAE.
>
> I heard from my colleagues at the old London AE company where I had originally earned my credentials. They do not have landscape architects and they need a landscape architect to put together an island hospitality destination.
>
> We have civil engineers (our chief civil is a Brit and he is down there) and they have marine engineers, and architects on site where a contractor is already building the island. They have an office in the UAE and an approved program. It would be three months' work.
>
> Does that interest you? And if it does are you free? Let me know, we need someone now and you are the first choice.

Here's how it works. I needed to keep my professional reputation fresh. I needed to be seen as a can-do professional ready to take on anything at any time. I knew Jeff and he knew me. There would likely be no strange surprises. A short-term assignment for an unquestionably high-reputation UK firm. They needed a Gulf Region experienced landscape architect to interface with the client's team on the ground in Ras Al Khaimah.

I said yes.

***

Tolerating the Tough

It wasn't easy at all when I told Bree about my new job. She had shown concern last time when I was preparing to go to Bahrain. She made her feelings known in no uncertain terms.

"It's time we talk about this."

"It's just another job," I said, maybe a bit too nonchalantly.

"But I do want to talk about it. I don't understand how you can work in such strange cultures. I was in Morocco with you. I know what that was like. It was hell for me from Casablanca to Tangier. Never a break. I was under attack even when I went shopping for food, veg, fruits, flowers, plants—it was all too much. And it was like that for all the Peace Corps volunteers around me. But everybody focuses on... pretends it is such a wonderful place. The climate in the northern third—Mediterranean like southern California—great! Fantastic plants, fantastic agriculture but so many of the people... are... under some kind of negative spell. Just not healthy. I don't care what the tourist brochures say! I live by my own experience.

"But here you go—North Africa and the Middle East—I don't understand how you can do it. How you can live in those MENA countries—dirty streets, poor water, insufficient food, harsh climate and Muslim?"

"It's not all like that. Morocco was tough—downright weird. But Bahrain? Away from the extreme Shia Ashura stuff, life was normal. Streets were clean. People didn't harass me. And there was a strong Hindu presence—even temples, restaurants and street food. I could get vegetarian anytime I wanted. And like I said, no young men harassing at all. It was the same in Saudi Arabia—no harassment. There we figured it was because of the strict laws—stealing meant your hand would be cut off in public. Leaves a strong message to would-be sleight of hand thieves. Hell, I remember Morocco—the mentality was you had to hold on tightly to your possessions because Moroccan youth said things like 'Allah left it for me' and boom, your backpack or purse would disappear if it was not in your hand or on your back."

"I still don't understand how you do it."

"What works for me? I am there for work. I am a guest in their home. I respect the sovereignty of the host country (nation). I am not there to change their culture. I may not like it. I may not get along with it; but it's their home. I do my work, get paid and return to the place and culture where I am most comfortable.

"Why don't I return to the US, you may ask—we've talked about that before. The US culture is intense, fast moving and in your face 24/7/365. I am more comfortable outside the US where I feel like I am five years and thousands of miles away from US wildly fluctuating cultural vicissitudes. I can stop and observe and think before reacting without the in-your-face pressure of American life in the US—especially in the big cities and university campuses."

"Yeah and I know that what you earn gives us financial security. But it is still a mystery because even here there are cultural subtleties that can get in the way of understanding—for example making a greeting before getting to business in any conversation—have to say in local dialect, good morning or hello. Without that the local response will be cold—even though cordial, it will be distant."

"Well, when I am meeting a Muslim in the Middle East, if I don't say *salem aleikum* I get the same coolness—they know they are speaking with a non-believer. Think I get an even break?

"But on the job, I do the work. I make it a point to know who has the money, who has the *wasta*—the cultural superiority—and that guides me to say what and how in order to succeed in getting the job done.

"But like your local example the subtleties are numerous and strange. And for some reason I can work with that in the Middle East and North Africa. Maybe I am just lucky. Anyhow, I'm off to the UAE for the first time. It's only for three months. I will be back before you know it. Please understand this is how it works. We'll be back together soon."

***

Ras Al Khaimah

I had a three-month agreement including transport to and from the UAE, a Toyota Yaris car, a furnished studio apartment to myself and a reasonable monthly salary, no bonus. The Brit firm, who joint ventured with Jeff's Kuwaiti firm for this project, had an office in Ras Al Khaimah, RAK.

I was eager on my flight into the UAE. This would be the closest I'd ever been to that monster the Empty Quarter, the Rub al Khali. I flew in to the UAE at DBX, Dubai International Airport, essentially in the centre of the city of Dubai. As we were beginning our descent, I could see only reddish blond sweeps and splotches with a wide dark red rib of naked rock mountains that separated that desert from the Arabian Sea. The towering red rock Hajar mountains started at the Strait of Hormuz on the Musandam Peninsula along the northeast coast of the Arabian Peninsula on the Gulf of Oman all the way to Muscat. That was before I could see the developed Gulf Sea coastal edge of the UAE, with massive urbanizations of Abu Dhabi, Dubai et al.

The Brit engineers met me at DXB. On the drive to their RAK office for 100km, it was one extended city, non-stop coastal development all the way from Dubai through Sharjah, Ajman, Umm al Quwain to RAK. RAK was the end, any further north along the coast would take me to Oman's Musandam Governate, the mountainous point on the Strait of Hormuz. RAK looked like the much younger sister of Dubai—in fact the coastal development gradually decreased all the way as we had driven northward from Dubai.

I was fascinated with the geography and history. Historical pirate coves everywhere north along the coast around the Strait of Hormuz. Our office was only 70km to the tip of the Musandam peninsula—just a stone throw from Iran and Pakistan. There were many Iranians living in the UAE—beginning long ago but the biggest influx came with the unseating of the Shah of Iran. Iranians sought freedom in the UAE and found it. Pakistanis were different. They came as labourers. Many were gardeners living in the Dibba area on the Gulf of Oman in valleys that are of an unusually amenable microclimate for plant growth. Many nurseries are in those valley mouths.

I did most of my work in their RAK mainland office. But I could go out with the marine engineers by boat anytime to see the island construction. The island was about the same size as Jidda Island in Bahrain. But the program and construction schedule were aggressive for international tourists and for profit—a private-sector venture.

The already established program featured a high-rise, Las Vegas-style hotel, the main architectural feature, with all recreational amenities—restaurants, cafés, indoor/outdoor swimming pool, and kids' pool. My task was to tie it all together via the design of an attractive island-wide vacation landscape development with gardens and walkway/cartway systems. There were numerous support infrastructure components because the island was to be self-sufficient in power, water and recycling.

There was a substantial maintenance centre to include desalination and power plant, irrigation and potable tanks, pump house and control centre, sewage treatment, composting and recycling components. Once under operation, there would be only electric vehicles on site—golf carts for guests and service. A purpose-built ferry would bring people to the island and provide circumnavigation.

Issues: beach and planting sand sources. Long lead items: date palms, mature trees. Identify possible landscape contractors.

When I arrived on site, my new colleagues gave me the works schedule:

1. Marine engineering construction complete in six months
2. Infrastructure/maintenance centre and hotel construction to begin in 12 months
3. Site underground infrastructure complete in 18 months.
4. Hotel complete in 36 months.
5. Site finishes begin in 24 months.
6. Opening in 42 months.

Busy, I would be very busy. I had to get approved plans for grading, site circulation, planting and irrigation in 3 months. The site finishes design and construction documents would be accomplished in Kuwait after my work was approved. I was in essence responsible for 15% conceptual design to enough detail to provide quantities for earthworks, paving, site lighting, signage and furnishings, planting and irrigation.

I worked in AutoCAD with the architects, civil and marine engineers. The government had approved inland sources for beach and planting sand. The architects helped with site lighting and site furnishings so that the island aesthetics would be of unified style. The evening lighting system was an unusual animal because most of the activity in the landscape would be at night. Night? Why? Because the temperature never dropped below 30C until after midnight.

The chief civil engineer and I became close friends as we had to "hide" the maintenance centre and shape the earth in the open space in the style of a rolling golf course, while overlaying a circulation system for pedestrians, bikes and carts. All of the Brits in our office were proper professionals. They got stuck into their work and got the job done.

I did have some long-lead items that needed sourcing—40 matching date palms, *Phoenix dactylifera*, with 6-metre clear trunks and 90 mature flowering trees, *Delonix regia*, multi trunk, with 5-metre height and 6-metre spread. The golf-course-like rolling landforms would require the contractor to employ a specialist earthworks person. There are two kinds of earthworks specialists—a ditch-digger who, once he knows the depth, works in a straight line—and a shaper. Good shapers are few and far between. A shaper is an earthworks artist, turning complex grading plans into seductive landforms. Encompassing all that, they wanted me to identify dependable landscape contractors to bid on the work.

The 15% design was actually closer to 30% to address all the quantities. I was able to use irrigation demands based upon the work I had done at Yenbo in Saudi Arabia. Similarly with the planting sand volume requirements. Marine engineers assisted me with beach sand quantities. And the architects handled all site elements within the confines of the high-rise hotel site.

Everything went smoothly in RAK, my colleagues were pleased with my efforts and our presentation to the client was approved without comment. The most difficult task was recommending landscape contractors, this being my first UAE project. I used two approaches. First, I visited, only had Sundays free, the largest projects in Dubai—mostly on the Palm Jumeirah, looked at their work and identified the contractors with the best-looking projects having mature trees at installation. Second, I called my old colleagues from SE Asia who supplied mature trees to high-value projects here in the oil-rich countries. Between those two efforts, I was able to provide a shortlist of four landscape contractors qualified for bid documents. Job done.

Three months had passed, my work was complete and now I was on my way back to Bree. I might get used to these short-term assignments. They were straightforward. No vacation. No holiday. Just get in there and crank it out. No flash expenses. Just save the salary and bank it. And I was back with Bree before I knew it.

***

Bree's Plant World

It was winter—the snow was already sticking to the ground, even in Zurich as I landed. Then snow all the way on the train via Bern and Interlaken to Grindelwald. And the air, cool, fresh, clean. I could not inhale enough. The air of the Gulf Region—30+C, salty, sandy, fines—never could get what I would call "fresh air". Glad to be back in the north, back in the mountains. And soon, back in Bree's arms.

I had a couple days in Bree's arms and more—renewing marriage vows. Put me in another world. It wasn't until a week later that I really emerged and began to see the world of Bree's winter garden and haybarn.

The first thing I noticed this time were the pots of *Aloe vera*—they were everywhere. She told me they provided the oily base for some of her market cremes. Another new world for me to explore.

But there was an old world. The world of her Mannlichen adventure and the wildings. I started, "We have been saying that the wilding legend about how to find that shaft below the Mannlichen was proven—we did it—but what did it actually prove?"

"What do you mean?"

"Well, that was only part of their legend, was it not?"

"Yes?"

"The rest of the legend was about ancient gold, no?"

"Yes?"

"That's where I get all cloudy. Anything that has to do with the Crusades, the Knights Templar, anything from that era—

anybody can make that up—it's too far back... and at night sitting around a campfire... a good story."

"What are you getting at?"

"Well just because we found the red-billed choughs and the ventilation shaft doesn't mean the rest of the story is true, does it? Can you feel my hesitation?"

"CJ we've been over that, and I am deep into preparing for and processing macerates now. Besides it's the dead of winter... we can talk about it after spring has come, can't we? When we start to see the dawning of spring, right?"

"Yeah..."

"Come over here and pluck some clovers from the pot on this windowsill. Tell me if you see any 4-leaf clover."

"Do you want any clover or only 4-leaf?"

"Just take a close look and tell me if you see any with 4 leaves."

And such was my time between jobs. Bree always steered me to the edge of landscape architecture—to a kind of twilight zone that she worked in. But we were both in the landscape domain. I wonder if it is up to me to try and link her activities with my activities—is this an unexplored area of landscape architecture? Yes, of course it is! She takes her landscape rides in the land of Faery and I take my landscape rides in the transcendent effulgences. Could those rides both be to the same place?

Before spring came, I heard from an old friend and colleague from my Yenbo times.

***

Queen of Sheba

It was an email from Marty, the guy from SE Asia who sourced and supplied plants for me while I was in Yenbo. He also, with his chum, set me up in his off-the-grid resort in Ban Muang, Northern Thailand. In fact, I had contacted him last year about landscape contractors in the UAE. I wondered what was up with him. He got right to the point.

Hey CJ,

Can you get into this? Palm Jumeirah Dubai, in the Queen of Sheba resort project. We have to make something happen in the next six months.

This has been a delayed project for a large grouping of five-star residences. Now they are upgrading a central rec area. They asked me to source 200 matching coconut palms. I told them that was impossible because of the nature of coconut palm growth and I sent photos to demonstrate. Nobody matches coconut palms—individuals that they are.

They listened to me and then they put it on hold because the designer was intent on making some kind of grid—with matching coconut palms. So she said go to hell and they said the same to her.

They asked me if I knew a landscape architect who, on short term notice, could design a layout sensitive to the individuality of coconut palm growth. Are you the guy? 200 coconut palms is nothing to me. I can do it. I have access to thousands.

But this is hot, this project has its A-level international celebrity 'Hollywood to Bollywood' opening media event in 7 months. So we have that pressure. Tell me if you can do.

I wrote back to Marty—count me in and asked for contact details, which he sent immediately.

Marty put me in contact with the Lebanese who were managing the project for the Emirati money men. My job was to fly immediately to Dubai, meet with the managers, review the design, adjust the grid plan to something more organic and make sure there would be natural-looking groves of coconut palms connecting the pool/rec area to the beach. Then make sure that the coconut palms matched the intent, arrived on time and looked "established" for opening in 7 months. Marty was right, this project was hot. We needed those coconuts on site yesterday.

The five-star residences were all 6-8 storeys tall. They looked like replicas of Sana'a old city, a UNESCO World Heritage—certainly in that style.

I signed a 6-month Memorandum of Understanding that covered all my travel and lodging plus a reasonable monthly salary and healthy bonus. The goal was to have the revised design planted and ready for opening before six months expired. Fortunately, the client already had under contract for this project one of the best landscape contractors in Dubai.

My furnished apartment and office were on the trunk of the Palm Jumeirah. Our design/construction on-site office was small—staffed with six Filipinos and two Lebanese managers, one an architect.

In the first week, I reviewed the design drawings and sketched out a new plan. The size of the pool and associated rec facilities had to remain the same. And so did the number of coconut palms. It was an easy problem and easy solution design-wise. Marty flew in and together we set trunk heights for all 200 coconut palms.

The next day he left for SE Asia to source the palms. A week later, he had sent me photos of the proposed palms. I, along with the local landscape contractor, made a quick trip out there to confirm. We agreed transplantation (careful limited cutting back of fronds, healthy sized rootballs) and shipping. The palms would be shipped directly, a six/ten-week process, to the Dubai landscape contractor who would immediately plant them on site. Marty had done well. We received 200 plus 10% in case of problems.

Getting those coconut palms in the ground was interesting. It wasn't one of those jam them into the ground as fast as you can. I learned a lesson way back in SoCal from a lady landscape architect, Ruth Shellhorn—the contractors hated to do her jobs because she took the time to rotate each tree on plantation to have its best side facing. Trees have a best side? Definitely. And these coconut palms proved that case—each had unique trunk diameter and curvature. So Marty and I worked with the contractor to make sure the installation, the coconut palm plantation was an unquestionably graceful visual treat. Took a little more time but the results were superb. I spent 18-hour days to get it right.

Once the coconut palms were in the ground, the contractor continued to install all the irrigation, lighting, paving, shrubs, groundcovers, lawns and furnishings. By the time my six months were up, the project was already looking sweet—that look all developers seek for the hi-vis grand opening. I was happy and the client was happy.

***

Back Home

It was early fall when I returned to Bree and the haybarn. We spent a week of loving frolic before the facts of daily life returned to us. She led me out to her garden and showed me all the ripe elderberries, *holunder,* fruit. She gave me the task of gathering the ripe fruit, then washing them in the outdoor trough. As she inspected them, I said, "I noticed that some of the elderberry shrubs were heavily fruited and others had no fruit at all—is that male vs female?"

"Not at all. I caused that. I vary the shrubs. Some I use one year for flowers only and those will have no berries. Then the next year the ones who had yielded berries will be for flowers. I alternate every year, follow?"

"Yeah." Made good management sense to me.

And we carried them inside for her to process. Syrups, jellies and liqueurs on the way.

While she was working, she said, "I saw the primroses up at the Mannlichen when we were there. Made me think twice about the land of faery and human greed. I was on the balance... the adventure at its most basic of proving a centuries' old legend true vs human greed to get hands on gold. So, I am all for taking any further actions up there very cautiously."

"Are you talking about me when you say human greed?!"

"I don't think so. I, like you, believe that working is integral to life. I've always thought one of material life's greatest mirages—like the grass is always greener on the other side—is that if I have enough money never to work a day the rest of my life, then I will be truly happy and satisfied. We are together on this, aren't we?"

"Yes, of course we are. But in life there are frontiers—frontiers of twilight, frontiers of mists where everything we think is clear is actually not so—and bewitching can charm humans..."

"I've felt that strangeness in the Sahara, the Sand Sea—but here and on my walks with you in this Jungfrau Region landscape, I've felt no such bewitching charms—no whispers—no strange noises. And I do keep my head on a swivel at all times—is there something you aren't telling me?"

"Let's cook *mittagessen,* lunch—replenish our energy."

Bree shut that conversation down; I was hungry. And preparing *mittagessen* was one other thing we enjoyed doing together. Having respect for the miracle of the soil, sun and rain that produces the food that nourishes us—and religious respect for every aspect of that process—growing, harvesting, cleaning, cooking and eating—including the recycling of compostable organics—a roundtrip lifecycle respect. Bree prayed out loud before each meal—simple but clear: Come Lord Jesus be our guest and let thy gifts to us be blessed. Amen. I first heard this prayer from her after I returned from my Egyptian walkabout.

I asked her and she said, "I always had a kind of Gaia respect for these miracles; but all that time in the church while you were gone—well, it enabled me to focus my respect for God's products from the earth."

There was hardly an activity Bree and I shared that did not include a climbable ladder to the spiritual—both of us relished that climb—and its examination of existential mysteries—searching for something true beyond faith. The Jungfrau Region and its Grindelwald bowl was landscape that invited our spiritual awe, our thanks to God for the little and the large. We were comfortable here, together.

***

Mangaf

B ree and I often relaxed a while after *mittagessen*. And when she offered to me a tisane, I had to ask, "Why is a tisane any different than a tea?"

"Good question. Easy answer—no difference. Proper answer requires discussion."

"Tell me the whole story—the long answer."

"Tea and tisane are the same in that they are both infusions. Infusions are made with boiling water and herbs (leaves, flowers), dried and pulverized—that's what all my mortars and pestles do—plus a little of my own elbow grease. Now the difference is that in tea (*Camelia sinensis*) the tea plant includes a stimulant—caffeine or theine. A tisane is any herbal infusion without caffeine." I sat quietly, relaxed and learning.

"I have some lemon balm from the garden. *Melissa officinalis*— which has a species name, that reminds me—*officinalis*—denotes a medicinal plant with a long tradition—many of the herbs I grow are traditionally part of a medieval monastery storeroom of medicines. Medieval monasteries? You may wonder, but maybe don't know that in our very own Interlaken there is a still existing 12th century Augustinian monastery."

She prepared the tisane as she finished her landscape history lesson. I sipped the tisane and relaxed till slumber—an afternoon nap.

We had many of these days as fall turned into winter. We were enjoying the non-glossy, clean whiteness of the fresh snow high above us in the Jungfrau Region mountains— Schwarzhorn, Wetterhorn, Shreckhorn, Eiger and many minor peaks.

Until another "jobs-is-on-the-way" email—this time from Jeff in Kuwait City about a new project in Mangaf on the Gulf, south from Kuwait City.

Jeff emailed me:

CJ might you be free to do landscape architecture design for a Kuwaiti coastal resort designed by a premier American architecture firm out of New York?

They have prepared a design for high-end Kuwaiti family tourism on the Gulf coast just south of Kuwait City.

Site plan is complete. Architecture is complete. Modern style meets classic Arab hospitality with views of the Gulf along 1.75km of private beach.

The American architect has given conceptual landscaping design guidelines. You would finalize the design using our Kuwaiti office staff.

We see this as a fixed contract, six-month assignment for a 6 acres site. You would oversee the preparation by our staff of construction/bid documents including planting, irrigation, site finishes and furnishings.

Can you assist us? If so, can you begin in 30 days?

Well, another short-term contract. I was into that. I told Bree, then I entered discussions with Jeff to hash out the details and in 30 days I landed in Kuwait City. And the new job?

Not long ago, I had worked with a large Brit AE company from London; and this job was with a large American AE out of NY. The Brits were real can-do colleagues. But this American architecture group... they described the project as modern style meets classic Arab hospitality.

During our design interactions it was for these New Yorkers— their way or the highway. They were stuck up and completely absorbed in their "modern-design-game", modernity writ large with all its design foibles. The Arab hospitality aspect? That was for operations well after construction.

I had another way to describe them—flying in from New York, then shouting, cussing and talking down to us—they were like seagulls; they flew in, crapped and flew out. They were always on the clock and never had time to listen.

I had already worked with Jeff's colleagues in RAK and in Bahrain. They were great, professional and very knowledgeable regarding local sensibilities—how to get the job done well.

This was a project aimed at affluent Kuwaiti families. The hotel had 200 rooms, 80 chalets, 60 villas; the villas had private pools. Only families could stay in the chalets and villas. Overall there were 1.75 kilometres of private Gulf beachfront, health club, sports club, beach club and plenty of kids' attractions. The rolling open-space landscape would be largely grassed and would be heavily used late at night well after dark when the outside temperature finally dropped into the amenable mid-upper 20sC.

We did it our own way as part of the final construction documents. So what did we do? The site was 6 acres or 150,000 square metres. Half in architecture and half in gardens and open space landscaping. The New Yorkers did the first 15-30% of the architecture and Jeff's company did all the engineering for infrastructure and architecture from 30% through construction documents, bidding, awarding and construction management.

We did 100% of the landscaping—finish grading, site furnishings, irrigation and planting design, construction documents, bidding/awarding and construction management.

After we finished the construction documents and my scope of work was drawing to a conclusion, Jeff took me aside. "Our Kuwaiti owners have asked me to offer you the opportunity to become the head of our Landscape Architecture group to help grow the business. Might that interest you?"

"I like the sound of that, Jeff, how do we move forward?"

"I'll tell the owners you are interested and arrange a meeting tomorrow morning before you return to Switzerland."

The next morning I met the owners and they offered me a renewable annual agreement with a healthy salary, 30-day home leave and return airfare. Thinking how could I see

Bree more regularly, I asked for three 10-day vacations/year with return airfare in lieu of 30-day home leave. Agreed. To commence as soon as I finished my R'n'R with Bree in our haybarn. We signed an agreement.

I was excited—a new job in the Arab world, in the Gulf Region. Kuwait interested me. Maybe it was the hard scrabble pearling tradition of the people. I liked this region.

***

Jobs Is on the Way

As always, I was eager to get home, to Grindelwald, the Grosse Scheidegg, Bree and our haybarn. It was a long, 3hr train ride from the Zurich flughaven to Grindelwald. I was impatient. But I did get relief in the last hour.

From the train the thrill of the landscape, along the Thunersee from Thun to Spiez and then on to Interlaken, enlivened me and calmed me with its beautiful lake, mountains, landforms, forests, pastures and villages. But that was only the aperitif.

Next came the exciting ride from Interlaken to Grindelwald. The cogwheel train carried me through a long twisting passage covered by dark steep forests, passing by numerous beautiful rushing streams and plunging, white bridal waterfalls. And then—breathtaking—the snowcapped imposing north face of the Eiger defined the edge of the sunlit Grindelwald bowl. I was almost home.

Bree met me at the Grindelwald bahnhof, a small, two-track end station. I was enlivened by her presence. And towering over us were three massive mountains—the Eiger, Shreckhorn and Wetterhorn. This was their valley. This was our valley. This was our home. Excited by the landscape and by being together, Bree and I couldn't stop talking as we walked to our haybarn.

We hardly finished one sentence, one topic, when we started another.

I said, "Every time I arrive here in Grindelwald it feels like I am an explorer beginning a journey—do you know what I mean?"

"Refreshing? That's it, is it not? I feel it too—it is a large-scale refreshment—a huge landscape refreshment, no?"

"Ever since I was a kid, I was an explorer, a seeker... as soon as I was old enough to ride a bike in the street, I rode beyond our neighbourhood to places I had never seen—but back home in time for dinner. The thrill of seeking had me and it still does. When I say 'jobs-is-on-the-way' it is my shorthand for being excited about going to a new place. Seeking where I've never been. And I get paid for it now."

We arrived at the haybarn. My eyes relished the coming of spring in Bree's garden. We went inside.

"Let me tell you about my new job in Kuwait."

"New job?! Didn't you just finish a job in Kuwait. What do you mean, new?"

"The people I have just worked for over the last 6 months, a large Kuwaiti Architecture and Engineering office, have offered me a job as Head of the Landscape Architecture Department—the best part is that I will be able to come see you every four months and my salary will allow my regular monthly wires to you. Good news, eh?"

"I suppose so. I'll miss working in the garden with you. I'll miss talking with you under the apple tree. I'll miss you... but once every four months... I'll get used to it."

She paused. I did not know what to expect. Then as she started unbuttoning her shirt she said, "Let's make the most of it, 'cause our time is short.'" She had me as excited as a 17-year-old teenage boy. She was smiling in her electric way as her eyes met mine. As she started undoing her trousers, I realized—renewing our marriage vows. The best part.

In my opinion, we did what we do best. Both of us were eager and by the time the morning had passed, we were exhausted.

Bree made a tisane. We took the two cups outside and slowly refreshed ourselves sitting in the sun under the apple tree, its leaves just beginning to emerge. Then she brewed a tea and we sipped it as we strolled around all the corners of her garden. Surrounded by the plants' early spring sprouting beauty, we talked.

"Feeling the warmth of this afternoon sun... made me think

of the other side of the Grindelwald bowl." She pointed across the valley toward the base of the Eiger.

"What?"

"In that area the wildflowers are a few weeks behind the sunny areas... I know a place near Alpiglen where some years, before the cows come up to the pastures, the pastures are full of gentians. It is amazing, the gentians and cowslips—we should go visit—the spring gentians are introverted, short, a lapis lazuli blue. You might have trouble seeing them at first. But once you focus on one of them, you will see their rich blue clusters and clumps of them everywhere. And the cowslips. They are taller and their yellow is as bright as the sun—they absolutely sing. They are joyful.

"If we take a train tomorrow about 10AM and bring a sandwich—what do you think? It will be great fun—if the sun is shining. Are you up for it?"

I was up for anything after the morning and there's little I like better than walking alpine pastures and observing alpine wild flowers. They open worlds for me like I first discovered in Tangier gardens. "Certainly, let's do it tomorrow!"

So the next day dawned clear. We made sandwiches, took some of last year's apples and we headed off to Alpiglen first via the Kleine Scheidegg train to Alpiglen, then on foot. It was glorious. It was still early spring and the cows were still in the lowlands. And after a short walk—all at the base of Eiger *nordwand*, we came across wildflowers glowing in the warm sun. Spring gentians dominated the pasture—clumps and clusters everywhere. Sprinkled among them were globe flowers and cowslips. They were all happy. They were stretching in the sunlight. Bree and I went our separate ways exploring for those special plants that demanded our attention. Fantastic day. Later we found a nice place to sit down and have the sandwiches and apples we brought.

Bree said. "I was thinking about your 'obsession' with what you hear—that Egyptian singer, the yodellers... there is something special about hearing... at least that is what I think. And you and I both hear things in the landscape, gardens, from the plants... things..."

"Things? Melodies? Or words? Or sounds," I asked.

"Let's just leave it at things... because I think they are special connections that reach beyond what we measure as the material world..."

"What are you saying? In Tangier gardens, I heard things from plants... I called them transcendent or effulgent glories..."

"I can't label..."

I interrupted, "I have tried so hard to find a label but everything I've tried always has so much history, so much confusion..."

"We can agree that our senses are limited—we've covered that before. But we also make mistakes. And that takes me to God, the supreme creator. And the church in Grindelwald that gave me shelter when you were gone for so long. It hurt so bad. And my prayers and surrender to the hands of God brought me some amount of peace that allowed me to carry on... all of it fits together for me... and now I am happy to walk these landscapes, and work in the garden with you."

"That's what we share."

"I think we also share service. We serve each other. I've also come to believe that the Ten Commandments are a simple outline of how to live with a minimum of complications— because complications and hurts do come—of their own accord—we don't need to encourage them..."

"I can't disagree."

"And I get fatigued talking about words, philosophy. Look at these flowers just next to us. How is it that these cowslips look like they are dancing—that they look joyful?"

"And how is it that I, we, can feel it?"

We both looked up at the snowcapped Eiger and the deep blue sky, inhaled deeply cool fresh mountain air, relaxed and sat quietly for I don't know how long.

These were the days. Before long it was time for me to return to Kuwait.

***

Q8

When I returned to Kuwait I had some things to do for my new job and my new home. I had to get to know the internal office, its processes and its couple hundred people. Plus I needed to find a place to stay.

Kuwait is a strange place. Following the discovery of oil, Kuwait modernized, Westernized early and then all hell broke loose—the Iraq-Iran war—within small-arms fire range. Then Kuwait was invaded and occupied by Iraq. The irrigation systems were destroyed. All public parks and landscaping died.

Maybe it will take generations to recover. Palestinians had become mid-level employees in the private and public sectors until they sided with Iraq. Then they became *persona-non-grata* here. After the war, Egyptians became the people of choice to occupy the mid-level posts. I found them everywhere. In the office, in the apartments. Everywhere.

There were still buildings which had their façade damaged by shelling. Visual reminders of the war that was long over.

The Kuwaiti AE, my new employer, was owned by two Kuwaiti partners—one an architect and the other a civil engineer. Neither of them working in the office, though they did walk through from time to time. They both used their connections to bring projects into the office.

Day-to-day operations were overseen by a Brit General Manager, finances were managed by a Kuwaiti and different departments, organized by discipline, were managed for the most part by Egyptians including an Egyptian woman as the Structural Engineering department head.

The two lead architects were one a Lebanese and second an American, graduate from Carnegie Melon University. Landscape Architecture department head—that was me. And I had two people on my team. Two landscape designers, Jen, a hardscape specialist Filipino guy from a suburb of Manilla; and Manjula, a plant-specialist Indian lady from Bangalore. Neither was a landscape architect, but they were both well-experienced designer/draftsmen. I was happy to be in a simpler job with no multi-level complications.

My company was one of the big 3 Kuwaiti AE firms. That meant we had a good share of high profile and landmark projects. In fact, it was back in the 70s when the Kuwaiti Architect partner brought famous landscape architects from the US, Sasaki Associates, to Kuwait to master-plan the waterfront.

Most of our projects were urban. Why? In Kuwait, land use had only two categories. Desert and urban. Desert was tough and intense. Sand and wind, daytime summer temps always in the 40s. I wasn't surprised. This was part of the Arabian Peninsula—all big-time desert—with subtle variations. Kuwait had *shamals*—dramatic sandstorms as shown in movies like *Mission Impossible–Ghost Protocol.* At least one/year. Winters in the 20s. Lots of sunshine but little and irregular rain, averaging less than 10cm/yr, but when it comes, it comes as huge electrical storms with an intensity causing local flooding.

Five months out of the year the average highs are above 40 and three months the average lows are below 10. Kuwait has no lakes or rivers. Freshwater resources in Kuwait are very scarce due to low precipitation, a high rate of evaporation and the dry sandy nature of the "topsoil". The water supply for landscaping is on its own citywide system and is brackish groundwater. While Kuwait is part of the Tigris–Euphrates river system basin, Kuwait has no source of nor access to that fresh water.

The process of typical large urban projects was that we would joint venture with a well-known large American architectural office, often from New York or Chicago. They would drive conceptual and preliminary design and turn it over to us for intermediate, final design and construction documents. We would oversee construction. But for certain Kuwaiti clients we would perform 100% of their projects.

Kuwait City was not large—but it had its neighbourhoods. Years ago, long before the Gulf Wars, the last of Old Kuwait City was destroyed when its residents tried to overthrow the King. So all of Kuwait City is "modern". Expatriates in Kuwait account for around 60% of Kuwait's total population. Some neighbourhoods are labourer dominated, others are Middle East expatriate dominated. All of those are apartments.

Kuwaiti neighbourhoods were definitely Kuwaiti family only. They were all single-family villas. Islam allows four wives, and Kuwaiti men with four wives often have compounds with four individual villas, one for each wife. And the man has his own *diwaniya*—a place in the compound where males only, friends and new acquaintances alike, can discuss politics, business, sports and any other topic that may arise—a bit like what Americans call a man-cave.

Looking for an apartment, I learned about the different parts of town, the sizes of apartment rooms, their layout and the behaviour of families. To summarize—in the neighbourhoods where Middle East (ME) expats dominated, the apartments were not open plan and had smaller rooms easily segregated between family and public entertainment.

The Western-style were open plan with larger rooms. For car parking, ME-style did not have underground parking whereas Western style always had underground parking. And in the ME-style apartment buildings, the public hallways belonged to the kids and the hallways were always noisy at all hours. Western? Hallways quiet, never filled with kids.

I found a place in a neighbourhood called Salmiya. The building had a swimming pool and an underground garage. From my apartment I had a view out over the waterfront, to the Gulf on one side and out the other side I saw central Kuwait City, its landmark water towers and the Grand Mosque. I had plenty of shops nearby and a 10-min drive on local roads into our Hawally office.

I settled in easily, working in a relaxed environment. So

different from Bahrain, from Saudi Arabia. Daily activities moved ahead smoothly. I did most of my shopping at the Sultan Centre, a large grocery and home goods store about 4 blocks from my apartment. My office projects included a modern souk using traditional architectural forms, downtown office buildings, plazas and university expansions.

Two things they all had in common—hardscape elements closely coordinated with adjacent architecture and—simple planting. Why simple planting? We had only minimal numbers and few species of plants. The government regulated the carefully restricted volumes of landscaping water use. And we had a limited plant palette because of winter and summer climate extremes combined with the very few plants that could thrive on the salt level in the irrigation water. We had no opportunities to improve plant options. Decades of experience had fixed the palette of sustainable plants.

I learned about the Kuwait Institute of Scientific Research (KISR) that was dedicated to improving the environmental conditions and increasing the diversity of plant life in the urban areas. I liked what I was finding. Everything, my work and my personal life here, seemed simpler and straightforward. The climate was hell, dusty, hot, dry and humid (both within a 24hour cycle), no mitigating refreshment, but I was busy and enjoying my time in Kuwait City.

Before I knew it, four months had passed and it was time for my vacation visit to Bree, in Switzerland.

***

Deeper into the Legend

I felt a comfortable routine starting. Nice job in Kuwait. More frequent visits with Bree in the haybarn. It wasn't until on my way back to Grindelwald when my Swiss train was twisting up the steeply forested Grindelwald Valley that I realized how flat and tedious was the Kuwait landscape. It was an oppressed landscape—burdened into flatness by the intense sun and blistering temperatures. The Grindelwald Valley topography, on the other hand, was filled with the musical energy of mountains, forests, waterfalls and river.

When I arrived in Grindelwald, cleanliness was in the air. No dust. No oppressive heat. My breathing was not laboured—it was normal. I felt fresh again—recharged even before I got to our haybarn. The Jungfrau Region landscape had power, an existential cleansing power.

I was dancing as I climbed up toward Grosse Scheidegg and our haybarn. Before I got there I could see the gardens in flower—they had a glow of their own. Reminded me of the lesson the guys at the Hibiscus House in Tangier tried to teach—humans have to put themselves into their care of plants. Then the plants would respond—like taking care of a pet cat or a pet dog.

A vacation three times a year? It was like having a honeymoon every four months. This time it was a bit different. I was surprised as Bree brought up the "adventure".

"What are we going to do?" she asked. "Should we revisit the Mannlichen adventure? I have been thinking about it—how amazing it was to find the tunnel, the red-beaked choughs and all—I'd be happy just to walk up there again."

I thought maybe that was the way to approach what JeanClaude had emphasized was a potentially dangerous effort. "What do you want to do?"

"I thought we could take some pruning shears and actually look into the tunnel—what do you think?"

"I think we should be careful. What if that ventilation shaft has been modernized, what if it has sensors? We don't want to be caught trespassing, do we?"

"You might be right. But we didn't get 'caught' when we dropped a stone down the shaft last time, did we? Let's bring our leather gardening gloves and do, like before, a minimal amount of pruning and pushing those brambles about..."

"But we have to be careful not to make it look like we have disturbed the place..."

"I'm with you—do we have a plan?"

"Definitely!"

Now we had a plan—a just-look-and-see plan. We were going to revisit the Mannlichen ventilation shaft we found, when? 18 months, almost two years ago. You could say it was in our neighbourhood; but the Jungfrau Region was large. Getting there from our haybarn required taking at least two trains.

We left first thing in the morning. It was autumn—locally they called it *goldener herbst*—a golden autumn. It was cool in the morning and warm in the afternoon. The sky was clear—a high-pressure clarity in the landscape. I had the ventilation shaft Northing/Easting saved on my phone. We brought pruning shears, leather work gloves and lunch with us.

We had to verify that what we found was still there and untouched. We liked that this time of year, the majority of tourists had long returned to their home. Nobody on the early train. Changed at Kleine Scheidegg, then got off at Wengwald. We started our hike—about 45 minutes uphill. We found the dry brook and continued uphill till we found the clearing—just as we saw it before. The bramble clump had grown.

We did some careful bending of the brambles and selective pruning to finally be able to peer into the shaft. It looked just wide enough for one person to rappel down. We shined our flashlight down the shaft. It appeared to be straight; but we could not see a bottom. The rock sides looked rough but carefully hewn.

In the adjacent open patch of grass, we sat for lunch in the sun. At the edges of grass the ecotype changed to mostly large Swiss stone pines.

I said, "We have to ask, what are we going to do? Do we seriously want to take this a step further?"

"Let's just enjoy our sandwiches and the afternoon sun now. And on our way back let's go via Lauterbrunnen and Zweilutshinen to see just what's going on at those military offices down below."

Before we left we hid the branches we pruned under other wildly rambling brambles and left it looking, so we hoped, like no one had ever been there. And we made sure to carry out everything we had carried in.

From Wengwald we took the train down to Lauterbrunnen, changed and rode down to the next stop, Zweilutschinen. The train followed the Lutschine River and just before Zweilutschinen, at the base of the Mannlichen's steep forests and cliffs, the train slowly passed a number of three-storey barracks and an admin building. In the parking lots were a number of cars and a larger number of military jeeps and trucks. We didn't have any idea what was being done there, but there were a couple of large steel door entries in one of the steep cliff faces. Definitely large enough to provide truck or bus access.

We changed trains and rode up to Grindelwald. As we walked to the haybarn, I said, "I'm not convinced—too many military, we don't have the skills and I don't want to compromise our haybarn life."

"You make sense but this is an adventure, like my time on the edge of the Sahara. We just have to plan carefully. Planning carefully, isn't that what you landscape architects do?"

***

236

Failaka

Any time I was away for my 10-day leave, the office was without a proper landscape architect. I made it a task, when I returned from leave in Switzerland, to hire a Middle East-experienced landscape architect. When I started the search I found that the Brit who had worked well for me in Bahrain was in the market. He wanted to return to the Gulf region. I put everything in motion and in six weeks I had a proper senior landscape architect on board to cover and to guide Jen and Manjula when I was away.

Every Monday (work week Monday through Friday, 9-6, one hour for lunch) our general manager met with all department heads to establish status and identify any new actions for the coming week. On this week, the GM told me of a new project on Failaka Island. I had one week to familiarize myself and the next week Jeff and I would go out to the island to make an on-site assessment.

This was the first time I looked at the larger history of the region. Failaka had become the archaeological hub of Kuwait, because there were settlements on the island dating to 4,000BC. Alexander the Great occupied the island and made it a regional trading hub, connecting Africa and the Far East with the Middle East.

The island was approximately 40sqkm and only 50km southeast of where the Tigris and Euphrates empty into the Gulf. In fact, the rivers' sources are in Turkey and their entry into the Gulf is via an extensive natural wetlands ecosystem that, by natural forces, has shifted substantially over the centuries between present-day Iran and Kuwait.

Prior to the first Gulf War, on Failaka Island in a small village, there were 2,000 permanent inhabitants. They were forced to evacuate to the mainland during the battles, never to return. Now, though, there was a very small number of fishermen living there.

I wondered how it might be anything but an Arabian Peninsula desert atoll. But I read that the island has a microclimate that is the envy of all Kuwaitis and has always been a "countryside" destination for short relaxations particularly in the spring.

Our task? Review the deserted waterfront recreation facilities and evaluate the possibilities for updating them. The following week, Jeff and I arranged to take a company 4x4 on the ferry from Salmiya to Failaka. The only public connection, the ferry makes only one trip over and back per day, and is large enough to accommodate about a dozen vehicles.

We arrived 15 minutes early and we were the only vehicle on board. The Public Transport Company ferry took one hour each way. It was no frills—no passenger deck—just an open deck for the cars. Not a tourist trip at all. We got out and stood on the side by the railing. The ferry would stay on Failaka until late in the afternoon, giving us about 6 hours on the island to do our work.

The island was about 20km away and, just prior to departure, Jeff and I were straining to see Failaka on the horizon. All of a sudden, all hell seemed to burst loose—squealing tires, horns, shouting. We turned and a line of desert military humvees had arrived at the last minute. The ferry captain re-lowered the ramp to let them drive on. We watched. There were six of them. Out of each humvee came two to four soldiers—couldn't tell if they were Kuwaiti or American—all in desert camo fatigues. Didn't make any difference, we turned our glance back out to the Kuwait Bay horizon searching for Failaka as the ferry shoved off. Slow and steady, we crossed.

We had just entered Failaka's small and somewhat ramshackle marina, docking in a few minutes, when a couple of the soldiers stripped off their shirts, climbed up on the rail and dove into the water. From the side of the ferry the rest of the soldiers cheered them on. Raucous it was.

As we docked, the swimmers had climbed out of the water and were waiting for the ferry's boat ramp to go down. That is when I did a double take. One of the swimmers was Gordie's brother Garrett, who had visited me in Grindelwald.

As I drove out I stopped next to Garrett. Got out. Greetings began.

"Garrett!"

"CJ! What the hell are you doing here?"

"Landscape architecture takes me around the world—what about you?"

"We're using the abandoned village for urban warfare training of Kuwaiti soldiers. Are you working in Kuwait or just seagulling in?"

"I live in Salmiya, how about you?"

"We are here for three months—we should get together."

"You got a mobile? I'll send you my details, call me and we can meet at my place," I said.

"Sure thing."

Jeff had no idea what was going on, so as we drove, he asked.

I said, "A long time ago, I worked in the Western region of Saudi Arabia with Garrett's twin brother—unfortunately his brother died there under unusual circumstances. Sometime later, Garrett looked me up in Switzerland to uncover the details. That's how we got to know each other.

"Jeff, is this where we turn to find those old waterfront chalets?"

"Take a right here and stop where those military guys are blocking the road."

I rolled down the window, an armed soldier advanced. He spoke American English. "What are you guys doing here? We have 'live-fire' tomorrow. No visitors!"

I explained our tasks and said we would be taking the afternoon ferry back to Salmiya. He waved us on and said, "Don't miss it!"

And we didn't. We photographed the remnants of what looked like a 1960s low-budget waterfront recreation project.

Thirty chalets, a swimming pool and an indoor rec-centre—all in one long, narrow strip. We took a lot of extra photos to make sure we captured the extended landscape context.

On the inland side we were careful because on the road behind us were tanks and armed humvees moving up and back the whole time. How long does this war-thing go on? I was glad to return to the mainland.

A week later I got a phone call from Garrett. He came by my Salmiya apartment that night. We connected. He had enjoyed hiking the Jungfrau Region and hoped to get back there sometime. I asked, "Just what are you doing—still working out of Belgrade?"

He said, "Yeah, this Failaka thing is my typical gig. But you, what about you and what was her name, Bree?"

"All is good, I'm on an annually renewable contract here with generous leave provisions—much easier working conditions than in Saudi. Do you work full time or do you have lots of down time?" I figured Garrett had the kind of fitness and can-do skills that Bree and I needed on the Mannlichen. I was thinking maybe I should see if he would like that kind of adventure. For the moment I kept those thoughts to myself.

"Oh, I do have some down time—but I like it that way—lots of personal freedom."

"In three months I go on leave back to Grindelwald... if you have some free time, why don't you come visit us and we can hike together?"

"Yeah, yeah, that's a good idea... three months from now? That should work. Let's keep in touch and we'll look at the timing when it's closer."

***

Garrett's On Board

My vacations never came quickly enough—especially since I was on bachelor status. But this vacation was special because we just might be taking a step forward on the Mannlichen adventure. In my mind I wasn't sure, because I had taken JeanClaude's warning seriously. I figured we'd see what Garrett, who was experienced in "covert" activities, would make of the proposed adventure.

Garrett did come to visit us; and he stayed as he did before, rough, sleeping outdoors. We told him the wilding legend about the ancient gold stores and he showed some interest. He said he'd look into it and took off on a hike.

Five days later he returned. He told us about old, no longer used forestry paths as separate from farm paths, *wanderwegs* and *bergwegs*. They were paths little used and they led him into a chance meeting with a wilding who told him that he used to work for government at CERN in Geneva, on the Hadron Collider project.

Garrett learned that the project, years ago, had been done in conjunction with DARPA, Defense Advanced Research Projects Agency, part of the US Department of Defense. The wilding told him they worked with the Swiss military utilizing deep underground storage and access to earth core heat to support a tunnel system of ultra-high-speed maglev rail to the Lauterbrunnen valley.

Garrett said, "My findings support your original wilding legend and I like this adventure. Can you show me that access shaft?"

"We'll have to go tomorrow because in three days I have to return to Kuwait."

"So let's do it; but you have to understand whatever is at the end of that shaft, whatever is going on down deep, it is of national and international significance—that is likely to be highly protected. This will not be like a hike in the mountains. But let's look at the shaft first." I liked Garrett's take on the project—similar to JeanClaude's.

The three of us made the trip via Wengwald the next day. Garrett assessed the shaft entry, its nature and size, plus the surrounding forest, topography and geology. We spread open some of the sprawling bramble so he could look at the entry to the shaft. After we headed back, the three of us sat around the table in the haybarn as Garrett outlined what he thought the plan should be.

"We have going for us that the ventilation shaft is old and obviously not accessible to daily public activity. That means we should be able to enter without causing any disturbance. But from here on it gets very dangerous. We don't know what we will find. It would be nice to think we can just rappel down the shaft and enter a room with open treasure chests packed with Middle East gold from the time of the Crusades, right?"

Bree and I looked at each other while Garrett watched our reactions. I said, "Yeah, that's the dream."

"Dream," said Garrett, "... dream and you never went any further than that, right?"

"Right."

"Well this is the 'fish or cut bait', the 'shit or get off the pot' moment because from here on it is hairy—danger of death hairy. Let me summarize. We need two people—me and someone else to rappel down that shaft. You guys need to stay on the top away from the action. We need secure rappelling, we need communication, we need to be ready to encounter danger, we need an escape plan and we need to have a way to retrieve gold if there is any. Are you guys still game?"

I listened carefully. I looked at Bree—she was up for the adventure. I said, "Garrett, could this be a two-phase effort? The first to rappel to the bottom and observe what it is, then if it still looks doable we return for a second phase with the goal to remove some of the gold—I mean removing gold—that's a logistic nightmare kind of challenge. What do you think?"

"There is some logic but once we are down there and it looks doable? Once in and once out is, to me, a better solution. Hell, we were never going to do a 'Fort Knox' gold haul—practically a couple pieces in each of our back packs in your first phase and we are out—we all end up with a bit of historic gold and one hell of a story. That's how I see it."

He made it sound doable but the realities... the chances...

Garrett said, "Let's think about this some more. CJ, when you leave for Kuwait this time, it will be four months before you return, right? I have another 3-month gig in Kuwait at the same time. We can meet in Salmiya again and take this further. In the meantime, I'll give you a list of things to prepare in your go-bags. I'll leave it to you guys to plan your go-route— you know this place well enough—you may have to leave the country—or maybe not—maybe you just have to quietly return to your haybarn. Me? I'd have to leave the country. Anyhow, take this list as a guide for preparing your go-bags and if all goes well in four months we will give it a go."

"Just a minute," Bree said. "This is my home, the Jungfrau Region, Grindelwald, my haybarn—go-bag? I'm not going anywhere. I'm not betting my home for a gamble in a tunnel. I don't care what's at the bottom. I love an adventure but in the garden outside my haybarn, every day is an adventure. I'm in on the dream—the pot of gold at the end of the tunnel—but if we're going to do it, my home must be protected."

I was stunned as Bree spoke. Stunned? Well, she did have form speaking her mind. It seemed often she was just along for the ride on this adventure but now...

Garrett said, "If I am involved, I would do it clean. There would be no connection between me or my movements with you or your haybarn. That I can do. But on the day, if something happened down in the tunnel, you would need to have a pre-planned route back to your haybarn without using public transportation. Then just go on the rest of the time like nothing happened—spend your time in your garden."

I could tell from Bree's face and eyes that she calmed. "Have we covered everything? Are we clear?" Garrett asked.

We nodded.

With that Garrett got up and left. Bree and I looked at each other and smiled, nervously. But inside I was glad to have already a go-route that JeanClaude had given me.

***

Cross-Cultural

My return to Kuwait brought me a new project. A wealthy Kuwaiti man, having Persian roots, for whom my company designed a high-rise mixed-use project, wanted his home villa landscaped. The job was handed to me. I took it—a valuable client. I learned some lessons.

First, before there were state boundaries for Iran, Iraq, Kuwait and Saudi Arabia, tribal groupings moved amoeba-like on this landscape. That means that many of the Kuwaitis have family roots in Iran. That in turn means that while Kuwait is mostly Sunni there are fair numbers of Shia.

And my client was Shia with Persian roots. I hadn't done a residential landscape since California—what—30 years ago? So I lapsed into my own SoCal-based design approach. First step was to understand how the residents plan to use their home gardens.

Well, that didn't work. I got cross-culturally side swiped. I was told by the client, in no uncertain terms, that I would never be able to understand his lifestyle, he wouldn't answer any questions about how he and his family would use the garden. I felt like the infidel that I was.

I didn't even get to first base. Lost the project. I was too much the unfaithful Westerner. Our GM gave the project to Manjula who worked directly with our client's wife to design and build the garden. Lessons learned.

Speaking of lessons learned, I have always had difficulties understanding gross and subtle cultural differences in the different foreign countries where I have worked. Maybe it is my own cultural roots that are so strong they prohibit my comprehension of foreign, but in the big picture, I do relish the challenges of a foreign place, city, environment and its people.

My head floods with images. Middle East and North Africa images from places I have lived and worked.

Here in Kuwait and in so many other countries the mid-level and labour level were expatriates away from home in how many different countries from the Middle East, the Sub-continent and SE Asia. That all adds its own range of conflicts and challenges. On the job site: Bangladeshi vs Pakistani, Brit vs Kuwaiti, Palestinian vs Egyptian, Pakistani vs Indian and it was all written on the porta-potti WC walls; but language and culture barriers kept me shielded from Shia vs Sunni.

I wouldn't want to bore you with the tedium of my daily activities; but in summary, everything has been challenging—from the largest to the smallest. Where can I buy groceries? What do they have there? Are things fresh? Are they safe to eat? What is popular and in season? Is there any fast-food? Is there any street food? Will I get to know any local people? Visas, driver's license, healthcare, apothecaries? Where to stay, conditions of lease? Fixtures and furnishings. Personal and household cleanliness. Post offices. Digital connectivity. Utilities. Am I the only one who speaks English? When to eat. How to eat. Right hand or left hand. Who and how to greet.

That's a thick paragraph. But that has been my fun in every country: Morocco, Saudi Arabia, Egypt, Turkey, Bahrain, the United Arab Emirates. Lessons learned? Their country, their rules. Learn them as best you can. No guidebooks, no tourist sites and the US Embassy does not have all the answers. On my own. Make it work. I've loved the challenges. And my time in Kuwait? More of the same. Every project had a unique cast of expatriate characters.

But hanging above all my office projects was the plan that Garrett was putting together. About 2 months later, he called me. He said, "Remember that day on Failaka when you saw me swimming with a friend? That friend is Faf, a South African who works with me out of Belgrade. He's the ideal guy to partner me and us for that Mannlichen project. We ought to get together and talk this through."

In my apartment, over the next couple weeks, Faf, Garrett and I went over the plans in detail. Faf was a mountaineering/rappelling genius. He had been to the Berner Oberland many times; and above all he saw this kind of adventure as pure fun. Faf said, "Damn the results, let's do it."

6-Adventure

The Final Plan

My every-four-month vacation was due and the adventure was afoot.

Garrett and Faf had arrived a couple days early to "recce" (reconnoitre) the site and get all their equipment together. Upon my arrival from Kuwait, they met me at the Grindelwald train station with their report. They had good news.

Garrett summarized. "We spent a lot of time day and night around that ventilation shaft. It is an old, well-crafted, rough-hewn shaft—no signs of modernization—no signs of use—no signs of monitoring—no unusual electrical, digital or sonar sensors, no electromagnetic radiation, comms or cameras. We can use adjacent mature pines to secure our descent rope and the shaft is wide enough for our rappel. It's a go." I was relieved but also a bit nervous.

We hiked up to the haybarn together and spent the next day testing the equipment, going over the plan.

The weather was rainy at night and drizzly during the day. I asked them if that might be a problem. They said the overcast and light rain would be no problem, maybe even an advantage—less people around.

Bree and I had our local go-route planned and our lightweight hiking backpacks ready. On the side, I had my international go-bag ready as JeanClaude had suggested. Professionally, I had always prided myself on planning for the unexpected. But this was a bit different—a lot different. I felt nerves like I never felt on a job.

I asked myself what if something happened? What about Bree? What about my Kuwait job? I figured if push came to shove, my right-hand man, the Brit senior landscape architect, could handle my job but hell, this was all a step too far.

And Bree? She was not convinced there might be trouble. And furthermore, she would never leave her haybarn. I lived with that; but I always thought there was an outside chance for trouble. I figured we'd cross that bridge if we come to it. I hadn't really thought about what she would do if I had to take my international go-route. I was lazy on that. Maybe she would just carry on in her haybarn while I was away—kind of like another international job. Anyhow, it was too late to re-think anything.

Garrett and Faf were going to attach their line to an adjacent deep-rooted, mature, healthy tree and both would single-rope descend. They had night vision goggles, helmet-mounted mini-cams and earwig coms devices linked to us. They made sure we didn't handle any of their equipment.

We were to stay on top and, with gloves, make sure the rope was protected, cushioned over the edge of the shaft. Plan was solid—one time only—in and out. These guys were strong and in excellent shape. They had already ditched their extra gear in one of the many bins around town that receive cloth, clothes, shoes and boots for peoples in Africa.

Their backpacks were sized for this adventure. Down and up. Easy in and out with just enough extra space to collect from the bottom of the shaft, "souvenirs", if they found any.

On the way in, we found the previously dry creek now running with rainwater—just a smooth flow, nothing substantial. We walked along its edge. No problem arriving to our destination. The massive bramble clump had the look of never being touched despite our previous visits. We had been careful in our handling of the brambles. We were just as careful as we opened a path this time.

They started with 200m of rope and each carried another 50m in their backpacks. They worked like a well-practiced team as they set up for the rappel. They wore gloves all the time, showed us what to do with minimal talking; after all, we had trialled it, dry-run it earlier before we left. Most of the time they said nothing.

Our comms set up was simple. Quiet meant steady progress. They sent their depth every 50 metres. If they would find something, they would message and image it. Otherwise all quiet. The cancel word was ROCKSTAR. If we heard ROCKSTAR we were supposed to get out, disappear onto the go-route, then ditch all equipment and notes.

They looked at us, gave us a thumbs-up and down they went. They cushioned the rope as it went over the edge of stone and rock. We were to make sure the cushioning always stayed in place. They sent images to my phone every 50m. Bree and I were giddy with enthusiasm. The shaft was tight but they made progress. They descended to 200m and still hadn't reached bottom. We waited anxiously on top—peering down into the shaft, even though we couldn't see anything.

On my phone—nothing but black.

***

Mannlichen Debacle

At nearly 220 metres they appeared to reach a landing. They sent an image—solid rock with a heavy-duty concrete frame holding a heavy-duty cast-iron grate. Could this be it? The entry to the ancient gold storage?

The image made us peer all the more intently—though we couldn't see anything down the shaft. Actually, we were telegraphing our hope in their direction.

Then, without warning, shouting came through our comms—ROCKSTAR, ROCKSTAR, ROCKSTAR!

Bree and I froze staring down the shaft. Seconds seemed like minutes. I started to stand up and as I was starting to tell Bree to come with me, there was a huge burst of gunfire from down below echoing up and down the shaft. Bree was still looking down the shaft and I, standing right behind her, froze, too. Action was required but we took none.

The rappelling rope went slack. The gunfire continued. The echoes were ear shattering. Then Bree screamed. Blood was spurting from her neck. She rolled flat on the ground. I finally started acting, I grabbed my hiking backpack, found the first-aid packs to absorb blood from major wounds. I rushed over to Bree. It appeared a bullet must have come up from the shaft and hit her carotid artery. I held all the packs against her neck. There was too much blood already. "Bree, Bree, talk to me!" She said nothing. Her body went limp. The packs were soaked with blood from her neck. She died in my arms.

The gunfire from the shaft had stopped. I had had no comms since ROCKSTAR.

It had been cloudy all morning; but somehow the sun broke through and a ray shone on a sturdy Swiss mountain pine at the edge of the clearing. With much effort I strained to pick up Bree's body. Oh, the mind and body have so many unexplained... so many surprises. In my mind I suddenly saw the simple altar of marigolds and basil from Vrndadevi's ashram in Ban Muang Thailand. And, in the mountain quiet, I knew what I must do. I carried Bree to the base of the Swiss stone pine.

The pine and the forest floor would be Bree's altar. I set Bree down at the base of the pine. Then I sat her up straight with her back and head braced against the tree trunk. I closed her eyelids. Despite the wound on her neck and despite the blood splattered over all her clothes, she looked peaceful. I stepped back in a strange, kind of in-the-moment reverence.

In shock are seconds minutes or hours? We were supposed to be running out on our go-route... but... Adrenalin had to be pumping for me to carry her body. I looked at my gloves, my jacket, my pants... I had her blood all over me. And as I was thinking what to do... I heard bells—large brass bells—the kind mature Swiss cows carry in the pastures. But the ringing was not sporadic and chaotic like from a herd of cows. It was more rhythmic, steady like church bells, like the local *trychlers.*

But I was tens of kilometres of distance and hundreds of metres in elevation away from the nearest village and there was no wind. The bells brought me peace—a peace absorbed deeply into my inner spirit.

I looked up to the sky and drew a very long and deep breath. Was the shock wearing... off...? Then I looked over at Bree, peacefully sitting at the base of the old Swiss stone pine. And I couldn't believe my eyes—they were fixated on her as I saw... the splattered blood all over her gradually disappeared. Then the carotid artery wound disappeared.

I was in a trance. I couldn't think. My intelligence couldn't ask... then Bree herself began to disappear ever so slowly, as if the tree was absorbing her body and spirit. I blinked and she was gone.

I was immobile, like a statue—still dazed. I snapped out of it. A clarity returned. I looked at the pine—just a pine. I looked at my gloves and clothes—no blood stains at all. I was in disbelief—a twilight zone in broad daylight. I could hardly say whaaa... when I heard a helicopter in the distance coming closer. Reality—big time—hit me like a ton of bricks. I had to move.

Before I left I examined the Swiss stone pine tree where I had placed her body. There was absolutely nothing there except the old pine needles; but the air... it carried the fresh pine aroma... a deep healing scent. I inhaled deeply. I could have stayed there forever. Except for the sound of the approaching helicopter.

I took off along the forestry paths I had identified as our escape go-route. I had only got about a hundred metres when I heard in the distance the helicopter getting closer. My path was through a heavy forest, dense with overhead foliage. I crossed a burbling brook and even though there were no signs of blood any longer, I washed my hands. Erased my iPhone data, removed the SIM card (threw it downhill into the blueberry shrubs) and tucked my gloves, iPhone and earpiece beneath a large rock under the flowing brook, then continued speed walking.

I worked my way down the Grindelwald side of the Mannlichen over toward the Gletscherschlucht then toward the Oberergletscher. From there I stayed in the forest all the way back to our haybarn. Adrenalin had wrapped up my emotions. But my emotions were pulsating with hurt and pain. My heart was in my throat. My muscles were already aching and my pulse rate must have been in the 140s.

***

CJ's Dream

An old LA (landscape architect) went desert walking it was a cloud-
less, windy day
On a burning sand dune he rested, as he pushed along his way
When all at once he saw afar, the path to all his dreams
A dancing in the shifting sands
Down into the salty seams.
Mirages in the sands

He saw other LAs flummoxed, struggling, looking
For the same as he.
They were working hard to find that answer, not yet found indeed.
They are bound to seek forever, for that answer just o'er there,
Veins bursting on their straining heads
As they seek in death's despair.
Mirages in the sands

As the bedraggled LA team ran by
He heard one call his name,
"If you want to save your soul from hell, searching always ever,
Then CJ, change your aim...
Or with us be doomed forever

Chasing that devil's curse o'er endless dunes and skies
For that n'er to be found answer,
And always in a ceaseless search we ever hope to die."
Mirages in the sands

Pounding and pounding—then with one last horrendous ear-splitting pound, I fell on the floor... and the dream was over.

I had been asleep in my bed in my room on the freighter. The ship was rocking violently. Someone was pounding on my door. I struggled to stand. Could not keep my balance. Fell toward the door. Grabbed onto the handle to keep upright. Finally unlocked and opened it. The shouting began.

"Sir?! You alright? Come with me. Make you safe."

We were somewhere where the Adriatic meets the Med and we had been accosted by a small but very aggressive low-pressure centre. And me? I was on a general cargo freighter to the UAE.

Four days ago a Slovenian shipping agent booked passage for me and as soon as I got on board I collapsed on the bed in my small 2.5 by 3.0 metre room. And I had been in that bed for 18 hours when either the dream or the storm or the pounding finally woke me.

In my head was a tune from my Southwest USA childhood—Vaughan Monroe singing *Ghost Riders in the Sky*—couldn't stop the song from repeating over and over.

The Filipino seaman led me upstairs to the commons room where, for our safety, I and the other three passengers were buckled into secured chairs. The captain came and told us the rough seas would likely be finished in the next four hours as the storm was moving northward and we were moving southward.

Didn't bother me. Not like my dream—not like my last two weeks. I had been running hard—real hard—non-stop.

Before long the seas calmed, the captain returned and said it was safe to walk around. Back in my cabin I collapsed in deep sleep again on the bed. When I awoke and went up on deck... Suez Canal, Egypt, blistering sun, blustery winds and... the haunting, the looming... the sands.

Exposed by the harsh desert realities, my dream had been the folly and fantasy of my lifetime searches—design—landscape. They were professional cocoons to protect me from the hurt of my personal life. My personal life? Now?

My old nemesis—sand desert and blistering sun. Maybe I was safely away; but I was all alone. All alone. All alone. Shock had not left me. Pain had wrapped me.

Time to stop hiding, let it all out. What had happened in the Swiss forest below the Mannlichen? I had a ball of emotion so large I feared opening it, letting it out. But something inside told me I had to let it out—relive it to the reality of it all. No more cocoon. No more hiding. I had to get into my real life.

I had 10 days of hell. I had 10 days of adrenalin mixed with the most painful emotions. On the day, I think Garrett and Faf were shot dead deep down in that ventilation shaft where they must have been discovered, unauthorized entries, and engaged by the military in a firefight. In the midst of the firefight a bullet came up through the shaft and hit Bree's neck, exploding her carotid artery. Her death was quick, bleeding out in less than a minute.

On the day, shock overtook me immediately. I acted on instinct. I don't know where that instinct came from. I had to leave the clearing and I had to take care of Bree. Bree was first. The adrenalin gave me the strength to lift her lifeless body and carry her.

How was I able to see an adjacent mature Swiss stone pine as an altar? Altar? Why did I feel it was important to place her body against that thick broad trunk as if she was sitting there? Instinct?

That is when, that day, it went one step beyond. I was in shock. I was in a daze after I placed her against the tree trunk. I stepped back and just stood there looking at her. I did not even process that she was dead... that my life... without her.

I wasn't thinking. My intelligence wasn't working. I just stood there looking at her and the tree trunk. That's when the strangeness happened—I saw a bright aura grow about her, then... the disappearing blood, the disappearing wound, and then Bree herself disappeared. Slack-jawed. I was not believing, not processing—slack-jawed.

Until I heard the helicopter approaching. Then I remembered the go-route—the emergency escape route we had planned. I started jogging.

I remember getting back to the haybarn where I dropped my backpack. Took off my clothes and showered. Dressed quickly and grabbed my international go-bag. I climbed over Grosse Scheidegg and began walking the path that JeanClaude had programmed onto the burner phone.

Without using public transportation, on foot and with rides from some helpful farmers, it took me almost a week to get to my Austrian crossing point. JeanClaude's note made clear the exact place and the time of day to make the crossing. It was a forestry haul road—no border patrol, no gates, just me and the forest.

Once in Austria, I started using public transportation, the Postbus system. It took me three days, travelling 400km, to reach the local area where JeanClaude recommended I cross on foot. Same as Switzerland, a minor Forestry service road with no gates or guards. That got me into Slovenia and the same day only 100km via buses to Port Koper.

I found a hostel just by the port and the next day I contacted the freight agent JeanClaude had noted. In two days I was on a general cargo freighter bound for Bombay, approximately 25 days at sea as scheduled, with multiple stops along the way to what would be my final stop Fujairah in the UAE.

But I would be remiss not to describe what I felt during the two days I stayed in the hostel while awaiting my freighter out. I had been running almost two weeks. I was physically exhausted... but in the Koper hostel I could not sleep.

With distance I can analyze now. It wasn't fear of being caught. It wasn't fear of a criminal trying to escape. Maybe a bit of that, but JeanClaude's route and notes on the burner phone had given me confidence of my personal safety.

Why couldn't I sleep after the physical exhaustion? In the hostel, when I laid down, grief and hurt filled me—my body, my head, my mind, my intelligence. Grief was my all. It wasn't the Mannlichen event. It was the loss of Bree. It was the loss of my tether to fullness. I was like a spaceman outside of the spacecraft safety and having the tether break. I was drifting without hope into eternity with nothing.

Over and over when I closed my eyes, an emotional reality overwhelmed me. Words? None. Hurt choked me. My mind? In knots dripping with hurt. Forty-eight hours straight. No sleep. The arrival of my freighter ride out had saved me.

***

Port by Port

And then on the freighter deck—in daylight the first time... I looked up at the relentless Sahara sun—the sun and sand that had, on my Pharaonic landscape walkabout, demanded I give up all emotional realities.

But I felt the full reality of emotions in charge. The brightness of the sun. The heat of the sun. The rasping sand of the wind. They all beat my emotions into a frenzy. I felt my real emotions whip me—meanly whipped as the dunes are by the relentless wind. My emotions had hurt whipped into them. My attempts to recover?

Relentlessly stripped away. Hopes? Little by little robbed. Shredded, buffeted and blasted into the unreachable eternal— by sun and sand, by life. Words weren't enough. The loss of Bree. Losing everything. That reality sunk me deeper still. I had to open up...

She had been a healer. She had been a lover. She shared everything—plants, landscape, her life, her haybarn. With her death these things were ripped away from me.

But I wasn't crying. I had been married twice and had both wives die in my arms. Something inside me said I had to carry on. I had to recover. But not before I tried to understand. Did Bree actually get absorbed by that tree? Or did I imagine that whole scene? Are Garrett and Faf really dead? Or...

Garrett and Faf knew what they were doing. They knew how to take care of themselves.

And Bree? She had decades of interaction with the land of Faery. But she was a Christian. And... Christianity is not without its magical, mysterious miracles. I saw what I saw. After she disappeared I walked up to the tree trunk and examined carefully the ground and adjacent plants. Nothing. Everything looked normal and healthy.

Maybe sometime in the future I can return to the Jungfrau Region to Grindelwald, to the haybarn, the Mannlichen and see... see what? If what? I don't think I should ever enter that country again. All that gunfire in the ventilation shaft—something was going on. The military did not want unauthorized personnel near whatever it was.

For Bree it was an adventure—a look-see. For Garrett and Faf? I don't know. They were on their own adventure. Nobody thought it would be some kind of massive gold heist. Heck, who knows if there was any gold? It was just a thousand-year-old legend.

For Bree it was fun. I thought there was danger but I went along with it because of Bree. I never thought I might lose her.

And now I am without Bree. I looked out on the Egyptian countryside—the unforgiving sands. I shuddered, choked and dizzied. I was alone with no one. My heart ached, it hurt... deeply, without pause. I was sickened... but...

I had to re-build my life. How? What? I was hurt. Constricting throat hurting so much. Thinking maybe I will wake up and the hurt will be gone. But it took years for me to get over the loss of Sachy and our kids. And now Bree...

I had been healthy again with the love, service and care from Bree. I thought I had recovered from the loss of Sachy and our three kids. And then Bree died in my arms—just like Sachy.

The Jungfrau Region, my landscape of love, was the scene of Bree's death.

I was hurting from my loss—emotional hurt. Did the landscape have anything to do with it? I had always speculated that the landscape feeds human emotion and in the case of my northwest Africa evileye episode the landscape "poisoned" my logic and crippled my emotion. Could the landscape be faultless in relation to human social behaviour?

Am I going to be a victim of the landscape? Am I going to blame the landscape for my own bad choices?

I have struggled all my life to understand landscape and its realism. There has always been more than Gilpin, Price and Ruskin's picturesque. Ruskin did write about the inner truth of landscape, but that is so shallow in comparison to the breadth of the marvellous magic unveiled by the landscape every hour of every day in reality.

Ruskin and many other academics make so many rules—there is in my opinion only one rule—when the landscape speaks to you—you have found its remarkable beauty. Landscape speaking the truth. What truth from the landscape spoke about Bree's death? Beauty in the landscape?

How can anybody separate the actions of humans from the landscape that feeds them, that supports them, that is always under their feet?

I remember Uncle Alp's words about the Jungfrau Region— love the *alps*, fear the *berg*—he had lived his 70-plus years in the Jungfrau Region. And me, an *auslander*, I saw them as Ruskin might have—God's perfect definition of beauty, of beautiful.

I struggled with the inter-relationship between man and nature—was there a physical (like the O_2-CO_2 cycle) meaty link, an existential link, a mental or intellectual link, an auric link or... no link at all? Something must be there... like JB Jackson speculated.

Did the Jungfrau landscape take away from me my most valued, most cherished joy in life? Bree. And the mountain climbers—did not the Jungfrau landscape take away their lives? And Uncle Alp's words again, "love the *alps*, fear the *berg*"? Where do I stand on all that now? Is that something like both sides of the same coin?

Landscape, gardens and plants had linked my personal world to my professional world. Now I have lost Bree... my personal world.

My professional world is all I have left. I have no personal life. There will never be another Bree.

My professional world? I may have lost that too on that

debacle of a Mannlichen adventure. I've had to ditch my Charles Jacobs ID and re-started my Christopher Janus ID. Where does that leave me as a professional landscape architect? I am still CJ and professional colleagues who have appreciated my work in the past may be interested to hire me as is. Still, it is weird. No way a government job in the US. No way an academic post anywhere. And my Kuwaiti job as department head? That's a problem—likely all over—finished.

My professional world... Jobs? Not in the USA, not in Europe, not in the Western world. MENA most likely. The Arabian Peninsula most likely. The Gulf Region? Not Kuwait or Bahrain... UAE, Oman, Qatar possibly.

With Bree, jobs had become no longer primary but secondary. And the subcategories of cocoons—culture, landscape, design—had become subjects for discussion rather than obsessions. Healing... I had been healed. Bree had been a miracle for me.

Culture was unusual because I found that in strange cultures I needed a cocoon in which I could shelter from the culture around me. Culture was also a subset of the landscape cocoon because I was intrigued by what I figured must be a linkage between human culture and the landscape—a 2-way link—with "energy" flows going both ways.

Now I am chancing another strange landscape/culture reality, the Empty Quarter—on shipping lanes that have existed as long as dhows—millennia. And me in the 21st century—floating in the salt waters surrounding that sand monster. I feel like a hunter circling my Arabian Peninsula prey... or maybe the Rub al Khali is sizing me up as it has every prey on every dhow since before written history. I've heard so many stories and now I'm on my way to the UAE to forget, start anew or dip my toes in those empty yet sinister sands.

Another foreign country, foreign landscape, foreign culture... another mystery... maybe that is just what I need. But will it be healing?

My route took me through the Red Sea, the Bab al Mandab Strait, the Gulf of Aden, and the Gulf of Oman. Those are just names. Where have I really been? My route took me through an emotional hell. I have tried to reason myself through it. But who has reasoned through the emotional pain of losing your closest loved one? Anybody?

Just before the Strait of Hormuz, we arrived at Fujairah.

Illustrations

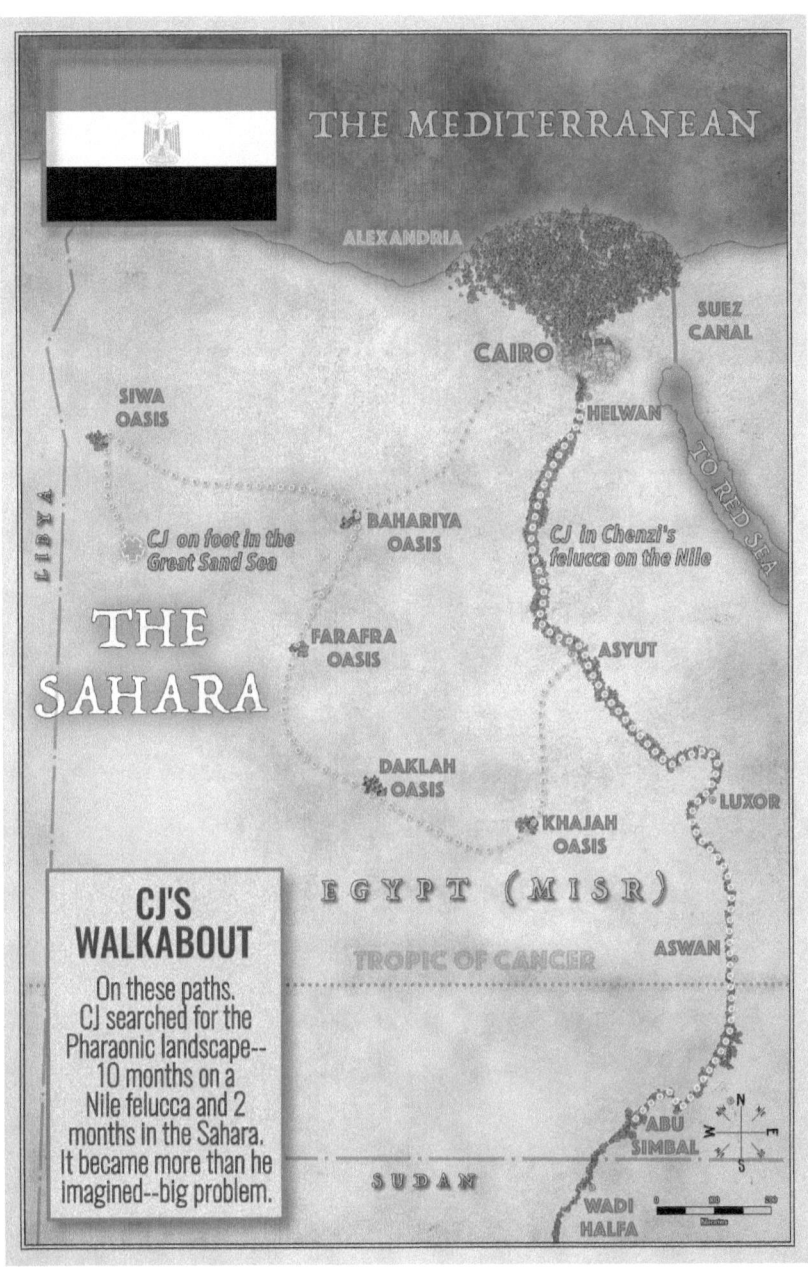

THE MEDITERRANEAN

ALEXANDRIA

SUEZ CANAL

CAIRO

HELWAN

TO RED SEA

SIWA OASIS

LIBYA

CJ on foot in the Great Sand Sea

BAHARIYA OASIS

CJ in Chenzi's felucca on the Nile

THE SAHARA

FARAFRA OASIS

ASYUT

DAKLAH OASIS

KHAJAH OASIS

LUXOR

EGYPT (MISR)

ASWAN

TROPIC OF CANCER

ABU SIMBAL

SUDAN

WADI HALFA

CJ'S WALKABOUT

On these paths. CJ searched for the Pharaonic landscape-- 10 months on a Nile felucca and 2 months in the Sahara. It became more than he imagined--big problem.

269

GIZA PYRAMIDS

Dwarfing humans, these pyramids sit on top of the Giza plateau just west and above central Cairo and the Nile,

DAVID ROBERTS' CAIRO

In 1838-9, David Roberts made this urban record. And it still drives Cairo's modern international touristic character.

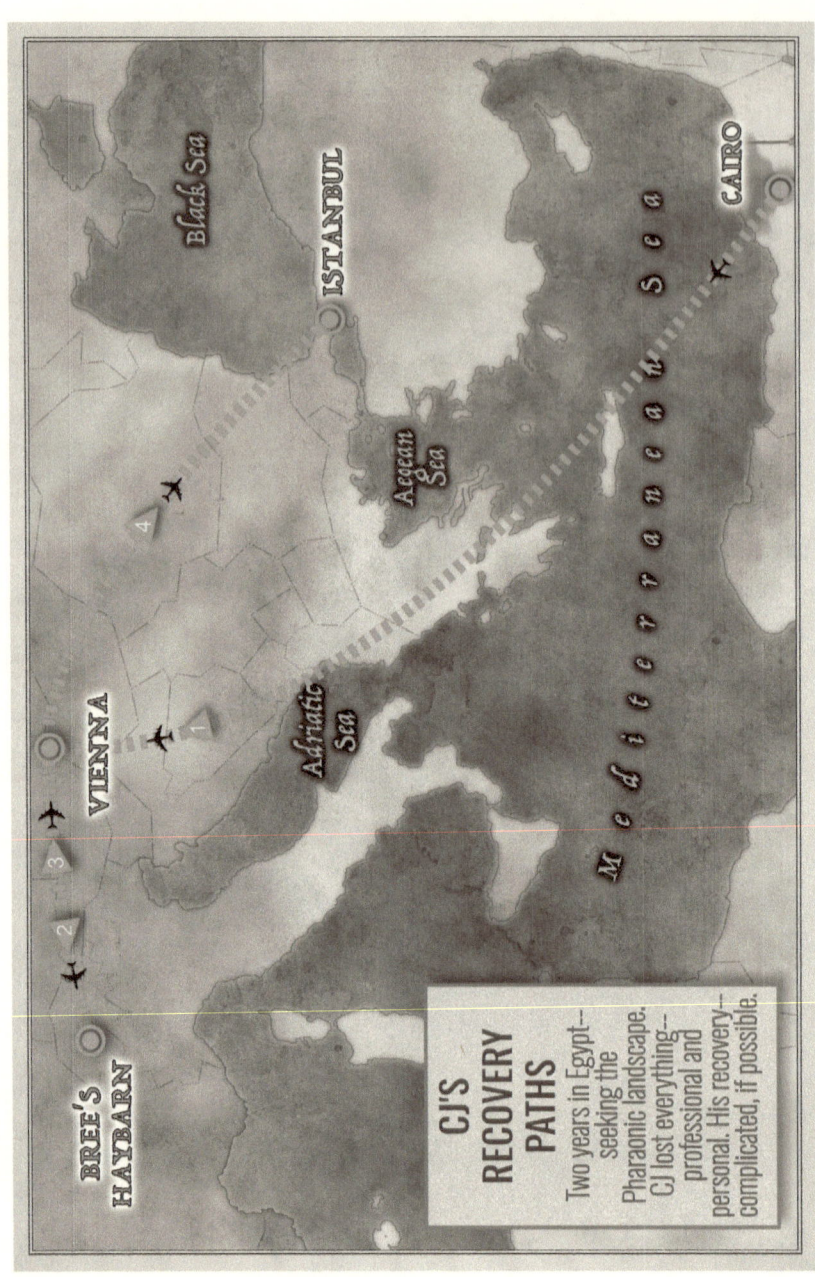

BREE'S HAYBARN

VIENNA

Black Sea

ISTANBUL

Aegean Sea

Adriatic Sea

Mediterranean Sea

CAIRO

CJ'S
RECOVERY
PATHS

Two years in Egypt—
seeking the
Pharaonic landscape.
CJ lost everything—
professional and
personal. His recovery—
complicated, if possible.

272

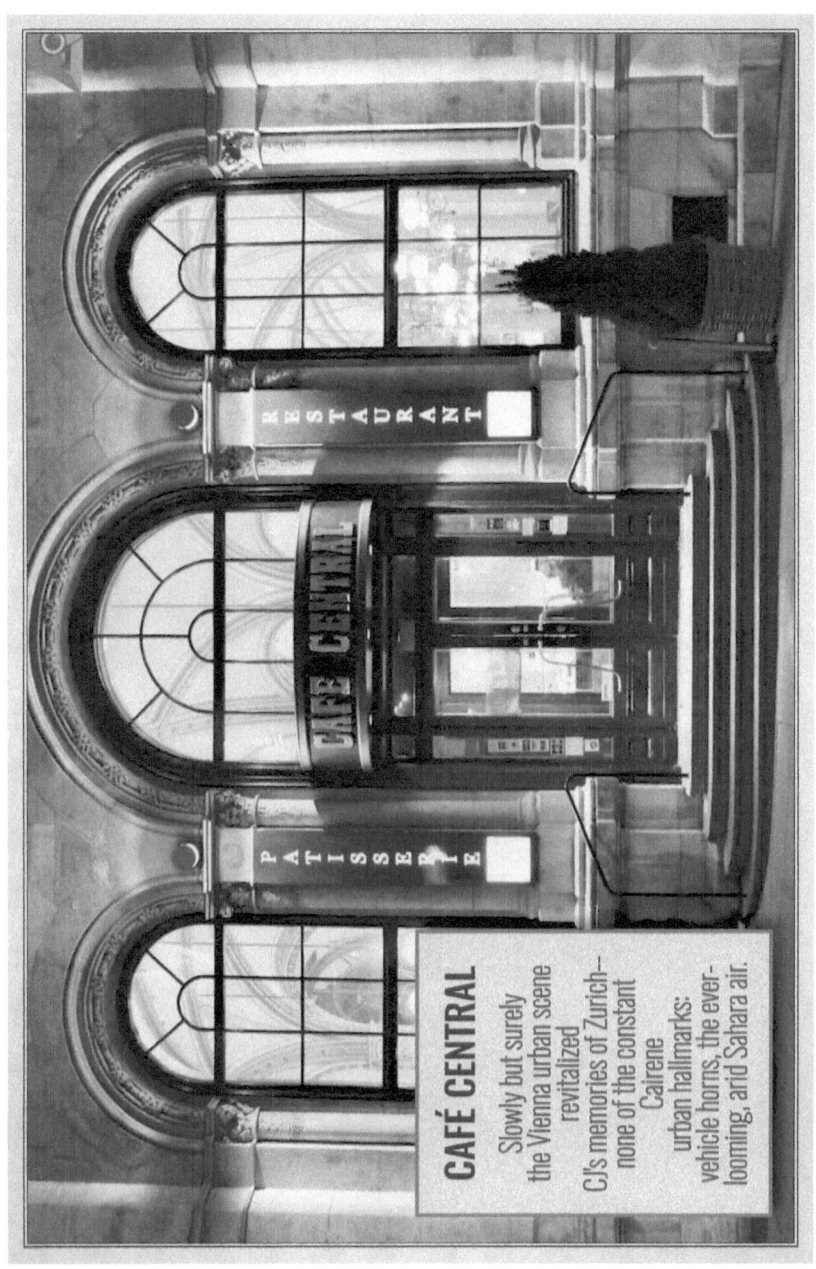

CAFÉ CENTRAL

Slowly but surely
the Vienna urban scene
revitalized
CJ's memories of Zurich–
none of the constant
Cairene
urban hallmarks:
vehicle horns, the ever-
looming, arid Sahara air.

273

HELVETIA

CJ often travelled from Zurich to Interlaken. Along Lake Thun he divined the enigmatic "summum bonum" roots of landscape design.

Zurich

Berne

INTERLAKEN

Geneva

WETTERHORN
3692

SHRECKHORN 4078

Grindelwald
1034

EIGER 3970

JUNGFRAU 4158

MÖNCH 4099

Lauterbrunnen
802

Interlaken
566

Lake Thun

Spiez

But it was on the train from Interlaken to Grindelwald that the Jungfrau Region landscape unravelled its "holy grail" mystery, revealing to CJ, through its magical music, a weaving enchantment that changed his life.

THE REVEAL

Eiger 3970m

Shreckhorn 4078m

Wetterhorn 3690m

GRINDELWALD BOWL

The Three Kings—
Eiger, Shreckhorn
and Wetterhorn—
mountains
watch over CJ,
Bree, the alps, the dorf
and the entire
Grindelwald Bowl.

GROSSE SCHEIDEGG 1962m

BREE'S HAYBARN

BLUMISALP STUBBE

DORF 1034m

CHURCH

SWISS STONE PINES

In the Jungfrau Region, Pinus cembra occur on acid soils just below the alpine zone.

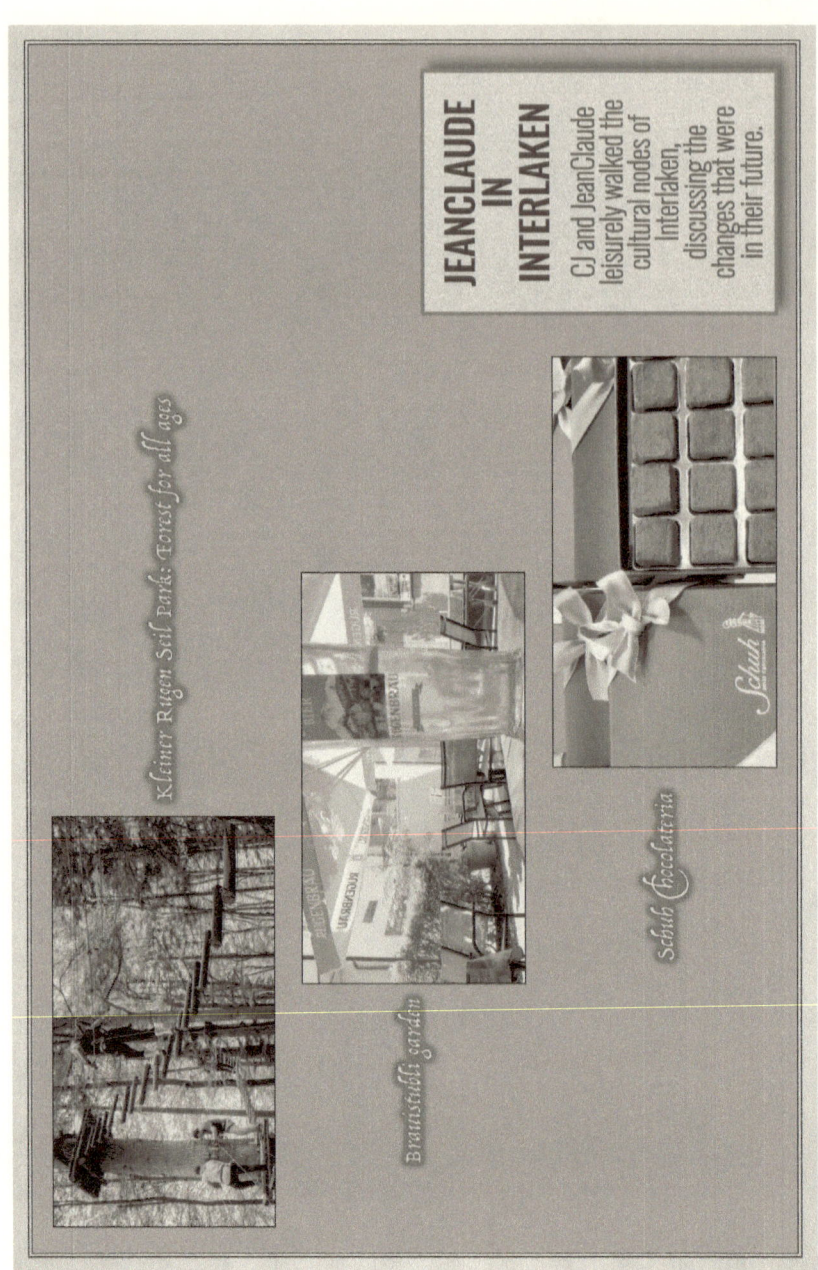

JEANCLAUDE IN INTERLAKEN

CJ and JeanClaude leisurely walked the cultural nodes of Interlaken, discussing the changes that were in their future.

Kleiner Rugen Seil Park: Forest for all ages

Braunstubli garden

Schuh Chocolateria

JEANCLAUDE RETIRES

CJ and JeanClaude walked a 5km loop from Interlaken West. In case of emergency, JeanClaude gifted CJ with an international go-route and burner phone.

Jungfrau 4,158m

WILDERSWIL

BRAUISTUBLI

Kleiner Rugen 733m

Interlaken 568m

SCHUH CHOCOLATERIA

INTERLAKEN WEST STATION

Legend:
1-Kitchen;
2-Private;
3-Stair to loft;
4-Botany;
5-Bookcases;
6-Campfire;
7-Gardens;
8-Forest.

THE HAYBARN

CJ and Bree lived in this re-furbished haybarn. CJ spent his time between international projects working on Bree's many garden plant projects and reading her hort books.

THE
LEGENDS

In the
Jungfrau Region...
Zwergs(gnomes?),
Trychlers,
Harder-Potschete...
Don't believe?
Come, see and
learn.

Black Sea

ANATOLIA
(Asia)

**BOSPHORUS
& ISTANBUL**

The Bosphorus is a
waterway connecting
the Black and Mamara
Seas.
Old Istanbul has Mimar
Sinar's skyline
mosques, Emminonu,
Topkapi, the covered
and spice bazaars.

TUZLA

ANATOLIAN
ISTANBUL

USKUDAR

PRINCES
ISLANDS

İSTİNYE

THRACIA
(Europe)

NEW
ISTANBUL

GOLDEN
HORN

OLD
ISTANBUL

Marmara Sea

20 kilometers

N

MIMAR SINAN SKYLINE

At the 16th century height of the Ottoman Empire, Sinan was the royal architect. Today his world renowned mosques still mark the Old Istanbul peninsula skyline.

283

THE SULEYMANIYE

Hilltop mosque in Old Istanbul. Built in the 16th century by Mimar Sinan, the royal architect.

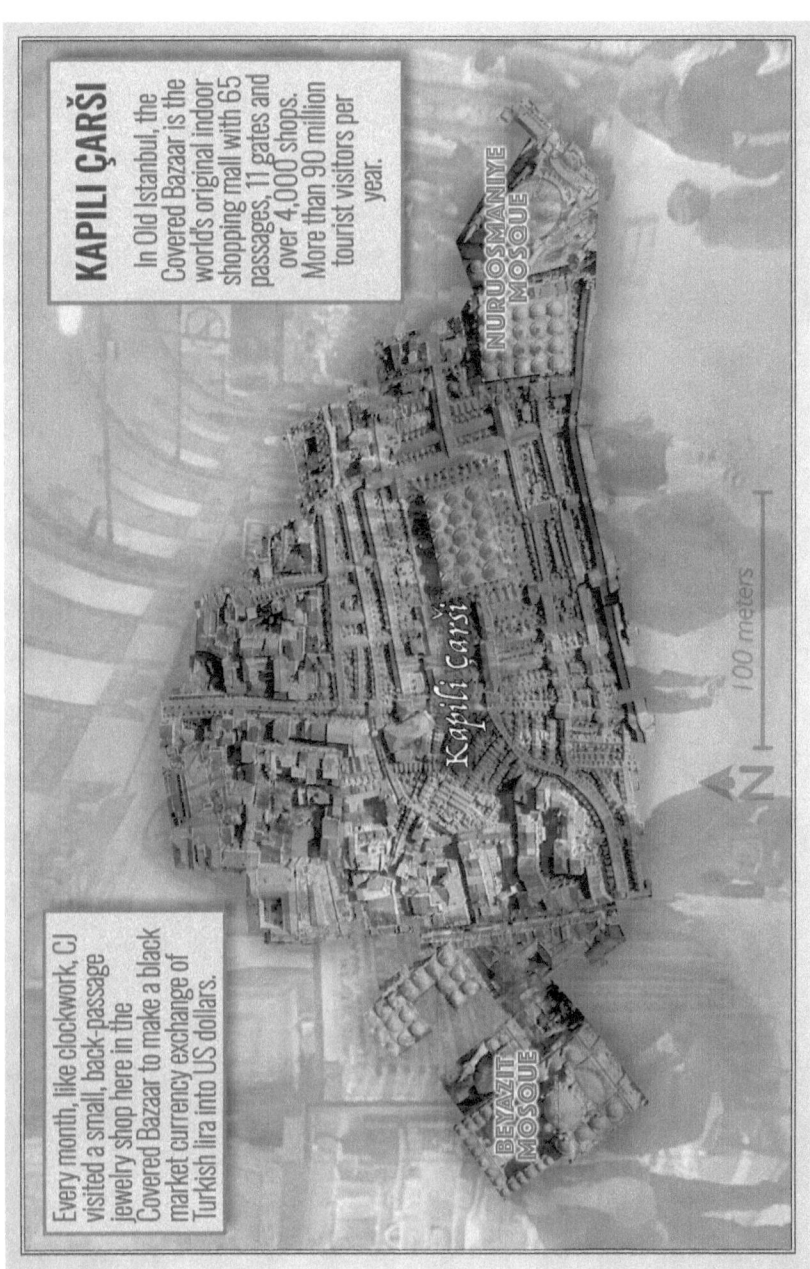

KAPILI ÇARŠI

In Old Istanbul, the Covered Bazaar is the world's original indoor shopping mall with 65 passages, 11 gates and over 4,000 shops. More than 90 million tourist visitors per year.

NURUOSMANIYE MOSQUE

Kapili Çarši

BEYAZIT MOSQUE

100 meters

N

Every month, like clockwork, CJ visited a small, back-passage jewelry shop here in the Covered Bazaar to make a black market currency exchange of Turkish lira into US dollars.

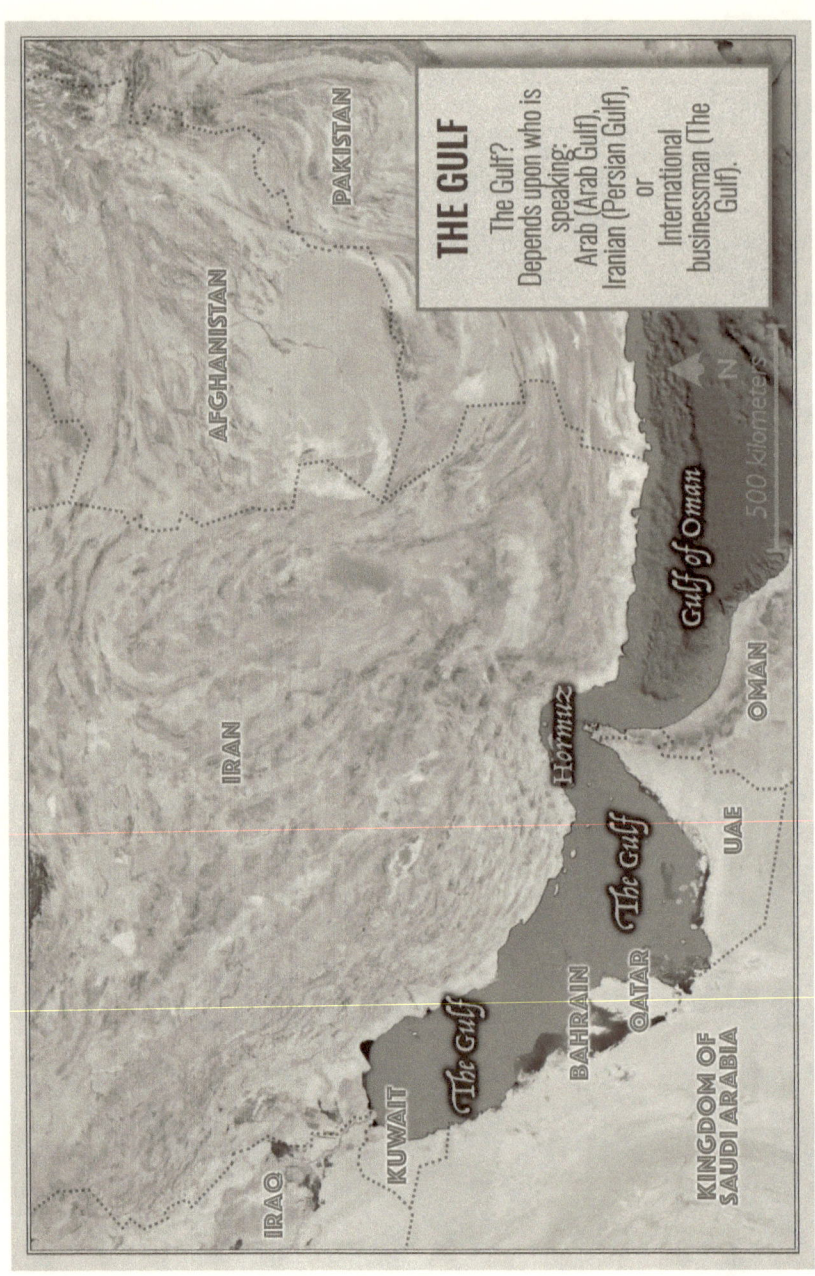

THE GULF

The Gulf?
Depends upon who is speaking:
Arab (Arab Gulf),
Iranian (Persian Gulf),
or
International
businessman (The
Gulf).

PAKISTAN

AFGHANISTAN

IRAN

IRAQ

KUWAIT

The Gulf

BAHRAIN

QATAR

The Gulf

Hormuz

Gulf of Oman

OMAN

UAE

KINGDOM OF
SAUDI ARABIA

N

500 Kilometers

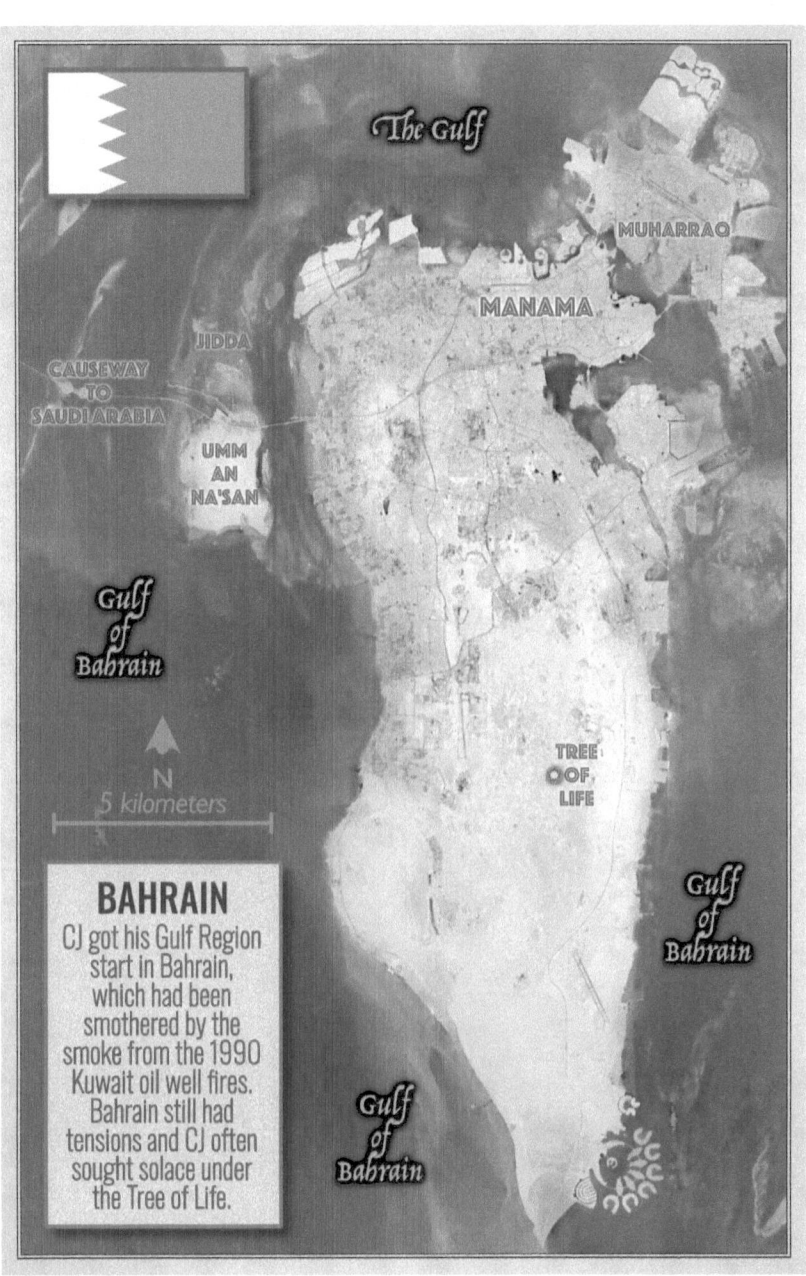

The Gulf

MUHARRAQ

MANAMA

JIDDA

CAUSEWAY
TO
SAUDI ARABIA

UMM
AN
NA'SAN

Gulf
of
Bahrain

N
5 kilometers

TREE
OOF
LIFE

Gulf
of
Bahrain

Gulf
of
Bahrain

BAHRAIN

CJ got his Gulf Region
start in Bahrain,
which had been
smothered by the
smoke from the 1990
Kuwait oil well fires.
Bahrain still had
tensions and CJ often
sought solace under
the Tree of Life.

TREE OF LIFE

The southern 2/3 of Bahrain is classic Arabian Peninsula desert--aridity writ large.

Except...except the Tree of Life. A cultural and landscape landmark for over four centuries.

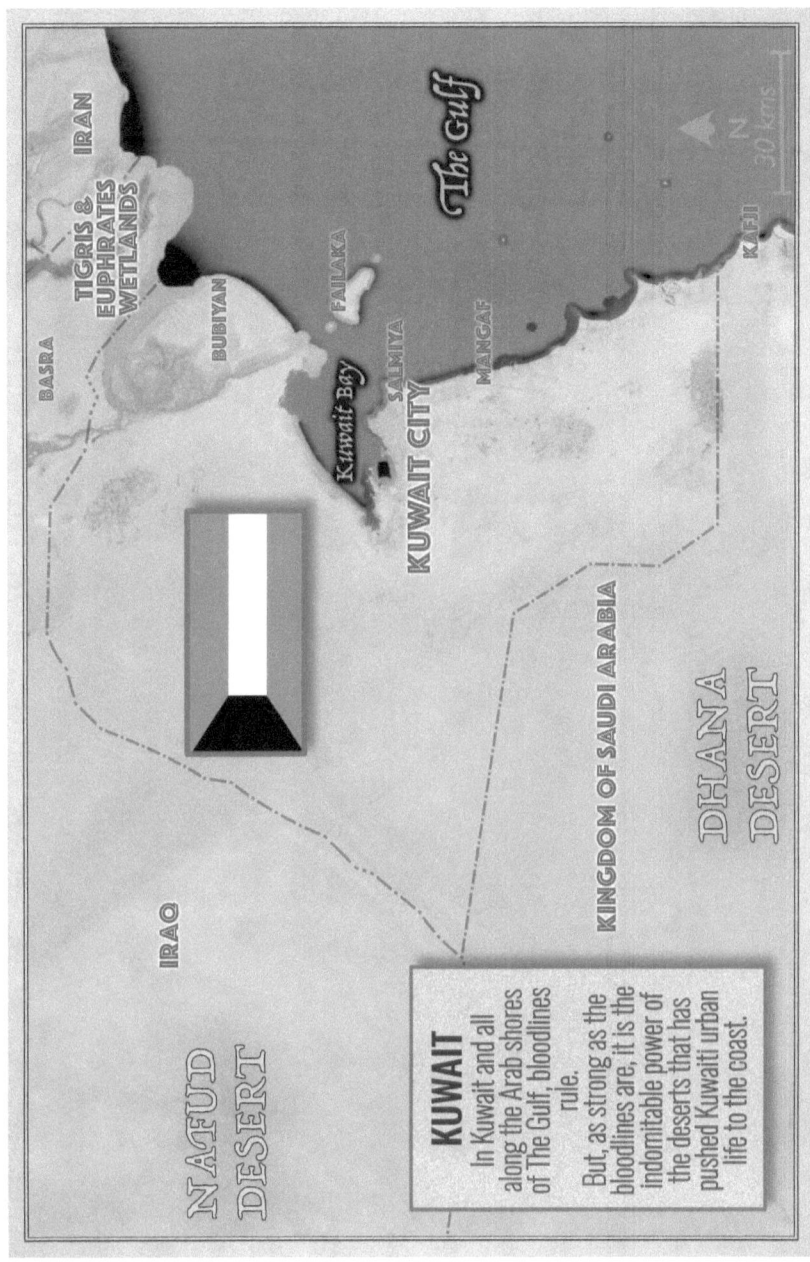

IRAN

TIGRIS & EUPHRATES WETLANDS

BASRA

BUBIYAN

FAILAKA

Kuwait Bay

The Gulf

SALMIYA

KUWAIT CITY

MANGAF

KIFJI

N
30 kms.

IRAQ

NAFUD DESERT

KINGDOM OF SAUDI ARABIA

DHANA DESERT

KUWAIT

In Kuwait and all along the Arab shores of The Gulf, bloodlines rule.

But, as strong as the bloodlines are, it is the indomitable power of the deserts that has pushed Kuwaiti urban life to the coast.

289

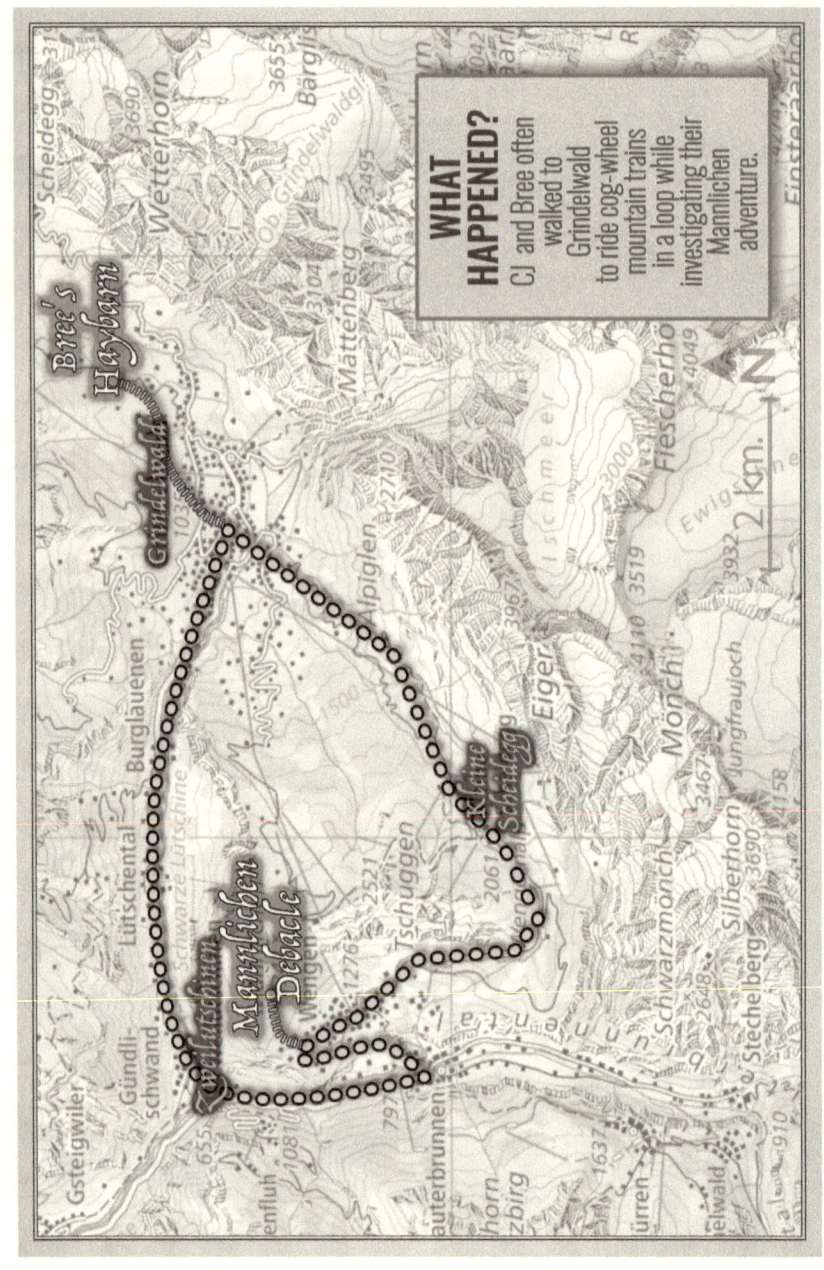

WHAT HAPPENED? CJ and Bree often walked to Grindelwald to ride cog-wheel mountain trains in a loop while investigating their Mannlichen adventure.

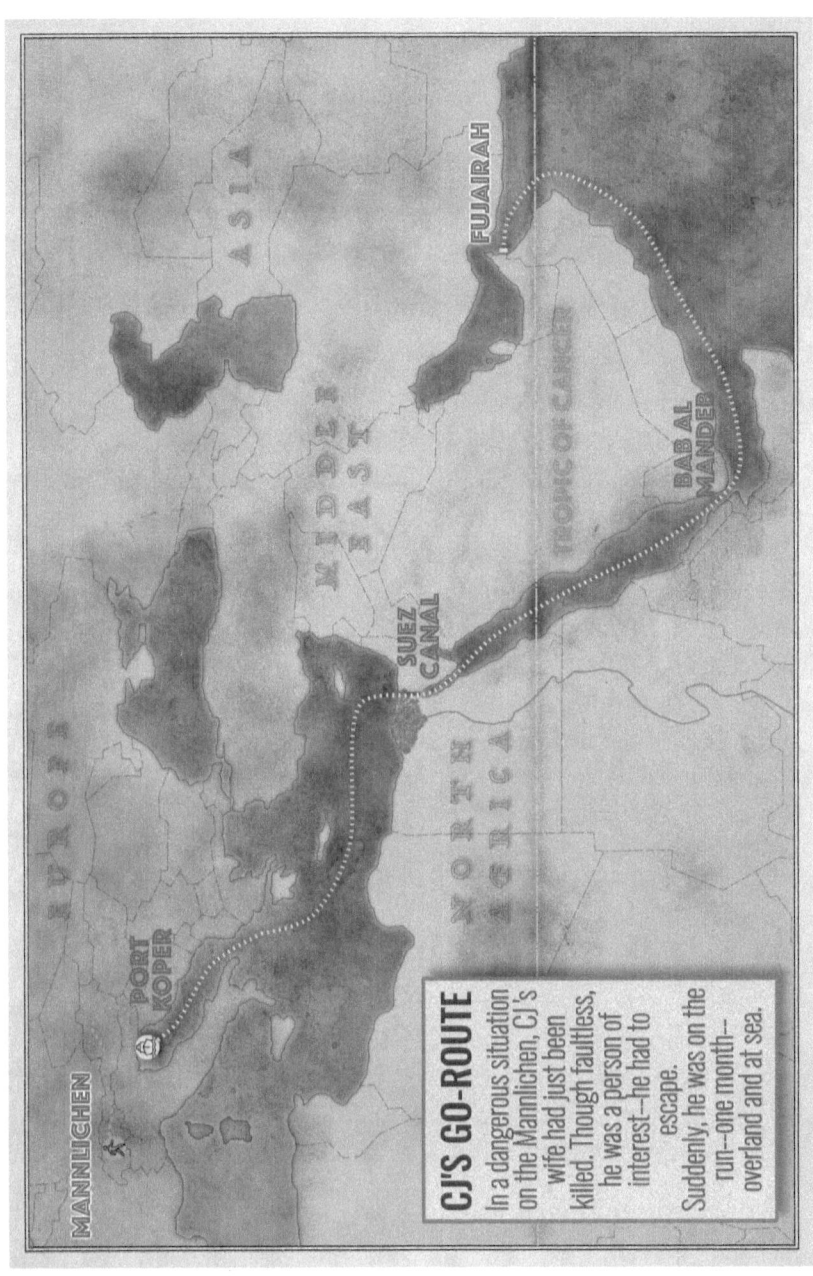

CJ'S GO-ROUTE

In a dangerous situation on the Mannlichen, CJ's wife had just been killed. Though faultless, he was a person of interest—he had to escape.

Suddenly, he was on the run—one month—overland and at sea.

MANNLICHEN

PORT KOPER

EUROPE

ASIA

MIDDLE EAST

NORTH AFRICA

SUEZ CANAL

TROPIC OF CANCER

FUJAIRAH

BAB AL MANDEB

"The Landscape Architect" Series

In this Book 5, *Orient Espresso*, we follow CJ in Egypt, Vienna, the Jungfrau Region of the Swiss Alps, Istanbul, Bahrain, Kuwait and the United Arab Emirates. CJ's professional career flip flops—a combination of his own fateful choices and the capricious nature of international landscape architecture work in the Eastern Mediterranean and the Gulf Region.

The Landscape Architect series is about CJ, Christopher Janus. He wrote it all. The six stories are his collected memoirs. He was into asking questions, discovering and writing. And above all he was a landscape architect deeply intrigued by foreign cultures, landscape and design. The six stories track the arc of his beginning interest in landscape architecture followed by his growth in the profession.

Who is CJ? CJ is an American, born in the Midwest, raised in New Mexico—a hard worker who found his muse in the landscape. At university in the late 1990s he grew to embrace landscape, literature and all the fine arts with humanitarian, environmental and spiritual sensibilities. He became a landscape architect and despite his heart-felt attraction to the New Mexico landscape—inspired by the works of Ansel Adams, Georgia O'Keeffe, and the writings of JB Jackson—he travelled the world because, like it or not, life had its own plan for him. CJ's personal life and professional landscape architecture career are woven through with drama in landscape, foreign culture and design—all presenting him with unrelenting dilemmas.

The series reveals the twists and turns in his professional

landscape architecture development. But the series explores further. CJ, drawing upon his fine arts history, becomes obsessed with experiences in nature and the landscape beyond the five senses. Beyond the five senses? The paranormal? He recognizes his limits yet always strives to achieve more.

CJ chases nature, its landscape and plants to their existential roots. He describes his interactions with cultures, landscapes, gardens and plants of the world—where the unexpected and downright strange become daily facts of life.

CJ, like his landscape architecture profession and its practitioners, obsesses over design. In one of the major themes in the series, he tries to get to the root of a gossamer, ever-evolving landscape design theory.

Unique in this series, CJ, not a tourist, uses his expatriate life across the Middle East, North Africa and Europe, attempting to weave the threads of his foreign landscape and cultural experiences into a pragmatic design theory.

Throughout his adventures and to his surprise, he discovers, on the good days, not the normal landscape architecture world, rather an enlightening and exciting ethnobotanical world influenced by the likes of Lord Byron, HG Wells, Algernon Blackwood and Rod Serling. And then there are the "not-so-good" days... strange cultures and even stranger landscapes.

Previously in Book 4, *Crystal Vision*, CJ, after six years in Saudi Arabia and having lost his job and his best friend, had embarked on a personal quest that took him deep into the Swiss Alps Jungfrau Region where, in the intertwining local culture and landscape, he discovered hope and a way forward.

In Book 6, *Dubai Sands*, CJ will be in the United Arab Emirates—Fujairah, Dubai, Abu Dhabi. Struggling to overcome personal and professional disaster, he takes one last project—a 5-star hospitality destination deep in the infamous, death-dealing Empty Quarter. Can he survive in this landscape?

Copyright © 2025 by Edward Flaherty

First edition 2025

Final illustrations and cover art by copyright owner.

Edited and formatted by Lin White, Coinlea Services, http://www.coinlea.co.uk

ISBN: 979-8-9851600-9-3

Published by copyright owner
https://flahertylandscape.com

Acknowledgements

All illustrations prepared by author. Base photos by author. Base maps from 2022 Google Earth: https://earth.google and from 2022 Swiss Topo: https://www.swisstopo.admin.ch/en. Some portions of base images from *Traditional Crafts of Saudi Arabia*, John Topham, Stacey International, 1981, were post-processed by the copyright owner. The following illustrations base images have been provided in 2024 as listed below:

Illustration: 2-Pyramids from https://historyfacts.com/world-history/article/7-facts-about-the-seven-wonders-of-the-ancient-world/

Illustration: 3-Cairo from https://artcollection.dcms.gov.uk/artwork/16013/

Illustration: 5-Café Central from https://lokalfuehrer.stadtbekannt.at/restaurants/cafe-central/

Illustration: 15-Sinan Skyline from https://www.behance.net/gallery/12747415/Home-is-where-I-am-with-you-charity-exhibition/modules/448177795

Illustration: 16-Sinan Mosque from https://www.researchgate.net/figure/Suleymaniye-Mosque-Side-Elevation-wwwsuleymaniyemosquecom_fig6_350618031

Illustration: 17-Kapili Çarşi from https://uclg-mewa.org/wp-content/uploads/2023/01/Local_Goverments_in_Middle_East_and_West_Asia.pdf

Illustration: 20-Tree of Life from https://worldlist.vision/eurasia/bahrain/tree-of-life.phtml

Colophon

Books are crafted. Colophons are the end credits of literature.

Books have a typographical tradition that to this author go nearly as deep into human culture as does the landscape.

The cover typeface represents a link to the Viennese Secessionist art movement.

Baskerville and Skia are the primary manuscript typefaces—cleanly bringing a Mediterranean aura to the manuscript—that is how the author thinks of it. These typefaces are for simplicity, clarity and ease of reading—things that CJ could never find in his Middle East and North Africa landscape experiences.

Ends of chapters are indicated by the author's line drawings of a typical cup of espresso.

Cover Art

On this book's cover, upon examination, you will find an urbane coffeeshop image representing the central point of the recovery CJ has to make following his sand-scoured walkabout in the Egyptian Sahara.

Dedication

Dedicated first of all to my wife, her photographs, support and understanding. Then to everyone who has interest in landscape, culture or the profession of landscape architecture.

About the Author

An international award winner and frequently invited conference speaker, Edward Flaherty practiced landscape architecture over the past 5 decades on very large projects where he has lived as an expatriate in Africa, Europe and Asia.

In the eastern Mediterranean and the Gulf Regions, he made his home with his family for years in Istanbul, Kuwait City and Manama.

Professional details at LinkedIn, https://ch.linkedin.com/in/edflaherty1

Discussion Guide for Orient Espresso

As I wrote this story, a couple big picture items kept me busy. I never fully resolved them, so I ask you, the readers, to discuss them and share your thoughts with me by commenting on my blog via this link: flahertylandscape.com.

1. Does human culture relate to the landscape? If so, then how?

2. What is the power in plants, gardens and landscape that induces peace in humans?

3. How do human cultures change? How do ecotypes in nature change? What happens at the edges of adjacent ecotypes and the edges of adjacent human cultures?

   I look forward to hearing from you. Thank you.

Call to Action

Orient Espresso is the fifth book in the fictional autobiographical series, "The Landscape Architect". In the series, CJ tracks the intriguing events he experienced in his personal and expatriate professional career in landscape architecture amid the strange cultures and even stranger landscapes of Europe, the Middle East and North Africa.

If you enjoyed reading about CJ's *Orient Espresso* adventures in Cairo, Istanbul, the Gulf Region and the Mannlichen then please write a short review and share it on my blog flahertylandscape.com.

You might also enjoy reading my fourth book *Crystal Vision* about CJ's personal recovery, design and landscape adventures in the Jungfrau Region of the Swiss Alps.

www.ingramcontent.com/pod-product-compliance
Lightning Source LLC
Chambersburg PA
CBHW060601030726
47498CB00005B/1496